Praise for Light of Evanora: Book One

This book is full of romance, fantasy, and dynamics that we could only hope to be challenged by in our lives!! Worth the wait for the next books in the series!!!

— LAVI, AMAZON

If you like finding new worlds to get wrapped up in, you'll love this book. I really enjoyed learning about the characters and the places they travel to, and I can't wait to read the future installments in the series!

— DANIEL, AMAZON

This book is a great read for anyone! I don't really read much anymore and not usually fantasy novels, but I loved it! The characters are amazing and journey of this story is incredible! I absolutely recommend this book!

— KENDRA, AMAZON

PRAISE FOR APPARATUS FROM ARUNA: BOOK TWO

This one was quite a page turner just as the last one did. I wasn't disappointed no bit; not until I finished it myself after a week of reading it, haha. But in all seriousness, this book is phenomenal and amazing in every way. Totally worth reading if anyone is looking for a coming of age fantasy book series because this is it! Tiffany has done it again!

— SEAN, AMAZON

This is a worth reading story. The language is simple and easy to understand. This book is recommended to the children above 16 years of age. The story had end number of twists and turns. The story was very interesting and intriguing. Don't miss this masterpiece. It had more suspense than the first one.

— VANSHIKA, GOODREADS

Fantastic! Well paced, dying for another book! The attention to detail in these books is great. And i love the stories of these characters as a fellow dnd nerd. Perfect indie read.

ISBN: 979-8-9922605-0-2

Represent
Publishing

Cover Design by Lidia Puccetti

Edited and Formatted by Represent Publishing

SONGS

FROM

HALDORIS

BOOK THREE

THE LEGENDS OF LIMORIA

SONGS

FROM

HALDORIS

T R NICKEL

For my nephew, Bentley,
The inspiration for the things that go bump in the night or
threaten to swallow my readers whole. You are my creative
collaborator, buddy. Thank you for keeping me a kid

"The voice of the sea
speaks to the soul."

The Awakening by Kate Chopin

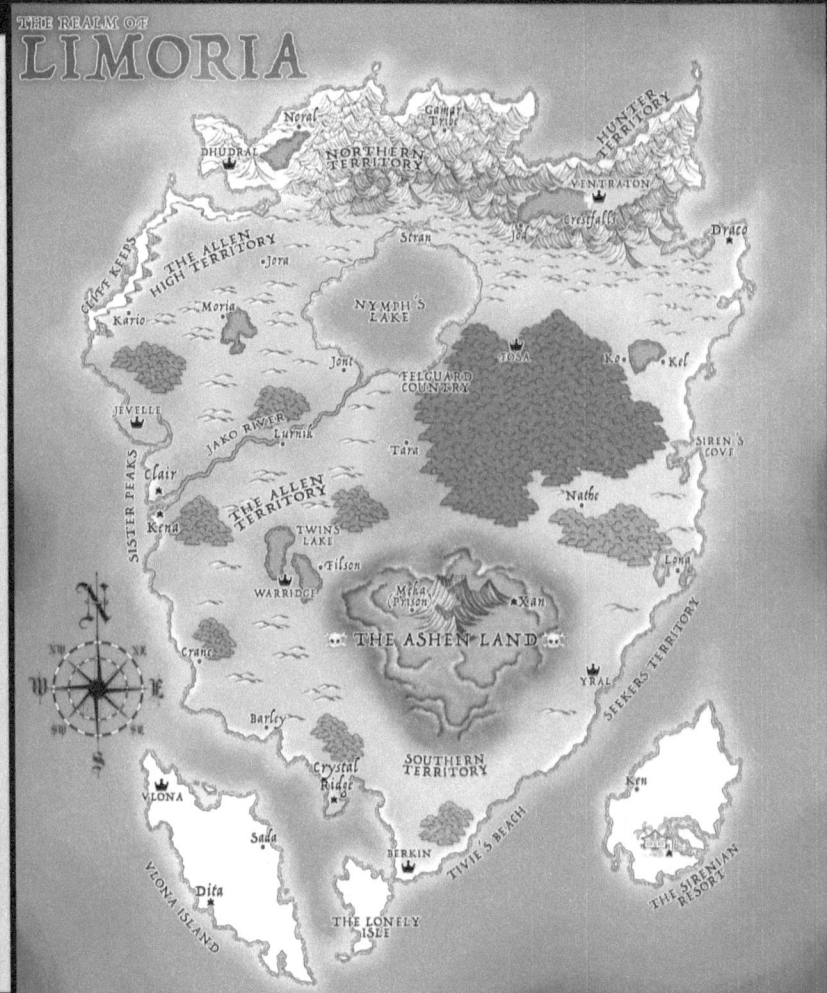

Author's Note

The creative process is anything but a simple one. What pulls our brains and hearts more towards one story or another is a fascinating mystery. I am a firm believer that you should only ever write what is true to your heart. Some truth that exists within you as the creator, or truth that lives in the life of someone you care about. It needs to come from a truth that exists in our lives for us to write about it with such authority. Those are the stories that people end up being drawn to, end up writing, end up completing and publishing. There are outliers, for sure, but the greats are the ones who always have something to say. I don't consider myself a great – no – I have too much self depreciation to ever think that and see too many imperfections in my work to probably be considered one by anyone else.

I am a truth teller though.

Mazu's story is one that has been eating at me for a long time. All of the Limoria stories have, each of them coming from a real place inside of me. The question of love (platonic or romantic) and what that looks like, feels like, is such a jumble in my head. I have ideals, daydreams, but it's different when it is not just in my head, but right there in front of me. I often don't even see it, but when I do, it scares the hell (or should I say infernum) out of me. Love is dangerous. The way it can make us do things we otherwise wouldn't normally do. Push ourselves harder than what we ever have. How if they call, you drop everything and run to their side. My heart is only open to so many people, and that has always been a flaw of mine, but I hope I have some development left in my story, because I like to think I could fall in love one day in the way people often talk about. Though, if I am really being honest, I'm okay if that doesn't happen. Why? I just don't think I was built for the everyday kind of love, but something I make all my own.

That is what this story is about. How far you are willing to go, and some of the forms it can take.

I hope you enjoy the world I created, and the chaos that I've put inside of it.

At the end of the book, you'll find an index that helps explain the unexplained and brings you closer to understanding the Legends of Limoria.

CHAPTER ONE

THE SEA BREEZE sweeps my hair around me, tangling it thoroughly, just as it always does. I set her blue-rimmed teacup down next to her gravestone, placing my hand against the smooth, arched stone.

You always said that when it was your time to go, it would be to a place where the sun always shines. On a beach with endless time to drink tea and watch the waves rise and fall.

"Mazu," Father calls for me, like my name is actually a command word to follow the order he is giving me in his head.

'We are leaving, now,' or 'Wrap it up.'

I look over my shoulder at him, his body already half turned away from Mother's grave, head hanging low, and his hand gripping Marinus' collar tightly. My brother's little face is scrunched up, trying to choke back his sob. I turn to my mother, kissing the cold and somewhat salty monument before standing and facing him.

"Okay," I whisper, following him on the weaving path down from the cliff side where most of our dead go to rest.

Looking back, I see the distant waves crashing in the background. Though she is littered amongst many, she stands out to me; just as she always had. The lavender-coloured sky, an homage to her calm and always beautiful demeanour, makes me want to believe in the stories she had told me about the Seasire. That somehow her devotion to the goddess earned her this blissful sight.

Though, I would have preferred if a goddess could have just healed her ailment.

I close my eyes, blocking out the view and turning away to leave her to rest. "**Sit tibi terra levis**, Mamma."

Biting the inside of my cheek, I make my way down to catch up to my father and brother, walking through the faint dust clouds kicked up from their feet. Marinus pulls away from our father's grip and grabs onto my hand. Hiding his face by leaning against my forearm.

Father sighs, "Take care of him."

I always do.

Taking a deep breath, I place my free hand on his head. "Shh, Ari. She wouldn't want to see our tears." He nods, sniffling, but his whimpering does not cease. "Mamma always said that our smiles brought her peace. Remember?"

Marinus lifts his head slowly, meeting my downwards gaze. "I'm trying." He cries, tears and snot covering his face, but a pathetic smile spreads across instead.

It falters, but he strains to put it back on.

Don't cry.

"There you go." I flash him the same smile right back. "That's how you do it."

It shouldn't have to be like this.

As we wander down to the road that will lead us back to **Berkin**, Marinus stays close to me, his little hands gripping onto my shirt tightly.

It'll take us well into the night to make our way home.

We remain silent as we walk down the beaten path, Father a few steps ahead of us. The surrounding hills, a mix of dirt and sand, the zoysia grass somehow finding it a suitable place to flourish. I watch as the slight breeze causes ripple-like waves through the strands that stick out of the sand.

Mother used to wonder if one could surf the wind. Each gust is like a perfect rolling wave.

I smile to myself, squeezing Marinus a little tighter, thinking of how he will never know our mother the way I had known her. Her strange but wonderful way of thinking and seeing the world, or how generous and kind she always was when she saw someone in need. Tears swell up, so I quickly face upwards, closing my eyes; hoping the tears will magically absorb back in.

Marinus will be my responsibility, to raise him, to tell him the same stories Mother once told me. He deserves to have someone nurture him, because I know Father won't.

He never has, for either of us.

"Focus on the road!" Father shouts.

My eyes snap open, and I see a carriage coming our way.

Father grabs my arm and tugs me towards him enough to not impede the carriage's path. "How could you not hear it coming?" he scolds.

I blink a few times, watching the carriage pass. It's expensive-looking. Definitely someone from the Cliff Keep. A royal blue with silver accents, the driver glaring at us as he needed to try to right his horse. The curtain moves slightly, revealing a woman with curled hair as white as sea foam and eyes the colour of copper.

The curtain drops and I feel a tug on my sleeve. "Zuzu?" Marinus looks up at me with a furrowed brow.

"Sorry." I shake my head, and Marinus reaches up to let me

know he wants to be carried. I pick him up while explaining, "My mind... it was just lost somewhere for a moment."

"Next time, don't do that in the middle of the road," Father scoffs, walking ahead.

I rest Marinus on my hip. "Are you alright?" I ask him as he lays his head on my shoulder, nodding.

Once we crest the hill, Berkin comes into view. The Cliff Keep's district to the right of the city climbs up the alcove. It belongs to the richest of us, allowing them to look over the city in its entirety. Merchants, traders and residents all reside within it, while the fishermen live on the beach lining the bottom tip of our city. Berkin is really just layers and layers of city, and the closer you are to the sky, the more wealthy and powerful you are. The only exception is our fishermen, such as my father. We are a primary source of food for everyone. We don't live in fancy houses or have carriages, but we get a lot of things for free as part of the service of providing meat to the city.

"Check that the nets are secured for tonight." Father mutters over his shoulder to us, "Smells like a storm."

His nose is turned up to the sky, the short greying curls on the top of his head rustle in the powerful gust hitting us. Ari clings tighter, the summer wind feeling chilly.

"I checked it this morning," I state.

Father runs a hand through his messy hair. "And I'm telling you to check them again, to be sure."

I take in a deep breath. "I'm positive that everything is secure—"

Father cuts me off by waving his hand up. "Just, just stop talking," he mumbles, lowering his hand and putting it into his pocket.

'You were positive when we lost the large casting net in that

one storm years ago, too.' That's what I imagine he is thinking right now.

The lavender sky quickly turns into one of twilight. Marinus' breaths are slow and steady as he sleeps. I carefully adjust him to my other side as my arm grows sore.

Father watches me. "If you would stop babying him, he would walk and strengthen his legs."

I ignore the comment, letting the boy rest.

He has been through enough today. It was already hard enough for him to walk out here.

A trader's cart passes us on the way into the city, but slows to a halt, noticing us. "I see you got a youngin in your arms. Do you need a lift into Berkin?" the trader asks as they dismount from their seat and step towards us.

I stay silent as my father looks them and their cart over before approaching. "That's awfully kind. How far into the city are you headed?" The horse stomps its hooves a few times.

My father gives me a nod, letting me know it's alright.

The trader offers their hand to help me step up into the front of the cart. "Just to the town circle," they say, stepping back up to take a seat at the reins.

Father nods. "Right, we have that trade show tomorrow." He shakes their hand. "I'm Hugstari, and this is my daughter, Mazu, and son, Marinus."

"I'm Lenn," they introduce themselves. "Your little guy looks so tuckered out, felt awful just passing you by."

Giving my most convincing smile, I say, "He had a long day."

Father heads to the back of the carriage, getting settled on the trailer's edge. I give Lenn the okay to continue the journey. The black and white stead quickly resumes its march to the city with little fuss.

A comfortable silence falls amongst us, the swaying movement of our transportation nearly lulling me to sleep.

"Do you know of any cheap but nice places to stay?" they ask, bringing my focus to them instead of the feeling of my drifting mind.

I adjust Marinus as he has fallen slightly to the side. "Nothing in the town circle will be cheap, but if you head down a few steps further, the Pleasant Inn stays true to its namesake," I inform them, and they turn to me with a smile. "We can walk you there once you check your cart in. We have to pass it anyhow."

Marinus stirs before settling back in my arms.

Pulling up to the city, guards step up, dressed in their yellow tunics with the symbol of the Southern Territory. An upside down crown, with hands reaching upwards out from its band.

I recognise the guard, Kellen. She waves at me, with a slight gesture, having noticed me as well.

She comes to my side of the cart, taking a step up. "Hey Zu," she greets, using a hand to balance herself on the cart. "How was the service?"

Lenn hops off the cart to show the other guards the goods and to talk. My father follows in his stead, the guards all recognising him.

My brow furrows. "Good, I guess. Weather was just how Mother likes it."

Kellen nods. "Sorry I couldn't get off."

Shaking my head, I give her my best smile. "Don't even worry about it. I had Ari," I say, smiling down at him cuddled up and sleeping away.

"You look like shit," she points out, tilting her head as I meet her green gaze.

How sweet of her. I'm trying not to have a complete melt-down is all.

I let out a slightly pained laugh. "Yeah, right." Kellen looks away to watch her colleagues checking the cart contents. "I'll be fine. Just been a long day."

Kellen looks back at me. "Can I help with anything?"

"Wanna check the nets for me tonight?" I ask, with a quirked up eyebrow.

"Hard pass, but how about I come by with a drink once the lights go out?" she offers, stepping down from the cart.

Nodding, I say, "Works for me. The pier?"

"Would we meet anywhere else?" She turns and waves goodbye as all the guards head back to the city entrance.

The short stone pillars with golden sculpted vines run upwards from them into an arch that reads *Berkin* overhead.

There wouldn't really be a point in having a grand gate like Yral. We live in a pit.

Lenn whips the reins, the stead guiding our journey, lurching the cart forwards. As we pass under the arch, the large city of Berkin is truly visible, the amphitheatre-like city streets. The town circle is clearly visible from here. There are only two other roads like this one. The one for those who live in the Cliff Keep and on the opposite side of that.

All pointing and leading to the ocean.

"Well, isn't that something?" Lenn says with a wide grin, looking out over the city.

I nod. "There is no other city quite like it, from what I hear anyway."

A chuckle escapes Lenn as they guide the cart down the hill, carefully and at a slow pace. "I've been nearly everywhere, and I can say that statement is as true as can be. It's like an onion."

Despite my heavy heart, a small chuckle leaves my lips. "An onion?"

"Lots of layers." They tip their head towards me.

FATHER HOPS off the cart to show Lenn where to check his cart at the Inn, while I carry Marinus home. I carefully step down the steep staircases that get us from one level to another.

"No bouncing," he grumbles, his arms tossed over my shoulders.

"Sorry, bud, the stairs," I mutter in a hushed tone, not to wake him completely.

As we pass the homes stacked against one another, the cobbled stone litters with specks of gold. The wind carries up sand from the beach, along with the salty taste and smell. I turn right, the beach a few layers down yet, the swinging lanterns in the distance illuminating the long and large decks going far past the shoreline. There are only two **trabucco** on this end of the beach, one owned by my father. Further down, that one is owned by Crey, a lively older woman who regularly teaches the younger fisherman some of the trade. The sound of my boots walking on stone shifts as I turn to begin my trek down the dock. The sound is hollow and nearly drowned out by the waves.

"Almost home," I say, lifting Marinus up again as his body starts to get too heavy for me.

Reaching the door, I carefully lean back so I can free one of my hands to reach onto my belt and pull the house key from its clasp. Marinus' eyes flutter open, hearing me work with our heavy metal door.

He raises his head and rubs his eyes tiredly. "Zuzu, are we going to bed?"

I slowly lower him down to stand on his own two feet, and I push the door open. "Yeah, buddy." We head in and I use my body to shut the door and lock it. "Take your shoes and clothes off before you lay down," I say as Marinus treks off to his room.

"Okay," he mumbles, and I follow him as he leaves his shoes in the middle of the floor.

If Father were here, he'd be scolding him about being lazy, acting as if we didn't just bury our mother.

Tossing his shoes over towards the door, they land upright, just slightly overlapping. Marinus disappears into the softly lit room, illuminated by the soft rays of moonlight making their way through. Outside of our bedrooms, bathroom, and the few support beams, the rest of the home is wide open.

"Checked the nets," I say out loud to myself, disregarding my father's instruction, and head into the kitchen instead.

I throw a log into the stove, taking a match from the side of the stove to light it. I walk over to the water basin and fill the kettle enough for two cups before placing it on the stove to boil. Reaching up, I open the cabinet door and pull out two tea mugs, along with the Ventraton mint tea bags. Mother got gifted them from her family in Draco for her birthday in the last sidereal year. I bring one of the bags up to my nose, smelling the sweet aroma. I plop one in each cup and put the tin back.

I wonder if Father sent word to her family yet. He said he would, but I can see Father putting it off. I'll have to ask him in the morning.

The kettle screeches, and I rush over to pull it off the stove before it stirs Marinus awake. I pour the water over the tea bags, letting them steep for a few minutes.

A loud clunk sounds from the door, the latch moving to unlock it, and Father pushes the door open.

"Welcome home," I mutter, bringing the cups into the living area and setting one on the side table next to Father's normal perching spot.

"Yeah." He kicks off his boots and sets them next to mine and Marinus'.

He walks over, sits in his chair and puts his feet up on the ottoman that Mother and I reupholstered two sidereal years ago, after he tore a hole in it.

Father picks up his cup, taking the bag out and sets it down on the saucer. "Check the nets?"

I nod, removing my tea bag and taking a sip. "Of course."

He nods, looking down into his cup and breathing in deeply. I watch him for a moment, his expression blank.

There are rare moments like this where I can't read him. That I have no idea what it is he could be thinking.

"You plan on heading out yet?" Father asks, finally taking a drink of his tea. His eyes meet mine. "I figure you are meeting up with Kellen."

I rip my gaze from him to look ahead of me and the dead fireplace, the mantel still decorated with a bunch of Mother's seashore findings.

"Mhmm," I hum.

He stands, grabbing his saucer and cup with him. "Lock up before you leave and be back in the morning."

Father walks away, disappearing into the darkness of his room, the door creaking slightly as he closes it.

I sigh and take another sip. Turning my head, I look out the glass window, the open sea nothing but pitch black, no lights beyond what lanterns we keep lit on our pier to avoid shipwrecks. The moon must have retreated behind some clouds. Closing my eyes, I hear a soft melody being composed with the wind brushing against the windows; the waves muted through the walls and creaking of the floorboards. Bringing the cup up to my lips, I hum a soft tune alongside the accompaniment.

SLOWLY, I make my way down the pier. The waves pull back for the low tide. The moon is the only light I need. I turn around, walking backwards to look at the sleeping city. The bright colours are muted and dull in the dead of night, most lights snuffed out and everything quiet. Turning back around, I finish my walk to the end of the pier. I take a seat on the edge, my legs feeling the exhaustion of all the walking I've done today.

My face turns upwards to face the moon. "Are you still watching, Mamma?" I ask, my words are carried up and out by a cool gust. My raven hair circles around my face and shoulders.

So many people believe in the goddesses, but the last time anyone ever travelled through those doorways was around 500 sidereal years ago. If it is even real. People think we get reincarnated and sent to the plane that best matches our morality. Who we are as an individual, but who knows if it's actually real, if the historians lied to give the future some sort of peace after the monstrous actions of man? Maybe it was a ploy to just get us all to follow the rules, be too afraid to be sent to the fiery world that supposedly created the Ashen Planes.

"Zoning out again?" Kellen asks as she sits down next to me, a bottle of cheap port in her hand.

She puts the cork in between her teeth before ripping it up and dropping it into her hand. "It's the only thing I'm good at, apparently." I grab the bottle from her and take a swig. My lips purse and brows furrow from the bitterness. "That is a really crappy port."

"But free." Kellen cheers me, taking a swig herself. Her stoic expression not even faltering from the sewage. "What were you thinking about this time?" I shake my head, but she shoves me with her shoulder. "Come on now. No secrets."

Rolling my eyes, I lean back, resting on my elbows, looking out to the pitch blackness ahead of us. "About after we die."

She scoffs, "Yeah, that's a great thing to be thinking about right after your mother's funeral."

"Wow, don't sugarcoat or anything. You asked, and there it is," I bite back.

Kellen leans over to me, raising the bottle. "Open your mouth." I look from the bottle to her eyes before doing as she asks. She pours the port in. "There's my sugar."

I nearly spit it out, both amused and repulsed, but I swallow it down. "I hate that."

"Then don't complain when I tell you how it is." She raises a brow, taking another swig herself.

"Why am I your friend again?" I ask, shoving her a bit.

She smiles, her lips still on the bottle. "Because of my wonderful personality."

"Ah, right." I chuckle, sitting back up, grabbing the bottle from her to take another drink.

Kellen wraps an arm around my shoulders, pulling me to her side. I take a deep breath and rest my head on her shoulder. Her thumb rubs softly on my arm and my chin trembles. I close my eyes tightly, not wanting to shed any more tears.

"Hey, Mamma?" I call out, not having seen her yet this morning.

Father is shouting curses at something outside and

Marinus is in the living area playing with some wooden toys he got during the moonmatrum holiday.

"Mom?" I ask again, approaching her bedroom.

I open the door with a soft knock, seeing her still tucked into bed and sleeping soundly.

Approaching her, I give her a soft little nudge. "It's time to get up, sleepyhead. Breakfast is getting cold."

She doesn't stir, not even a flutter of her eyes or groan from being awoken. I furrow my brow and shake her harder, but still nothing.

All the air leaves my lungs, and a lump forming in my throat as I start to shove her harder. "Mamma! Wake up!" I shout.

I hear light, bare footsteps padding over, sharing my shout. Panic rising.

I turn quickly and walk out the door, stopping Marinus from coming in. "Go get Dad, Ari. Okay?"

He nods, giving me a confused look, his hand coming up to my face and touching my cheek. "Are you hurt? Cause I cry when I'm hurt too," he says, pulling back his hand; it's a tad wet.

I am hurting; my heart is in my throat.

"Go get Dad," I reiterate, and he runs off to shout out the open window.

Going back into the room, I can't lift my eyes to look at her. My legs shake and the room feels like it is spinning. I don't hear Father come in, but he quickly slams the door shut behind him. Marinus pounds it on the other side, upset we are keeping him out.

"Mazu, go run to the docs," Father commands calmly.

My feet stay glued. He sighs and heads out himself, closing the door once again.

13

"I wanna stay with Zuzu!" Marinus shouts, his voice growing quieter as I assume Father carries him away.

"Mazu," Kellen says, shaking me a little, pulling me out of my head once again. "You are really good at pushing out the world."

I sit up, her arm falling back to her side. "I told you," I mutter.

"Wish I had that talent." She takes another drink.

Shaking my head, I say, "No, you really don't." My words sound flat.

Kellen looks over to me and just hands me the bottle again. I take a few drinks. A tear slips past my waterline and slides down my cheek. She reaches over and wipes it from my face.

She looks at me with no pity, and I don't think I will ever be able to thank her enough for that. Cause if she did, I think I would fall apart.

"Drink up. We'll sit here until it's gone." She lays down on the pier, looking up to the sky.

CHAPTER TWO

THE SEA BREEZE eases the pounding going on inside my head.

Is it possible to remove my head from my body without dying?

I dig my toes further into the sand, my feet already properly buried. The waves slowly get closer and closer as the sun begins to rise above the horizon, twilight colours slowly fading into purples and pinks. Boats are already heading out to do some fishing. My hand grips the bottle, tipping it up for another drink, but only a small drop touches my lip.

Damn, I keep forgetting it's gone.

"Should have brought two bottles," I mutter to myself, looking over to Kellen, who is curled up next to me, snoring softly.

I lay back, leaning on one of my elbows to get a better look at my childhood friend.

Always showing up for crap like this, whether I want her to or not.

Her lips are parted slightly, her messy curls wrapping

around her face. The salt from the sea sticks to her brow and makes her hair stiff. Almost like she put too much holding gel in it. A smirk plays on my lips as I reach out and move some of her hair out of the way so I can get a better look.

She's always so stoic, but she looks all cute and relaxed sleeping like this.

There are bags under her eyes, and her lips are chapped. Her cheeks tinted with a soft pink. Her eyes flutter around, like she's searching for something behind her eyelids.

Kellen always has the most gorgeous lashes.

Her skin seems a bit discoloured, likely from how much we had drunk last night into the morning. At one point, she decided the pier was depressing her and had us migrate down here.

I think she just wanted to lie down on something that wasn't a hardwood surface.

She stirs. I turn and lay flat on my back; some stars are still visible even as the sky transforms.

Kellen mutters a few curses under her breath, her hand coming up to grip her head. "I'm done helping you grieve. Next time, drink by yourself," she mutters, moving her leg like she is trying to kick me.

I chuckle. "I'm not feeling all that amazing myself, Kel."

She grimaces. "Please, don't make that awful noise again."

I raise a brow. "You mean my laughing?" I ask, and she nods. "So hostile."

We sit there awhile, just letting the sun rise and shine over us, the waves becoming louder as they encroach. Kellen slowly sits up, her hair sticking upwards. I swallow my laugh and look the other way towards the stone steps that lead down to the beach. A man is walking down them.

Awemother save me.

"Mazu!" Father shouts, walking to us.

I sit up instantly, my head spinning from the quick motion. Kellen sighs and tries combing her hair with her fingers to get it tamed, at least somewhat.

He reaches us quickly. His hand grabs the bottle of port and flips it upside down to find it empty. "Can you even see straight?"

I pinch the bridge of my nose, closing my eyes and nodding. "Of course. I just need—"

"I don't care, Mazu. I don't care what you need. What I care about is that you weren't home this morning, causing your brother to come in and wake me up screaming saying that you were missing. Now I'm missing out on money because I had to come out and search for you!" he shouts, waving his hands around.

Looking closely, I can see his eyes are a bit red. "I'm sorry," I mutter, standing up and dusting the sand off of me.

"Mr Hali, it's on me. I dragged her out here." Kellen tries to defend, but my father waves his hand, dismissing her.

I smile down at Kellen. "Don't. It's fine."

My father gestures for me to get moving, and I do. Putting one unstable foot in front of the other as he follows behind me.

"Marinus is at the Relch's. You'll have to go pick him up," he spits.

Nodding, I continue walking, not glancing back towards him.

He doesn't bother to say goodbye when we eventually go our own ways, but I turn and watch his back for a moment until he disappears as one of the homes cuts into my view.

It's only a few minutes' walk before I see the familiar structure of the Relch's abode. The white-washed walls, salt stains causing small discolouration circles all over. The orange outlined windows and an orange door to match.

Whenever Mother and Father would go out, the Relchs

would watch us. They were the closest things to grandparents we had.

I walk up and Mrs Relch opens the door, giving me a soft smile with a furrowed brow. "Hi dear," she says, opening the door wider for me to slip through. "He was all worked up."

Marinus is curled up with Dodger, the Relch's black lab, on the floor. Dodger looks at me as I slowly approach.

"Buddy, it's time to wake up," I whisper, resting my hand on his shoulder.

His eyes open slowly, but widen quickly as he takes me in. "Zuzu!" he shouts, startling Dodger. Marinus sits up and hugs me tightly. "Where were you?" he asks, not letting me go.

I shift him slightly so I can pick him up. "Just at the beach," I mutter, standing up.

"I had a bad dream, and you weren't there," Marinus complains.

"Buddy, I'm here now." I try to soothe him, but his little body shakes.

"You weren't there!" he cries.

Mrs Relch looks at me in a way I nearly want to cry myself. So much pity and grief reflecting in her eyes.

"Marinus..." My words turn to vapour against his tears.

He nuzzles his wet face into my neck. "I thought you left, like Mamma."

My heart seizes and I close my eyes, hugging him back tightly. "I'm right here, buddy."

Gods, I am so selfish.

Turning to Mrs Relch, I say, "I'm sorry for inconveniencing you." My brows furrow, and I bow to her slightly.

She waves me off. "Nonsense. We help each other out around here. I was so sad to hear about your mother."

I thank her and take my leave, heading straight home, my eyes beginning to feel the lack of sleep. Luckily, most of those who are waking up are already out to sea or further into the city, leaving me to not have to do the polite smile or stopping to chat if they felt like giving me their condolences.

What's the point of that, anyway? To constantly remind me she's gone? To make them feel like they are helping me by saying that?

We make it through the door to our home, and I set Marinus down onto Father's usual chair. "Breakfast?" I ask him and he gives me a big smile in return.

I light the stove, setting the cast iron onto the heating plate and grab a few eggs from the bowl they normally sit in. Marinus hops off the chair and runs into his room, coming out with one of his wooden toy ships Father got him for his birthday this year. He pitter-patters over to the kitchen table, climbing up onto the chair and playing by himself as he waits. I smile a bit and crack the eggs into the warmed pan. Marinus hums a familiar tune, the lullaby I sing to him whenever he has a bad dream.

He notices me looking at him over my shoulder. "Can you sing it?"

"Well, I suppose I could." I smirk.

Clearing my throat while continuing to cook, I let the old tune slip from my lips in a soft and smooth tone.

♫

The moonlight gently kisses the sea,
A lullaby whispers, drifting to me,
Close your eyes, let worries depart,
In the cradle of waves, find rest for your heart.

Hush-a-bye, sail into dreams,
Softly, my love, where the starlight gleams,

Tomorrow awaits, with the morning light,
Sleep softly, dear one, in the arms of the night.

The waves, they murmur a tale of peace,
Serenading the worries that long to cease,
Stars above, like guardian angel,
Watch over your dreams and keep them stable.

Hush-a-bye, sail into dreams,
Softly, my love, where the starlight gleams,
Tomorrow awaits, with the morning light,
Sleep softly, dear one, in the arms of the night.

The sails of your dreams catch your strained breaths,
Guiding you to blissful calming in your mind's ocean depths.
To wake anew with the morning tide,
Embraced by the sun, your fears will all subside.

So, lay your head on the pillow of the sea,
Let go of sorrows, let your spirit roam free,
In the cradle of night, find sweet reprieve,
For tomorrow, my love, the sun will relieve.

Hush-a-bye, sail into dreams,
Softly, my love, where the starlight gleams,
Tomorrow awaits, with the morning light,
Sleep softly, dear one, in the arms of the night.

♫

After a few lines, Marinus sings with me, bringing a smile to my face. He kicks his feet that hang from the chair and sways his head to the beat. I grab some plates and serve up the eggs, setting his breakfast in front of him as the song ends.

He reaches to eat the eggs with his bare hands, but I lightly swat them away, turning back around to grab two forks. "Here." I hand it to him and he digs in right away.

MARINUS PLAYS on the living area floor as I struggle to keep my eyes open, sitting down on the ground with him; my back resting against my chair. I eventually give in to the weight of them, just listening to him play. His giggles and pretend noises lulling me into rest.

"Have you told him yet?" Mom elbows me lightly, a big smile plastered on her face.

I roll my eyes and shake my head. "You think I am going to tell him I want to sing? Sing instead of fish?"

She chuckles. "Your father is stern and not always the softest, but he does care about what you want."

"Yeah, I just don't see what you see," I explain, my grin slowly fading as our hands weave thread, trying to repair a few holes in a large net of ours.

"I think you are just scared. Not because of what your father will think, but because it's not an easy way of living." She points the needle at me before going back to work.

I hate when she does that. Make me the problem versus letting me blame someone else.

"Well, you loved to sing. Why didn't you do it?" I ask, glancing up at her.

She furrows her brow for a second. "I wasn't as strong as you. My family had a certain way of living and didn't want me to stray from that. By the time I met your father, that dream was out of the picture and we had you shortly after."

"Excuses," I tease, breaking the tension from her brow.

We chuckle and she nods. "I guess you could put it that way, but that means you know I know what it means to give up something you really want; and I am telling you not to give up on this. Even if you are scared."

"Fine," I say, biting the inside of my cheek.

The door slams shut, my eyes blinking open. A mess of dark curls resting on my chest, Marinus napping soundly in my lap, his breathing slow and steady. His body heat acts like a blanket weighed down on me. I lift my head; Father watches us as he removes his boots. He notices me awake and furrows his brows, opening his mouth to say something but quickly closing it. He shakes his head and goes straight to his room.

"May the goddesses have mercy on me..." I whisper under my breath, not looking forward to whatever conversation that might turn into.

I lay my head back to rest on the worn cushion behind me, looking up to the wood-panelled ceiling.

I never followed through with telling him. I'm sure that always disappointed her.

Marinus stirs in my lap and slowly stretches his little limbs. "I'm hungry," he murmurs, not getting up from his spot.

My soft chuckle disrupts the rhythmic breathing he was resting into, and he sits up with a deep-set frown. "Hop up, and I can make us all dinner."

He stands, a bit wobbly, allowing me to head over into the kitchen. Though standing up too fast brings a white light to the forefront of my vision, I push through it until I feel the counter jab into my side.

I hate when that happens.

A knock at the door sends a jolt through me, and Marinus eagerly rushes over to it. "Wait," I command, halting his little footsteps. "Don't answer the door without checking who it is first." My reminder earns me a nod. He walks over to the window and seems to recognise them as his face beams with a big smile and he goes to unlock it.

"It Ke!" he shouts, and I tense up, glancing at my father's room.

I rush to the door and help him finish opening it, Kellen sticking her head through. Her eyes quickly find mine and they furrow slightly before she looks down to Marinus.

She ruffles his hair and steps past him. "Hey kid."

"What are you doing here?" I ask, putting my body somewhat in the way of her entering. "He's not in a good mood," I say, hushed.

Kellen nods. "I figured, but I wanted to remind you about tonight. In case you forgot, with... you know, everything going on."

I sigh, shaking my head. "I didn't forget."

She nods. "Are you still coming?"

I close my eyes and pinch between my brows.

"No, I probably shouldn't." I point my eyes at Marinus, earning yet another nod from her.

The floorboards creak behind me, causing all of us to look at my father standing there. "Go," he mutters.

My eyes widen. "What?"

"Go." Father sighs. "Just be back before morning this time."

I look at Kellen, whose face mirrors mine with surprise at hearing him so relaxed. Marinus grips onto my shirt, and I glance down to see him shaking his head with his bottom lip pushed out slightly.

What's the point of me going?

My hand goes to the oval necklace hiding under my shirt.

I grip it slightly and furrow my brow. "I'll think about it," I mutter.

"Okay," Kellen replies, making her way back to the door. "You know where to find us if you change your mind."

Marinus releases me from his tiny grip and runs over to the kitchen. Father stands there, his brows creased and eyes staring through me.

"Dad?" I ask, taking a step closer to him.

His eyes tune in and focus on me. "I'll make dinner," he grumbles, making his way into the kitchen after Marinus.

Something is wrong.

"Okay..." I mumble, staring after him.

I watch him for a while, as he moves around the kitchen for the first time in months.

Since her health went further south.

"Papa is cooking!" Marinus shouts excitedly in the seat next to mine. I cross my eyes at him, hoping to divert his attention.

Father grumbles, hearing his squeal but continues doing his work.

I TUCK MARINUS INTO BED, caressing his sleeping face for a moment before standing and stepping carefully through his compact room. I close the door and let out my breath in relief. I was able to finally get him into bed.

He's too smart for his own good. It's like he knew I was planning on heading out after he fell asleep.

"Are you heading to the Siren then?" Father asks in a hushed tone, smoking his pipe in his chair.

The window closest to him billows the curtain lightly as the breeze finds its way in. It's cooler tonight than it was yesterday.

Perhaps that was just the booze.

I hum and nod my head, heading into my room. A twin mattress, with a frame to keep it up and off the floor, and a dresser is all that occupies the small space. I sit on the bed, leaning down to open the bottom dresser drawer, the sound of crumpling paper filling the room for a moment before I pull it back and see the beautiful material hidden inside.

This was your last gift to me, Mama.

Stripping off my basic trouser and puffy linen shirt, I put on the jewel-lined neck sleeveless top, a white line sewn straight down on the front and back. Its form fitting, but luckily for me, I pull out the white off the shoulder top, an intentional slit in the centre of it to give it slightly better form. Its golden-coloured hem pops against the plain colours it is surrounded with. The wind rattles my window a bit, and I peek out to see the city illuminated by the sunset glow. A small smile rests on my face as I quickly pull the burnt orange flowing shorts up around my hips, and then the thigh high black stockings.

I feel like a fool.

Bending down, I reach under the bed, pull out my light heeled black dress shoes and put them on.

"This better help us win," I say under my breath before heading out of my room. "I'll be back once it's over," I mutter to my dad, who glances towards me.

Was that a smile he just gave me?

I do a double take, but he's already turned his head. I leave the house and speed walk my way to the centre of the city to the Siren, where the performer competition is being held for this year's trade show. Events like this always come up around this time, but this is the only one I'd ever take part in.

It's taken me years to even do it, and she was supposed to be there. Front row.

My heels click against the stone, but it quickly fades to the background as the hollering of spirit-infused bodies crowd the walkways. I manoeuvre my way through, avoiding the mindless movements they all seem to make. Lanterns are lit everywhere, businesses that are normally getting ready to close have hired help for the extended hours they have specifically for the travelling troops, merchants, traders, guests from nearby villages and towns.

Just breathe, Mazu.

It feels like I am being swallowed by the waves of people, but I ride with it and find my way to the overflowing Siren. I force through a few large gents who don't understand that perhaps they should stand clear of a doorway. Every seat is taken, and a drink is in nearly everyone's hands.

"You came." Kellen grabs my arm to help guide me to a table she is sitting at with Lip and Mehl.

I greet them all with a smile, and they raise a glass. "We were holding out hope." Lip winks, chugging the rest of their stein, wiping their mouth to stop the small trickle of what mead slipped past their lips.

Mehl furrows her brow in disgust before laughing and patting the seat next to her. "We were hoping to have vocals. I don't think we would have had a shot at winning without you." She gives me a side hug that I pull out of before I think her flustered self was ready. "You are looking hot, by the way. You should dress up more!" She giggles.

"You should learn to watch your liquor intake," I tease. "Are you going to be able to play?"

Kellen laughs, sitting across from me. "You should know by now that she always seems to play better when she can't see completely straight."

We all chuckle, Kellen sliding the rest of her pint to me. I smirk at her and finish it off quickly.

"Excuse me!" a young woman shouts from standing on the stage. "Quiet down!" she shouts again, gaining most of the patrons' attention this time, though some are mindlessly chatting away. "The Sea Sing Song is officially on!"

The crowd erupts with shouts of excitement and laughter. All ready to be entertained and eager to play. My stomach drops and the feeling of dinner wanting to reverse itself is suddenly very present.

"We have the five finalists here, ready to give you a show!" The crowd hollers again, Mehl and Lip joining in. "Let us give a warm welcome to our first act, Seafarers!"

I clap along with the crowd as a group of six cram their way up onto the stage, picking up their needed instruments. Their tune is quick and erratic, my heart wanting to speed up just from the pace. A little loud for my tastes, making it hard to hear any of the words they are saying, but the crowd is bouncing around and drinks are spilling everywhere.

Mama, I hope you are here with me.

I carry in a bowl of clam chowder soup, Mother looking out the window. Her gaze is so far beyond the bed she is now confined to.

"I brought you soup." Her eyes turn and focus on me before she smiles and sits herself up more on the bed. "It's a bit hot."

She flattens the covers, and I set the bowl in her lap. "Thank you, darling."

Her hand comes up and caresses my head for a second before her brow furrows.

"What's wrong?" I ask, seeing her smile fade.

Mother shakes her head. "Nothing I want to burden you with."

I take her hand in mine. "Let me care for you. I promise I can bear it."

She sighs and nods. "I am–I am just sorry, Mazu." Her voice quiets and she drops her gaze. "I'm leaving this all on you."

"You're going to get better, Mama. You're not leaving," I state, firmly.

I squeeze her hand and she puts on a smile, meeting my gaze once more. "Right."

"I don't mind taking care of Dad and Ari in the meantime. I think Dad would work himself to illness. He doesn't know when to stop lately, it seems." I chuckle, and her smile falters. "He says he's saving up for a surprise for all of us." I quickly add on to try and reverse the worry.

"Mazu..." she mutters, reaching up with her other hand to grip the midnight blue oval pendant hanging from her neck.

I wince in pain; my hand automatically reaches down to caress the bruising dent in my shin. My eyes flicker up to see Kellen with a mug smile.

"Really?" I hiss.

She laughs, "Now's not the time to daze off."

Rolling my eyes, I focus on the stage where a different group is already ending their song.

I really was somewhere else. Wow.

"Sorry," I breathe out, earning another laugh from Kellen.

The young woman from before jumps back up on the stage and tries to quiet the crowds cheering for the band that just filed out.

"Hey," I say, turning to my friends. "I want you to do me a favour."

Mehl's eyes widen. "That's a first!"

Lip and Kellen wait to hear what it is.

I clear my throat. "When we get up there, can you play the same melody as Windbreak?"

They all furrow their brows. "Windbreak? That's not really a tavern song," Lip says, looking to Mehl before back to me.

"I know, but I have a song I want to sing," I explain.

Kellen nods. "Okay."

Lip and Mehl instantly nod, hearing Kellen's agreement to my sudden suggestion.

"Thank you." I smile, and Mehl just leans in, earning a head shake from me.

"Look at you, asking for stuff," she teases.

I shove her off and focus on the next band. The singer, an orcish male, closes his eyes and nods his head along with the beat of the drum before he starts singing. The song is talking about the first time he walked into a tavern, falling in love with the maid who brought him his drink. The guys holler and Kellen rolls her eyes in my peripheral.

We all clap as they wrap up and head off the stage, the young woman appearing once again. "Alrighty! We have come to our final band of the evening." The crowd all boos, but chuckles underlying their disapproval of the night coming to an end.

I swallow the lump in my throat, now regretting not staying home.

"We got this!" Mehl says to the lot of us.

"Please welcome The Waves!" The crowd hoots and hollers, and we get up and head towards the stage.

Now this is where I need to not pass out.

People move out of our way, Kellen taking the lead to guide us there. A few folks pat our shoulders, likely as a good luck gesture.

What if they all hate it? Why did I suggest for me to do a brand new song on a public stage? I am such an idiot.

Kellen looks back as she reaches the stage and raises her brows at me with a smile. "It'll be great."

I take a deep breath and follow her up on the stage, Lip right behind me.

Once Mehl reaches her drum, and Kellen settles with the lute, Lip smiles at me with the flute raised to their lips. I turn back to Mehl and nod my head. She leads us in with a soft beat, like rolling thunder in a storm cloud headed towards us.

♫

In a world of storm and strife, I set sail,
A heart too young, a face too frail,
But the ocean's call, it knew my name,
Tossed me in a game where the stakes were not the same.

Too young to bear this load,
Through the tempest's rage, my soul was towed,
Strong ain't the word, for my heart's been bruised,
In these waters deep, my youth was used.

Faces weathered, tales untold,
In a sailor's heart, the memories hold,
Battles fought on an endless sea,
A tale of strength, but that ain't a word to describe me.

Too young for this strife,
Navigating storms that cut like a knife,
Not strong, but tethered by the tide,
In these haunted waters, my innocence died.

Through the night, I've sailed alone,
Bearing burdens that weren't my own,
Trauma's anchor dragging deep,
In the shadows, where my dreams would sleep.

Too young to bear this load,
Through the tempest's rage, my soul was towed,
Strong ain't the word, for my heart's been bruised,
In these waters deep, my youth was used.

So, through the storms, I find my way,
A sailor's heart, a price to pay,
Not strong, but forged in the crucible,
Traumatised soul, yet somehow still usable.

Too young for this test,
In the ocean's arms, I lay to rest,
Not strong, but resilient through the strife,
A survivor's heart, navigating life.

♫

As the words leave my lips, I grip the necklace Mother gifted me days before her passing, hoping it brings me closer to her. The tavern stills, the joyous nature evaporating as they all look towards us. No one raising their drinks or swaying. My heart would sink, but it's elsewhere while singing this song. I close my eyes, hoping to block out all of their wide eyes or furrowed brows and just let the song release me from the grief.

I'll do what I have to do, Mama.

The raw emotion of these words slip past my closed lids, a single drop rolling down my cheek. It leaves me bare and open to every stranger intently watching. I open my eyes and see some of their mouths agape; their faces matching the turmoil this song speaks to.

It'll be enough just to give Ari the life he wants.

My voice fades as the song ends. I turn to Kellen, whose normally stoic expression is contorted, and she takes in a deep breath as she stares at me.

Quickly, I step back from the front of the stage and look to the crowd, where no one claps. They all stand there, still watching. My hand drops from my chest, Lip and Mehl moving around behind me. Turning to Kellen, she sets down the lute and gestures for me to get off the stage. As we take a step down, one person starts to clap somewhere in the back. Slowly, the rest of the room comes back to life and starts clapping, but it seems all too solemn. No hollering or shouting. Some raise their glasses to us as we make our way to the front of the tavern.

The young announcer gets back up on stage, her eyes a tad red. "Well, I think it's time to wrap it all up. The judges are finalising their decision now!" she shouts, trying to put energy back in the room. Some of the drunker folks fall right back into place and cheer.

People start talking again and finishing their glasses as we wait. Kellen and the rest keep glancing towards me, and my face reddens from the attention. A tall man, with grey hair curling around his ears and glasses resting on his nose, stands and hands the young woman a piece of parchment.

She gives the crowd a big smile before reading it. "Everyone played incredibly, but we have selected the winners!" Everyone claps. "In third place, we have The Waves!" The crowd claps.

"Third place? Her voice was so mesmerising though," a woman, sitting at the table where we were first seated, complains.

She really thought that?

I put on a smile and look happy to have at least placed.

"In second, we have The Sea Wenches!" The girl group all raise their fists and cheer. "And for our winners of this year's contest is, The Tavern Hearts!" The orcish singer from before jumps up on stage and raises his hands, clapping above his head, enjoying his victory.

I chew on my inner cheek, the guilt of ruining this for my group growing intensely. The people around us congratulate us and compliment our playing – my singing – but we lost.

She wanted me to win.

Kellen wraps an arm around my shoulder, and I shake my head as we all pile out of the tavern.

I couldn't even win for her.

"Stop, you're overthinking it. You had everyone tranced. So what if we didn't win," she says.

A scoff leaves my lips. "I should have just stuck to the plan. It's my fault for changing the song."

Mehl pinches my side. "We could have told you no, but we agreed to it. Heck of a new song, though, Zu! I was trying not to cry the whole time." She smiles, grabs Lip's hand and they dance around the street, bumping people's elbows as they go.

The ground begins to shake beneath our feet, the whole town circle silencing, the lanterns rattle and trees creak from whatever this shifting is. Kellen's grip tightens on me, and I glance at her now alarmingly sober appearance.

"What the infernum?" she mutters, looking around.

I glance with her. Everyone is confused and unsure of what is happening. My heart is in my throat. I look to the cliffs, but they are steady. Everyone is frozen in their place as the shake intensifies before quitting suddenly.

No one mutters a word, like we are all waiting for the cause to suddenly answer itself. Some set their drinks down and start filtering out after us.

Kellen lets go of me. "I need to go to work. Make sure that wasn't some attack or something," she mutters.

I grab her hand as she walks away. She looks back, locking her eyes onto mine. "Be careful," I say.

She smiles, the kind where her eyes squint. She nods and I release my grasp on her hand. Mehl and Lip return to my side.

"We will head home," I tell them. They both return with a solemn nod.

"Yeah, looks like the guards are about to make us," Lip says, pointing with their nose as some of the off-duty guards are in action, just as Kellen ran off to do.

They are pointing and gesturing for people to clear the circle.

"Kellen will let us know if they find anything out," Mehl chips in with a brief smile.

We quickly say our goodbyes and go our separate ways.

I wonder if Father and Ari felt it all the way out on the pier.

"Damn," I grumble under my breath, realising that if they did, it means that Marinus is likely awake.

Picking up the pace, I jog through the streets and down the steps as quickly as I can. I miss a step, and roll down the rest of them, a sharp pulse radiating from my knee. I ignore it and stand up just as the rumble starts again, but the sky lightens. My breath catches seeing the blackness of night turning a soft shade of grey, muting the bright stars to merely a whisper. Turning around, the grey gradually lightens, but the source seems far beyond us. The light flickers before it fades away.

My feet carry me home as I sprint across the pier. Gasping for air, I take out my key to unlock the door. The latch is already undone, so I open it.

"Dad!" I shout, not seeing him in the living area.

I close the door and walk in, not bothering to kick off my shoes. I walk into Marinus' room and see an empty bed.

"Dad? Ari?" I call out, leaving his room and heading to Father's.

Please tell me they didn't rush out trying to look for me.

I quickly turn around, heading back out. Pulling the door open, something swings towards my face. My instincts of watching for the swinging sail kicks in and I duck. But a fist grips at my hair, pulling me up. A man with a thick black beard forces my gaze to focus on him.

"Aren't you fast." He lifts the club he swung at me upwards and drives it back down hard.

CHAPTER THREE

My brain aches worse than a hangover, and my back is stiff. My eyes slowly flutter open, but there's nothing to see. Despite not feeling anything on my face, everything is completely dark. Like I got locked in a room with no lights, but I smell the sea water, and hear waves crashing, even the faint heat of the sun beating down on me, but my eyes can't take anything in.

What is happening?

Images of that man come to mind and I start to panic, thrashing against the ropes keeping my arms and legs tied behind me.

What did they do to me?

"Hello?" I shout out, grunting as I fight to get out of my binds.

I hear footsteps in the distance, approaching. The sound of dirt or gravel crunching under them.

"Who, who's there?" I shout again, stilling my thrashing.

I hear a chuckle. "What are you being so noisy for?" a man grumbles, kicking my side.

I try to hunch into myself, but the ropes restrict me as I seethe through my teeth from the sudden impact. He grabs my binds, pulling me upright so I am resting on my knees.

Why?

My head is reeling, not understanding what, where, who or why any of this is happening.

Some sick freaks who just want to see someone hurt?

"Colby, you can cut it out!" the man hovering over me yells out.

The thug holding me talks with his hands. He jerks my body along with the motion of how I assume he normally would when having a conversation.

I feel like a puppet.

"Why?" I hear a sigh from somewhere to the left of me.

"Because... I... Just do it, idiot!" the man next to me demands.

There's a moment of complete silence between them before I hear a faint, "Fine," from the guy apparently named Colby.

My vision instantly returns to me, like a fire was just lit inside my brain allowing for me to see.

I'm so confused.

"There, now she can see," he mutters, leaning forward to rest his elbows on his knees as he sits on one of the boulders.

Was that magicae?

A cliff west of Berkin, overlooking the ocean. I turn and see a roguish man, dressed in a black shirt, the lacing left undone and open. His hair is short but kept long in the front where it nearly covers his steel blue eyes glaring towards me.

He raises a brow as I continue to scowl at him.

The man hovering over me leans further so I can see him. "Goodie." He shows off his toothy grin, his teeth pointed like rugged daggers.

He's bald, has his large and hairy chest out for anyone to see, and is wearing old and dingy trousers that are stuffed into laced up brown leather boots.

"Why are you doing this? Who even are you?" I ask, my eyes darting between them, pulling at my binds again.

The man behind me shoves my face down into the dirt. My breath makes it fly up and into my eyes. As I inhale, the coarse and fine dust burns my throat and lungs.

Colby stands up from where he is sitting and says, "What's the point of making her see when you shove her back down, blinding her?" His voice is gruff.

"Cause I feel like it. Makes her more scared, putting a face behind the actions." He chuckles.

"I would disagree," Colby argues, walking up and squatting down in front of me.

The pressure being put on me lessens enough so I am not actively inhaling the earth.

Where is my father?

My eyes lift up to meet Colby's once more, and he tilts his head, as if waiting for something to happen with such a bored stare.

"Why bring me out here?" I ask, much quieter this time.

Colby furrows his brow for a second. "We're using you for money," he states before standing upright and looking behind him, hearing the sounds of hooves approaching us.

Who do they think is going to be paying for me?

I can see a navy box behind the horse, blurry as they are, barely visible from where I am.

"Boss is coming," the large man says, earning a glare from Colby as he looks over his shoulder at him.

"Really, Biggie? I would have never guessed that we would be seeing the boss at the specified location we agreed to meet at"—he faces back towards the carriage—"crazy."

"You don't have to be such an arse," Biggie growls.

I hear a low chuckle coming from Colby.

"You have the wrong person!" I shout, earning a kick from the oaf behind me. I let out a grunt. "My family isn't rich," I finish through gritted teeth.

"I don't think you even know who your family is," Colby retorts, stepping away from me.

The carriage pulls up, dust filling the air. Colby approaches and opens the door, extending a hand to help someone out of it. A pale hand grips his black-leathered gloved hand. Her silver curls bounce around her shoulders, her floor length blue gown brushes over the dirt and her copper eyes land on me. She smiles and takes a few steps closer. Colby reaches into the carriage, grunting from the strain of tugging out whatever he is fetching.

"Hi there," their boss says, her voice sickeningly sweet.

Colby reels back and pulls out my father before throwing him to the ground. My eyes widen, and my heart drops.

Do they have Ari?

She doesn't turn, hearing my father's painful wince, but continues to just smile plainly at me. "I hope they weren't too rough with you, dear," she starts, waving her hand at Biggie, who instantly picks me up so I'm kneeling in front of her. "It is unfortunate that we had no other choice but to involve you and your sweet little brother."

Fuck, fuck, fuck.

My eyes dart past her once more and see Ari holding onto Colby's hand as he steps out of the carriage. Ari's eyes are so red, his nose running. His free hand clutches onto his chest, but his pained expression changes as he sees me. His eyes widen, and he lets go of Colby's hand and runs to me. My lip trembles and they let him make his way to me, his little arms gripping onto me. I pull at my restrains again, instinctively wanting to wrap my arms around him.

"Hey, buddy." I try to say in the most calm tone I can manage. I lean my head to rest against his. "You okay?"

Their eyes are on us, watching our interaction.

Marinus sniffles, but nods his head, a little whimper leaving his lips. "They hurt Daddy."

I look over to my father, whose face is swollen, bruises already forming from where I am sure a club, fist, or boot were meeting his face.

What's happening, Dad?

I close my eyes tightly, wanting to blink this all away.

"Biggie, I don't think she really needs those binds anymore. I think she understands what's going on," the boss says, as I reopen my eyes and glare towards her.

"We aren't as rich as you might think," I state.

Biggie unsheathes a dagger from his belt and bends down to cut the rope. I nearly topple over from the release, but I catch myself and wrap my arms around Marinus.

The boss smiles widely, pulling a letter out of her brazier, holding it up like I'm supposed to recognise it. "You're correct. You are not all that rich, but your family ties are."

I shake my head. "You mean my mother's side?" Father is the last of his line of family after his brother died in a fishing accident. "If they were rich, they would have helped us out when she was sick."

My brows knit together as she just smiles wider, but she breaks our eye contact as her gaze shifts to my father. "Would you like to explain?"

His forehead drips with perspiration, his mouth glued together in a fine line and his eyes inspecting every speck of dirt on the ground.

"Fine," she sighs, "read for yourself." She tosses it down in front of me, and I pick it up without looking away from Father.

> *Sir Hali,*
>
> *I write this with the deepest of condolences hearing of Aunt Nami's aliment. From what the latest letter had stated, her condition has become irreversible. We apologise for our absence during this difficult time for your family. Seems your communications were not being delivered to the correct hands.*
>
> *My mother has since moved back to her family home in Draco, but I will be sure to notify her of any further updates regarding my aunt.*
>
> *In the meantime, please let me know if there is anything I can do to assist you.*
>
> *With my father's passing, there is an opportunity for us to mend the bridge of our families.*
>
> *I do hope you take me up on that.*
>
> *Best regards,*
> *King Kage Felguard.*

My breath catches, my grip wrinkling the parchment. Mother never mentioned this. "Dad... is this true?" My voice is a whisper.

He finally raises his line of sight, catching mine for a brief moment. "They were never going to help us, Mazu. We wrote them so many times but they—" His face gets kicked, the boss' heel connecting with his nose.

I wince, seeing him get hurt like that, my jaw clenching as I continue to stare like a look from me could kill them.

We're related to a king?

"No one cares about that," she states. "The important thing is that you"—she points towards me—"are going to take him up on his offer."

"Who the infernum even are you?" I ask, standing slowly, Ari gripping onto my legs.

She raises a brow, and Colby takes a step closer to me. "Little ol' me? Well, I'm Renna, but you only really need to know that I'm in charge."

Renna snaps her fingers and Colby rushes forwards, my eyes going dark for a split second. My legs pull out from under me, and Ari's screaming at the top of his lungs as his grip is ripped off of me.

"Wait, no!" I shout, turning in time to see Colby holding Ari over the cliff by his neck. "No!"

Marinus is sobbing, pulling with all his might, trying to get out of Colby's grasp. "Zuzu!" he cries out.

I scramble to my feet and run towards them, but Colby sighs and quickly pulls out his sword and raises it. I'm barely able to stop in time before the blade pierces me. A small prick stinging my chest.

The boss chuckles over Marinus' screams. "Feeling motivated yet?" she explains.

I don't glance back. Instead, I meet Colby's blank stare. "Please don't do this. He's a child."

Colby shifts his gaze, tightening his jaw.

"This is just to show you how serious we are, dear. Your father will be next if you don't pull through," she explains. My heart drops in realisation that this isn't just a threat. "Colby. Let's get this over with," the boss commands.

I glance behind me for a split second, hoping to plead, but she's already turned her back to this scene. Looking at Marinus, Colby already let go of his hold on him. I knock Colby's blade to the side, causing his gaze to focus on me, but my feet are already carrying me to the edge. Marinus dips past the ledge and my body slams down, reaching out.

I grip onto Marinus' hand tightly, my muscles screaming at me as his weight pulls me down, further over the edge of the cliff. My body strains and my arm shakes as I try pulling him up. Marinus reaches with his other hand to climb the edge, but any grip he finds breaks and falls down into the crashing waves.

"Reach further, Ari!" I shout, straining through the pain.

"Well, isn't that annoying," the boss says from somewhere over topside.

Colby leans down and grabs onto my arm, lifting us both slightly from the cliff's edge. The grip I have on Marinus loosens.

Colby grunts at the strain of lifting us. "You know, we will just throw him over again."

My eyes begin to water as I look down into Marinus' wide and terrified ones. "Zu!" he screams out, desperately still trying to climb up.

My grip weakens more as a soft sob escapes my lips. "I'm not letting you go."

Marinus nods, trusting me. Colby lifts us further up.

What am I supposed to do? How do I get us out of this? How can I save him?

My eyes lift above the edge, seeing her smirk, mocking our tears and desperate cries.

"Ari, I will never let you go," I say, giving him that pathetic tear-filled smile he gave me the day we buried our mother. "Never alone."

Colby's expression changes into panic as he sees my feet push against the cliff's wall. He releases his grasp on me, and Marinus screams as we begin to fall. I pull him close, wrapping my arms around him, squeezing tightly.

"Smile, Ari," I mutter into his ear, turning us in the air so my back hits first.

Marinus squeezes back, his body shaking viscerally. "I'm trying."

Looking up to the blue velvet sky, I let out my breath and close my eyes as the sound of the crashing waves becomes deafening.

CHAPTER FOUR

♫

The seas where shadows play,
A seafarer's soul in twilight grey,
Lost in waves,
An innocence given way.

Oh, the sea, a mirror true,
Reflects the dreams you never knew,
Oh, the sea, a sacred hymn,
An ancient tale, the origin,

The salt-stained breeze, a timeless song,
Awakens spirits, dormant long,
A dance with waves, a cosmic tide,
Unveils the self that seeks to hide.

Oh, the sea, a mirror true,

Reflects the dreams you never knew,
Oh, the sea, a sacred hymn,
An ancient tale, the origin,

Upon the seas of fate,
Let the soul and ocean mate,
For in their union, a story's spun,
Two become one.

♬

My eyes slowly blink open, my body feeling caressed and weightless. A soft light shines above me, glimmering and distorted through the water's surface.

I should be swimming up; I should be fighting for my life. I should be scared.

The water feels warm and welcoming. I open my mouth, bubbles of air making their way to the surface. My hair swims around me in tendrils, and a soft smile finds me. I reach upwards to see the glowing spots dance on my skin.

Is this what death is like?

My eyes flutter, my chest convulsing, but I shake my head slowly, pushing out the pain spreading across my chest. My hair is now obstructing the view.

"Mazu..." I turn my head towards the disembodied voice.

It sounds so far away, and I see nothing but the slow fade to black.

I convulse again, my eyes shutting firmly as I gasp.

"Mazu!" Ari shouts in my ear.

Opening my eyes, the copper colour of an eroded wet rock cradles me, choppy waves splashing against my back.

Coughing a few times, bits of mucus and sea water burn my

throat as it comes back up. I turn to see Marinus shaking under my arm, gripping onto the rock and my arm.

"I can't help," he whimpers, and I shake my head, trying to focus, but my vision feels cloudy.

A wave crashes into us. Marinus braces for it, but I slip further down, realising this is what he is referring to.

My muscles strain as I pull myself back up. "What happened?" I grunt, as I turn over to sit on top of the rock before reaching down and grabbing Ari's arms to lift him up next to me.

"You... swam us... here..." he chatters, his soaked body pressing into my side.

I raise a hand to my head as it spins, my eyes rolling to the back of my head from the pressure. I lean into him, needing some support. Glancing upwards, the peak of the cliff is hanging over us, shading us from the sun and leaving us to the cool breeze hitting us along with the sea spray.

"We're gonna be okay," I whisper in a hoarse voice.

Kissing the top of his head, he nods and says, "I know."

I'm not sure how many sunshifts pass while I try to regain my composure. A part of me still feels like I'm drifting out to sea while the other is sat on this rock, holding my brother whose lips are now chapped and skin dry from the salt. Our hair is stiff and clothes are still damp.

We need to get to the beach, or any shore, something that will not leave us stranded here. My body is sore, and I should feel lucky that's all I'm feeling. We both should be dead, or at least seriously injured.

Don't think about it.

I look out to the horizon versus my waterlogged shoes. No signs of ships, which is both good or bad. My guess is, they know we are still alive. I don't pretend to be fully aware of the people that just tried to kill my brother, but leaving things up to chance doesn't seem like it would fit their motive. Closing my eyes, I imagine the map my teachers showed us, an old one that showed us all the nooks and crannies carved into the cliffs along the coast's edge. Kellen and I used to say all the time that we would make one of them our secret hideout. A place to run away to when we didn't want to deal with the real world.

We need to move.

"Ari," I mutter, "do you think you could swim?"

I pull back from our huddle to look at him. His eyes are a bit swollen.

"Yeah." He nods, releasing me from his grasp.

"Breathe, Mazu," Mother says, rubbing circles on my back.

My hands clutch the sides of the small rowboat.

"Mommy, I'm scared..." I whimper, looking at the open sea around us.

She smiles at me. "Do you remember that story I told you, the one where the little girl is lost at sea?"

I nod slowly. "Yeah..."

"And can you tell me what happened?" she asks.

I stop myself from looking at the terrifying waters and focus on her. "She sang. She sang, and the Seasire saved her."

"Right, and do you remember the song?" She brings up her hand to caress my cheek. "Do you want to sing it together?"

"We just need to head that way, okay?" I say, pointing east.

There should be a sea cave just a mile or two towards the direction of Berkin. Even if they know about it, it's better than being stuck on this rock.

Marinus jumps in next to me, and I quickly pull him up above the water. "Don't stop swimming. If you get tired, you have to flip on your back and just keep rotating between those two. If you stop, it'll be harder to start again," I remind him, and he nods.

I pace myself, being mindful of his swimming speed. With a slower pace, at least, I can try to conserve some energy if he gets tired and forces me into needing to do the work for both of us. We swim a few metres away from the cliff wall, careful not to get cut on any rocks, and to try and avoid being caught in the waves breaking against the hard service.

"Keep going, Ari."

He just grunts back at my words of encouragement.

MARINUS CLUTCHES onto my back as I continue our swim; it's getting harder to fight against the pull of the waves. My body wants me to rest, but I know there has to be a bank somewhere close by.

"We gotta switch over, buddy." The words come out breathy. He lets go of me, and I flip over onto my back.

I grab his collar, and as he floats on his back and I pull him along with me, I kick again. The sun is now casting deep shadows as it prepares to set. I wish I would have known I was going to be thrown from a cliff. I wouldn't have worn these clothes. Then again, maybe I would have just brought a change of clothes since I needed them for the show.

Wow. I think I'm drinking too much of this salt water.

I just have to keep distracting myself, making sure I keep my body moving and not think about how every muscle in my body is straining to keep moving.

Think of anything else.

"Go get her." I hear my mother command from behind the white curtain.

Father walks past it, giving me a quick glance of her laying in the healer's bed.

He gives me one of those rare smiles. "Want to meet him?" His voice is quiet and solemn.

I nod and stand from the wooden stool one of the healers got for me. Tentatively, I walk forwards, pulling back the curtain to walk in, my mother holding a blanket. Her eyes have dark bags under them, sweat speckled across her forehead.

"Mazu, come closer. Let him see you," she whispers, as she repositions herself to sit up more.

I walk over, sitting on the bed next to her, peeking over and into the swaddle of blankets. His little curls stuck going in funny directions, and bright big brown eyes looking off into another world.

A chuckle slips out, and I put a hand up to my mouth to keep quiet, but his eyes flicker over to look at me.

"This is your brother, Marinus. Marinus, this is your big sister, Mazu." She smiles and sticks him out towards me.

My eyes widen, but I create a basket with my arms for her to set him in. I stare down at him. Everything about him seems so fragile. My heart hurts a bit, and my brow furrows.

How can something so perfect exist?

Mother's hand reaches up and wipes a tear from my face, making me lock eyes with her. She laughs, looking at my father, who has wandered to my other side.

"Welcome, Ari," I whisper, leaning down and giving him a small kiss on the forehead.

It takes the last of my energy to swim us to the closest rock cluster inside the cave. Pulling myself up onto it, Ari tugs on my shirt to try and help. I make it further up, where I won't be submerged in the water, but the moment I do, my body collapses.

That was further than a mile.

Ari shivers beside me, his teeth chattering echoes through the cave. I can feel my body respond to the cool breeze that passes over my soaking wet clothes and salty skin.

"Stay close, Ari..." My voice is barely audible over the waves that curl against the rocks. "I need to rest."

My eyes blink a few times, everything around me looks muted in colour, my lungs are on fire, my mind hazy and pounding. My eyelids grow far heavier than they ever have, but soft strokes on my cheeks pull them open. Ari's fingers caress my face, trying to comfort me as I fall to sleep just like I have done for him so many times. I allow myself to rest, a tear slipping past my lashes.

Chapter Five

Ari's body is pressed tightly against mine, our clothes and hair stiff from the dried salt water. My lips are chapped and my mouth dry. It is well into the day, the shadows on the rocks just outside the cave letting me know it is past noon. He's been complaining about being hungry, but I'm not sure how we are going to get out of this one. My body is achy from the strain I put on it just to get us this far. The next bank we could potentially climb our way to a main road is further than what I think we swam yesterday, meaning there's no way for us to get there. A part of me is waiting for some miracle, like the one that saved us from that fall yesterday, but how many blessings can a person have.

As time passes on, and no ships cross this way, I worry we shouldn't have been saved at all. That a death like that would have actually been more merciful than the one we are looking at right now.

"We are in trouble... aren't we," Marinus whispers, his arms tighten around my waist.

I want to tell him the truth, but I can't think of how I am supposed to actually say it. 'We're gonna die here' seems far too brutal, but not saying anything isn't an option.

"Yeah, buddy," I admit. "But we are not giving up yet."

He nods, and just him accepting that nearly breaks my composure. Ari doesn't deserve this. All the pain he has been put through at such a young age.

I should have protected him, been a better sister.

Closing my eyes, I try to imagine the map once again, but no matter how badly I want the bank to be closer, I know that it isn't. We've lost too much time today; we wouldn't make it even close by the time low tide came back in, which puts us at risk for being shoved up against the cliffs. We barely survived it coming into this cave.

"Zuzu!" Ari shouts, making me jump.

My eyes open and I immediately see what caught his eye.

A ship.

"Close your eyes!" I tell him, quickly shimmying my orange shorts off.

I run along the rocks to get as close to the cave's mouth as I can before diving into the water, ignoring my body's signals of pain and discomfort. Swimming as quickly as possible, I make my way out of the mouth of the cave and raise my shorts in the air, waving them around to hopefully attract their attention.

"Help!" I scream. "Help us!"

The ship isn't very far, but far enough where it would be humanly impossible to swim fast enough to catch it.

"Man overboard!" I scream again.

It's a small vessel, could hold maybe twenty aboard it, but only really needs two or three to run it.

"Help—" My voice cuts off seeing the silhouette of a person looking towards me.

They point in my direction as they turn around to likely speak to whoever else is onboard with them.

They disappear, and the sails quickly shift around to point them in our direction.

"Ari! Come jump and swim to me!" I call out to him. Turning around, I see him hesitate as he looks at the slight drop and the rocks surrounding the nearest edge. "You can do this. Get a running start, and jump as far as you can. The moment you hit the water, you need to swim as hard and as fast as you can."

I start making my way towards him, ready to grab him if he isn't strong enough.

"Zu, it's too tall!" he yells, shaking his head and taking a few steps back. "I can't do it."

"Yes, you can. We survived a much bigger fall, right? You can do this." His fists tighten at his side, hearing my words. "The ship won't be able to come into the cave, so we need to go to them," I add, letting him know he doesn't have a choice.

He disappears over the edge, but it's only a moment before I hear the hasted steps and his body leaping into the air. He grabs his nose a second before he hits the water, out of the visible rocks' paths. I don't realise I held my breath until his head pops up out of the water.

"Swim!" I remind him, and I can see the water splashing up from behind him as he kicks his feet.

I swim further towards him, grabbing his shirt and pulling him to me the rest of the way. He climbs onto my back, my head dipping underwater for a moment from the weight, but I kick harder to propel us forwards, closer to the ship.

Once we get close enough, someone throws a ladder over the ship's side. I have Ari climb up first, taking a moment to put my shorts back on, before climbing up after him.

"Thank you, you are saving us." My breath is heavy before I straighten up and face our saviours.

A familiar suntanned woman smiles and pats the wet head of Ari standing in front of her. "Well now, aren't you two soggy little dolls!" Her boisterous voice combats the despair we're bringing aboard.

"Crey..." I mutter.

As my eyes meet hers, every limb on my body feels five times their weight. The gaze I'm trying to maintain is going hazy.

"Mazu?" Arms wrap around me as I fall to my knees. "What has happened to you?"

The floorboards seem weathered. Father makes us reseal the decks every year. I always find it so tedious, but I understand if this is what it looks like when you don't. There are cracks running through the whole plank.

Ari starts crying, and I raise my head to see him kneeling in front of me. I reach out my hand and rest it on his head. "We're safe now..."

"Keep up," Father mutters, gesturing for me to run to remain at his side as we walk down the cobbled road. "We're already running late."

His long strides are hard to keep up with. My hand reaches for his, but he crosses his arms in front of his chest. Instead, my hand grips around the hem of his shirt, trying to help keep him at a pace I can walk. This is the first time he is taking me with him to the community meeting with the other fishermen.

I forgot to put socks on.

The inside of my boots are rubbing against the back of my heels and ankles, likely the beginning of blisters. Mamma normally helps me with getting ready before I leave the house, but she was feeling extra tired today. Father said I needed to leave her alone and get ready by myself.

My fingers hold on to the fabric of his shirt tighter as we approach a large building. It has two windows on either side of the weathered blue door.

The mail slot matches the gold colour of the knocker that Father uses as we reach the door. "Be a good girl and stay by me, okay? Don't get in anyone's way and be quiet."

I nod my head and shift myself behind his leg as the door opens. A woman with wavy red hair and bright blue eyes smiles warmly at my father, welcoming him in before her gaze shifts down to meet mine.

Hiding myself a little more makes her chuckle. "Don't be so shy, we're practically family!"

She's loud.

Father pulls me out from my hiding spot by the back of my shirt. "Say hi, Mazu. This is Crey."

"Hi," I mutter.

Crey just smiles and moves to the side so we can walk inside. The interior is filled with people who are already standing shoulder to shoulder. They pushed all the benches and tables to the far side of the room, allowing them to stand in the centre of the room. The red-headed lady pats my father's back before squeezing through the crowd to jump up onto the bar so she is overlooking all of us. I try to make myself smaller and cling to my father's side as I accidentally brush against some strangers.

"Mazu, you're going to make me trip," my father mutters as he takes a tiny step forward.

I let go of him and look up at the new faces, some of

which smile down at me. My eyes shift away from one of them, drifting my attention back towards the woman standing on the bar, trying to quiet everyone down.

Her eyes lock on with mine as the noise dwindles. "You, come here. You'll get crushed by these brutes." She chuckles and gestures me forwards.

"Go on," my father says, nodding his head towards the bar.

I stare at my father for a moment longer before doing as I'm told and squeezing through the legs of the folks in the room. Another lady helps me up onto the bar so I can stand next to Crey.

Her hand pats my head. "There, much better." Smiling up at her, she ruffles my hair before turning her attention back on the crowd that is staring towards us. "The guards have failed us more often than not. These pirates are taking advantage of us at every turn, and I know we all feel the rage of losing such immeasurable life as we have on the Trove's ship this past mooncycle."

Father had talked to Mother about some bad people attacking a fisherman's boat. I know he would be mad if he knew I listened to their conversation, but I was so bored being in my room.

"We need to defend ourselves. Let them all know that we will not just allow our own to be taken advantage of. When the call comes, we all must gather to defend our own!" Crey exclaims, bending down and grabbing a horn.

The crowd nods and shouts their agreements.

SHE'S BEEN the one who has held my father – no, our community – to a higher standard. Always the one to look out for others.

Crey had let us rest on her boat while they took us back to

Berkin. She was kind, not asking too many questions, though I could tell she was hoping I would just come out with it.

"We're about to dock," she says, looking down at us huddled together on the deck floor. "I'll have Lars walk back with you, if just to make sure you don't pass out on the way home." Her tone is mocking, but I can see the softness around her eyes.

There are probably scenarios running through her head, but I doubt she'd ever be able to come up with what really just transpired.

"I don't want to burd—"

Crey waves my sentence off. She points a finger at me. "You need to learn to just accept the help."

Now she kinda sounds like Kellen.

I smile and nod. "Thank you."

Though, a part of me still wants to fight back. Lars may be capable, but I don't want to put him in harm's way. He could very well be just someone to witness if those people come back and try to kill us.

Standing up, my heart warms seeing the familiar sight of the layered metropolis. I pull Ari up as they dock the ship. Crey gives each of us a pat on the back as we hop off the modest fishing boat.

"Crey, we owe you!" I shout up at her as Lars walks up from behind us.

"Write a song about my heroic rescue!" she teases, her red hair waving us goodbye as it blows in the wind.

Lars towers over the two of us, giving me some peace that he at least looks imposing. Though, in reality, he has always been quite shy. He doesn't say much on our way back to the house, but I'm very grateful for it.

"Are you alright to be on your own?" he asks softly, looking down at me.

I give him a smile. "Yes. Of course. I appreciate you walking us back."

He hums. "It's no trouble." His gaze shifts to my ruined and still damp clothes. "You were wearing those for your performance."

I grip Ari's hand tighter.

Lars' eyes shift back to meet mine. "If you're in trouble—"

"We will be okay... really," I say quickly, cutting him off.

"It's okay to ask for help if you need it, Mazu," he states.

A part of me wants to scoff. He has no idea the weight I would be putting on someone by asking for their help. I can hardly wrap my head around what has transpired, let alone allowing him or anyone to unknowingly be a part of this.

I furrow my brows. "Thank you, Lars, but you've all helped us out more than you know."

He nods. "Okay then."

We wave him off and I turn to my front door, my hand reaching into my pocket for my keys.

Of course.

I sigh and softly bang my head against the door.

"Aren't we going in?" Ari asks.

"I—" The unlocking of the door startles me. My instincts have me reaching down and grabbing my brother.

My breath catches though, as Kellen steps through the door. I set Ari down and run to her, wrapping my arms around her neck. She quickly returns the embrace.

"You were supposed to come home right away, you idiot." Her words are quiet.

I chuckle, the emotions I've been trying to keep at bay suddenly finding their way to my throat. "Yeah... I know."

Kellen pulls back from the embrace, looking me over and down to Ari, who is clutching to my leg. "What the infernum happened to you two?"

My lips tremble, my mind trying to grasp the situation we were in, the information I'm still struggling to even come to terms with. "A lot..."

The feeling of my salt ridden clothes and crusted hair finally becomes more obvious to me. The slight chill that has been creeping into my bones since we fell into the water is now making my hands shake ever so slightly.

She nods. "Clearly... Well, come inside."

We migrate to the living room, and I'm quick to lock the door behind us. I blink a few times to try and rid myself of the teary vision threatening to expose the heartache I'm really feeling.

Keep it together.

"Ari, we need to get you in the bath," I mutter, as I close the curtains around the house, only leaving small cracks for the sun to dimly light the interior.

"I'll take care of him. You go get changed for now and rest," Kellen states.

I furrow my brows, but she takes Ari's hand and walks off to the bathroom. A sigh leaves my lips. I head into my room and strip out of my clothes, finding some loose trousers and a blouse to put on for the time being until I bathe myself.

They will come for us.

My heart tightens at the thought, but I shake my head and walk into the kitchen. I have to take care of Ari, and myself, right now. Talking to the authorities will come once I can fill his stomach.

I start making lunch for all of us. Sandwiches, not the best choice, but something easy I can make, and a lot of.

You aren't going to be able to keep him safe. You're going to get him killed.

My grip on the knife tightens as I cut the bread.

"Stop it," I mutter through a strained voice.

Dad's probably dead or being forced to commit treason as we speak. You left him there.

I drop the knife and rest my head against the countertop, my hands gripping the hair on the back of my head.

"Stop thinking, Mazu. Stop," I whimper.

In. 1,2,3,4,5,6,7,8,9,10. Out. 1,2,3,4,5,6,7,8,9,10.

I smack my head against the counter lightly before forcing myself to stand upright and finish making our food. As I set the table, I hear the murmurs of Kellen and Ari talking.

She's good.

My feet carry me over to the bathroom door, being mindful as to not make my approach heard. I press my ear against the wood and close my eyes to try and listen in.

"It was... really scary, but Zuzu jumped right after me and saved us..." His tone is too sombre for a youngin his age.

Kellen is silent for a moment, and a part of me is wishing I could see her face. "She jumped?"

"Yeah. She hugged me super tight and there was this blue and white light that was swirling around us," Ari explains. "You know what... it must have been Mama!" His tone perks up. "Mama saved us!"

"Yeah, buddy... that must be it." Kellen's voice is quieter, but I'm sure she is putting a smile on for him right now. "We should get you out of the water and dried off."

"Alrighty," he says before I gingerly step back towards the kitchen with them wrapping up.

At least Ari doesn't know the real reasons behind why all of this happened. I can make something up, make him feel like this was an adventure that he's heard about in the stories Mother and I have read to him. Not to mention Kellen not having to find out. I don't want to lie to her, but I know if I tell her, she will force my hand and do something crazy. I'm not sure how I am going to save Ari from all of this, but I will figure it out.

The patter of my brother's steps plasters a smile on my face as I turn to look down at him. "Hungry?"

We all take our seats; Ari and I are quick to eat. His are cut up into mini sandwiches, helping him chew them easier.

"You guys are starved." We both nod in response to Kellen's comment as our mouths are full.

I chew my food enough to mumble, "After this, you're taking a nap."

Marinus furrows his brow at me and shakes his head. I raise a brow at him and he slumps in his chair.

Kellen's chuckle draws my attention though, her eyes shifting from Ari onto me. Her smile falls a bit as she takes in my appearance.

As we finish up, Kellen shoo's me off to take a bath. The cold water is not the most relaxing, but all I need it to do is get rid of the salt dried on my body.

What am I going to do?

Ari can't stay here. I'll need to take him to Mrs Relch, or maybe Kellen could take him to her place for a while. I'll go to the authorities and see what can be done. It'll be getting dark and I figure that is when they will come back.

I stand up and dry myself off, though drops of water still drip from my hair as I finish getting dressed.

"That was fast," Kellen says as I come out into the living room.

She is sitting in my chair, looking up at me as I approach her. "Kellen..."

"No." Her tone firm and gaze unwavering.

I furrow my brow. "You didn't know what I was going to say."

"But I do." She stands up, facing me. "You want Ari out of

the way so you can go and deal with these thugs who threatened you, right?"

I purse my lips and just stare at her.

"What did they even want? Does your dad have some debts or something? Why didn't you come find me?" Her normally stoic stature is more pleading as she grips onto the back of the chair. "I want to help."

"There was no time to get you, Kellen. I came home, and the next thing I knew I was tied up and laying down near the edge of a cliff with these people who are threatening my family for money because apparently we are related to the King of Felguard." It all comes out of me like vomit. "I don't know where my father is, and I honestly don't want to think about what could be happening or has happened to him." I take a sharp inhale. "When I saw that guy throw Ari off the cliff, I couldn't stop myself. I couldn't watch it happen. I don't know how we survived, but we did." My hand clutches onto my shirt. "And the fact that I know they are going to be coming back, I need to get him somewhere safe. I need him safe—"

Kellen wraps her arms around me tightly, her hand cradling the back of my head and fingers gripping lightly on to my hair. "Breathe."

I gasp for air and in my exhale, my body shakes and tears start running down my face. "I... I—"

"Shh." Her voice is quiet and her embrace tightens. "I know. We will get him somewhere safe. I'm not letting you do this alone."

I shake my head, my hands moving so I can return her embrace. "I can't let you do that..."

She pulls back enough so I can look into her eyes. "You don't have to be strong with me, Mazu..." My lip trembles, but I bite it to stop. "I... I can't even imagine how you are processing all of this in your head, but what I know is, I'm not leaving your side. Never."

"But, what if—" She tightens the grip on my hair ever so slightly, making my stance drop.

"I am good for more than just being the buddy you drink your sorrows away with. There is nothing I wouldn't do for you. So stop thinking about what could happen to me, because all I'm concerned about is what is actually happening to you." My eyes search hers, trying to find any wavering, but her gaze is steady.

What did I ever do to deserve her?

Closing the distance between us, I embrace her again, feeling the tension in my body relax a bit in her arms. Kellen drops the gentle grip on my hair and moves her hand to my back, rubbing circles while her other hand pulls me close against her.

As much as I want to stay like this...

I pull back slowly, watching her furrow her brow as she examines my face, like trying to determine my thoughts from my expression.

"We need to get Ari to the Relch's. It's going to be dark soon, and they will probably come here once it is."

Kellen drops her arms and nods.

I take a step back before turning and heading towards Ari's room.

"Then, you and I will go to the guard's centre and tell them what's going on," she states, obviously feeling the need to clarify my next steps.

The door creaks open slightly as I peek in. His black curls are a mess from not combing them after his shower.

"Ari..." I hum. Kneeling down next to his bed, I bring my hand up and pet his head. "We need to go."

His eyelids twitch before his little hand comes up and rubs

against his face. A quiet whine escaping him. A prick pierces my heart for a moment, a pain shooting through me as I watch him.

What am I going to say to him? How can I explain this when I don't even know what is going to happen?

I scoop him up and into my arms, earning whimpers of protest from him as his eyes slowly blink open.

"Zuzu?" Ari mumbles.

I carry him out into the living room and set him down on Father's chair where he sits up, but his head keeps falling forwards from the sleep trying to overtake him.

"Kellen?" I call out, as she is no longer in the living room.

A moment passes. "I'm grabbing some stuff," she calls back from my bedroom; its door ajar.

I grab Ari's shoes and put them on him before I put on my own.

Kellen had the right idea.

Walking back into Ari's room, I pull out some extra clothes and some of his favourite toys before packing them in an extra sack we kept in the kitchen.

"Where are we going?" Ari asks, his voice soft.

I smile at him. "To visit with Mrs Relch," I murmur as Kellen rejoins us in the living room with my pack on her back.

"Let's go."

CHAPTER SIX

"I AM SO sorry to be doing this..." My voice is soft and my head is bowed slightly towards Mrs Relch.

She sighs, her hand patting my head gently. "I can't say I understand, but I can tell that this is serious." I lift my eyes to meet her gaze. "We will watch after him, for as long as you need."

A kind smile forms on my face as I look at her. Kellen pushes herself back upright from where she was leaning against the wall.

Mrs Relch looks at her as she approaches my side. "Kellen, make sure to take care of Mazu. Even when she may not want you to."

Furrowing my brow, I open my mouth to protest.

"I will," Kellen states, cutting the words that were preparing to come out, giving me a smirk.

I give her a sideways glance. "We can talk about that later," I mutter under my breath to Kellen before I walk to the back room where Ari is laying down.

Dodger raises his head, his long drooly tongue hanging out as he lays at the foot of the bed Ari is occupying.

His little head pops up and I smile. "Zuzu? Are we staying here tonight?"

"You'll be staying here, but—" I place myself onto the edge of the bed, as he sits up with his eyes wide.

His little hand grips onto my shirt. "You are too, right?"

My smile wavers, my hand moving to rest on top of his. "Ari... I have to go make sure those bad guys never bother us again. Once I do, I'll be back."

His eyes start to water, and I close mine for a moment to make sure mine don't.

"Please don't go..." he whimpers.

I really don't want to.

Leaning forward, I rest my forehead against his. "I'm going to go find Father and ensure you're safe. I have to."

Not that I know what really ended up with our father. I don't think I even want to know; I don't think I could bear anything other than he is okay.

Ari's cries weaken my heart. I know this seems cruel, and he might never really understand, but I can't risk losing him. He is better off here than any life I can give him on the run. Even with the help of Kellen, we won't be well off by any means.

He doesn't deserve any of this hurt.

I gently guide him to lay back down. "I'll sing you to sleep." My voice is soft.

"I won't. I won't sleep until you come back!" he argues, sniffling a bit.

A sigh escapes me, but I keep smiling, my hand coming up to pet his head.

♫

The moonlight gently kisses the sea,
A lullaby whispers, drifting to me,
Close your eyes, let worries depart,
In the cradle of waves, find rest for your heart.

Hush-a-bye, sail into dreams,
Softly, my love, where the starlight gleams,
Tomorrow awaits, with the morning light,
Sleep softly, dear one, in the arms of the night.

The waves, they murmur a tale of peace,
Serenading the worries that long to cease,
Stars above, like guardian angel,
Watch over your dreams and keep them stable.

Hush-a-bye, sail into dreams,
Softly, my love, where the starlight gleams,
Tomorrow awaits, with the morning light,
Sleep softly, dear one, in the arms of the night.

The sails of your dreams catch your strained breaths,
Guiding you to blissful calming in your mind's ocean depths.
To wake anew with the morning tide,
Embraced by the sun, your fears will all subside.

So, lay your head on the pillow of the sea,
Let go of sorrows, let your spirit roam free,
In the cradle of night, find sweet reprieve,
For tomorrow, my love, the sun will relieve.

Hush-a-bye, sail into dreams,

Softly, my love, where the starlight gleams,
Tomorrow awaits, with the morning light,
Sleep softly, dear one, in the arms of the night.

"THE CARRIAGE IS the best piece of information you really have," the head of guards mutters to himself.

Once Ari was back to sleep, we headed straight here. The sun had already set, and time was of the essence. Kellen was able to get us in with the top brass right away, since she works for them. I told him my story twice, though the part that is hard to believe is the threat on life.

Ari and I walked away without a scratch.

Kellen sighs. "Are you seriously saying this isn't enough?"

She leans forward, her hands on the wooden desk sitting between us and him. It is littered with paperwork, all flipped over to conceal the information.

"I'm not saying that. You said there is no evidence of breaking and entering, right? No injury to you or your brother? Nothing but potential first names and the colours of a carriage with a crudely drawn picture to help us identify it," he states, leaning back in his chair and staring at me. "Your father missing is a concern, and we will have people looking for him, but in terms of the around the clock protection you are asking for, there isn't enough here to disperse those kinds of resources in this case."

The chair Kellen is occupying goes flying behind her. "This is the type of crap I have been telling you, boss. Of course people don't report, not when you tell them there's no point because there's no substantial evidence. Petty thefts, muggings, home invasions, assaults, they have all been on the rise." Her voice is harsh; the calm and aloof demeanour I've always admired is completely gone.

The head guard glares at her. "I'm not saying there isn't anything to be done, but regardless, you will watch your tone. I don't care if you are on or off duty."

Kellen's fists clench at her sides.

I stand, placing my hand on her shoulder while looking at her boss. "I understand. Regardless, I don't feel safe going back home. What would you suggest my next steps are?"

His shoulders relax slightly, hearing me reason with him. "Like I said, I'm not dismissing this, and we will look into it." I nod, happy to hear he is willing to do that at least. "Taking your brother to a close and trusted friend was the right move. I would suggest you either stay with them or leave town for a bit."

"Leave Berkin?" My voice is quiet.

"It's probably for the best," he confirms.

Kellen shakes her head. "Then I'm taking leave." We both look at her, eyes widened. "Sir, if she leaves town, I am going with her."

He stands up, leaning against his hands that lay flat on the desk. I lean back, a lump building in my throat as he towers over us. Kellen doesn't falter, though, her lips forming a tight line as he glares at her.

"Did I not just say that we can't afford to waste the resour—"

Kellen cuts him off. "Then I quit."

I gasp hearing her say those words, causing me to join them in standing. "Kellen." I grab her wrist and force her to face me. "You can't do that."

Her entire life has been so focused on her work. The only

reason she even joined The Waves was because Mehl and I begged her to. She has only ever wanted to be a guard, to provide for herself the way her father had failed to, to prove she could be more than the drunkard's daughter.

She rips herself from my grasp and just shakes her head. "Just shut up, Mazu." Her voice is harsh. "You seriously are pathetic at taking care of yourself."

"You are being foolish," he states. "I can't understand where this is coming from, Kellen."

Despite her bringing me comfort just by standing next to me, I agree with him. She can't uproot her life.

"Sorry, boss, but this is more important." Kellen's words are definite.

I'm not worth this.

My gaze hardens towards her, my hands balling into fists. "I'm not going to let you give up everything you've been working towards – your dream – to help me, Kellen."

Kellen scoffs, shaking her head as the palms of her hands press against her forehead. A groan escapes her lips as her eyes come up to meet mine again.

"You don't know me at all... do you." Her voice is a whisper. She turns back towards the head of guards. "I'm quitting; we will head towards Barley."

Kellen brushes past me and out of the office before anyone can say anything else.

"I'll send correspondence to the Barley's barracks if we find anything," the head of guards mutters, sitting back in his chair, flipping over some papers.

Nodding, I take a few steps back and follow after Kellen.

I don't know her at all?

The night air feels refreshing, a slightly chill breeze on my warm cheeks. My eyes search the street. Kellen's form is leaning up against the wall, looking up at the night sky. The stars twinkling far above us as the dark space around them feels vast. My feet carry me towards her, but she doesn't avert her gaze at the sound of my steps. I press myself against the wall, matching her pose as I watch the stars twinkling up above us.

"We will need a horse," Kellen says. "You are a slow walker, so getting to Barley will take forever otherwise."

Of course, it's straight to business with her. She pushes off the wall and starts walking more towards the centre of town.

"You really aren't going to explain what you meant?" I ask, not moving from my position.

Kellen keeps walking. "If you don't get it, then it doesn't really matter."

I furrow my brow and chase after her, trying to match her speed. She does this cryptic wording every now and again. I wish she would just come out and say what she means, because she pins it on me for not understanding her when I know that it's not true.

"You know, that is a pretty shitty thing to say to your best friend. Of course I know you!" My pace falls in line with hers.

She looks at me. "We can talk about this once your life isn't in immediate danger."

And she says I'm the stubborn one.

"This is more important," I argue.

It may not be a matter of life or death, but her giving up her dream for me should be just as important as whether or not I'll be around tomorrow.

A sigh escapes her. "See, you are damn sucky at caring for yourself."

I scoff. "Why? Because I'm trying to understand what in the infernum just happened back there? Because I want to understand why you would do something like that?" My tone turns more harsh as my frustration grows.

How can she possibly think this isn't important right now?

She just shakes her head and keeps walking.

"Answer me!" I yell.

Her eyes glance towards me. "You're an idiot."

I feel like my eyes are about to get stuck in the back of my head at how I just rolled them.

This is pointless.

I've known Kellen long enough to know that once she resorts to childish insults, the conversation is over. She won't budge on her opinion or view of whatever subject we are arguing over.

Does she really think I don't know who she is? What am I missing here?

We continue the walk in silence, though my glance wanders to hers every so often, hers remains focused forwards. The guards' presence around town has been scattered for a while now. When the council repositioned our city's protection to the country's borders, crime spiked. The new king of the Felguard Country had apparently pushed for higher security across the realm during the Limoria Court meeting that happened when he overthrew his father. I can't really remember why. I – along with the majority of people – was a tad distracted by the mention of an elf being a part of the coup d'état.

Suddenly, Kellen's eyes widen, and she stops in her tracks. "Mazu?" she whispers. "I can't see."

My heart sinks; the chocolate brown colour I like is now completely white.

They found me.

Before I can react, the feeling of cold and sharp steel is pressed against the small of my back.

"Careful now..." Colby's breath brushes against my ear as he whispers, so only I can hear him. "Making a scene will get your friend here killed."

Biggie comes up from behind Kellen, a big smirk spread across his face.

"Kellen. Just stay quiet..." I mutter, trying to keep the panic in my voice as unnoticeable as possible.

Her body is shaking, but she nods, likely already knowing we are not alone from the way her hand subtly shifts to her thigh holster where her dagger always resides.

The knife poking my backs retracts. "Good girl," Colby mutters. "Step back..."

"I can't see..." Kellen mumbles. I follow the man's instructions as I watch her pale eyes shift around, trying to listen to the noises around her.

"I know." The anxiety-inducing feeling of your vision suddenly disappearing is still fresh in my mind.

We could scream, try and draw attention, but by the time someone would get here, I think it would be too late. Kellen's agreement to be silent makes me feel more confident in that decision.

"I swear to the goddesses, I will kill you if you lay a finger on her," Kellen spits out, her gaze aimless.

Biggie chuckles. "Yeah right." Colby continues to have me step back, putting space between me and Kellen. "Just stay still or you both won't make it out of this."

She stiffens, the grip she had formed around her dagger's hilt loosens. Kellen is brash, but she isn't stupid. She is clearly at a disadvantage in more ways than one.

Colby turns me around to look over my features. "You going to listen?"

My lips tremble, but I nod.

He gestures his head to Biggie to follow us.

"Don't, Mazu." Kellen's voice is soft. "Please."

"I don't have a choice..." I whimper as I step in line with Colby, who is making his way back towards the sea.

Kellen takes a deep breath. My eyes widen; she is about to scream. I whip around, her hand pulling out her dagger and blindly charging forwards. Before I can plead for her to stop, Biggie's club is already coming down, smacking against her head.

My knees nearly buckle, but I reach for her, wrapping my hands around her before she collapses to the ground.

"She's fine." Colby sighs, grabbing my arm, pulling me up and away from my unconscious friend. "Someone will walk by and help her."

"You are a monster!" I yell, but he frowns and clasps a hand over my mouth.

"That's human nature," he hisses, forcing me forward.

CHAPTER SEVEN

I WILL NEVER FORGET TODAY. This is one of those life changing moments where I don't think I will ever be the same after it. Mother talked about them all the time. Meeting my father, leaving home, and having us youngins. My first was losing her, I didn't think my second would come so quickly after. I choke back the emotion, every feeling of fear, grief, misery, and pain just so I can try not to break down in front of these people. The quill glides over the paper as I finish signing my name.

Your Majesty King Felguard,

I regret to inform you that my mother, your aunt, has passed and in the wake, my father has disappeared, leaving me and my brother with very little and on our own.

Sadly, we have yet to meet, and I was hoping to seek counsel with you, or one of your representatives, as life has taken a downwards turn. I understand your time is highly valuable, but I would hope that our familial ties would be enough to obtain a small portion of it.

My brother, Marinus, and I have secured passage to Yral. Please send any return correspondence to their library. We will be on a boat the moment this letter is deposited, so I do hope to hear from you by the time of my arrival to Yral. If it is necessary to travel to Felguard, we may need assistance in securing further travel.

I apologise that due to our loss, this will be our first communications with one another.

With regards and respect,
Mazu Hali

"There," I mutter, sliding the paper towards the boss, who is smiling at me.

She adjusts her position in her overly large and decorated chair while the boat rocks slightly as we sit in her quarters. Her bed is in the far right corner, layers of blue and white fabric hiding the mattress and covers. The large desk we are sitting at is in the dead centre of the room. Colby sits on a short but long dresser against the wall opposite of her bed.

"See, look how smooth things go when you just do what you're told." Her voice is sickly sweet. The smile she wears sends a shiver down my spine.

I swallow the lump in my throat. "What happens next?"

"You'll likely get a seat with a representative, where they will, on the King's behalf, hopefully establish some type of stipend for living. Well, once you ask him for it. Then you will provide it to us. It's that simple." She rests her elbows onto the arms of the chair as she finishes, collapsing her arms in front of her.

"That's it?" The disbelief drips from my words. "Beg for money from a king and give it to you?"

She nods. "That's it."

I let out an exhausted laugh, shaking my head. "You keep saying it like he is actually going to care." I squeeze the bridge of my nose. "That family couldn't care less when my father asked for money. Granted, I didn't realise who that family really was, but they did nothing."

Mother would always excuse her family's absence, trying to reason that she was the one who cut ties with them years ago. She said it was due to a difference of opinions, but Mother was always the diplomatic type. She would never really talk poorly about someone, even if they did deserve it. Father was just angry she was sick, or at least that's what I thought. Now I can understand better. They had the means, but chose not to do anything.

"Well, let me put it this way. You better pray to whatever goddess that he does care, because if he doesn't, I don't see any need for you and your brother to live." She picks up the paper, folding it to fit into an envelope.

My heart tightens as I stare at her hands.

"I want you to take Ari out of this," I say, my eyes travelling up to meet hers. She tilts her head, waiting for me to continue. "Killing us might be the easier option for not getting your way, but it cuts out multiple avenues to where I could be useful to you."

Renna crosses her legs, her hands clasping together as she rests her elbows on the desk.

"I like this..." she chuckles.

Anything, I'm going to do anything to protect him.

I take in a shaky breath. "I'll work for you, do whatever you want me to. Just to ensure that he is safe."

Colby takes a sharp inhale.

Her smile widens. "Anything I say, huh?"

It takes me a second to will myself to nod in agreement.

Tilting her head, she sticks out her hand. "Deal."

I take her hand. "Deal."

"You can take her to the hold. I think she'll find it to be a fine temporary home." Her tone sounds perky.

My nails dig into my hands as Colby hops off the desk and makes his way over to me. I try to stand, but the strength in my legs is gone.

Did I really just do that?

The room seems to come in and out of focus. "Let's go." Colby's voice shakes the panic from me, reminding me that this is not the place to break down.

I don't want to give them the satisfaction of seeing my pain.

Using the desk to help, I stand, Colby scooting the chair out for me.

Just focus on something, anything else, Mazu.

Colby waits and watches me as I take a second to find my footing and move towards the exit.

We leave the Captain's Quarters, and his pace is faster than my own as I stare at his back. Unlike when we were at the cliff, he is wearing a short-sleeved jacket. His hair is longer than I realised.

He has to be hot in all the black.

He glances over his shoulder, the blue in his eyes is like staring into the stormy sea. Colby raises a brow at me before facing back in the direction of where we are headed.

I follow after him silently. He reaches for his side, the clinking of keys sounds off as he pulls them from a pouch on his belt. Colby unlocks the door that leads us down to the bottom of the ship. Cells align both sides. All of them are empty. He opens the nearest gate and gestures for me to walk in.

I stare into the small cage, nothing but a bucket inside of it.

"Once you prove yourself, she'll let you out," Colby mutters as I stand frozen a few inches from the entrance of the cell.

My eyes shift to meet his. "And how does one prove themselves?"

This guy just stares at me, his eyes fogging over. He blinks slowly, his eyes staying closed a moment longer than normal.

Is it really that bad?

A knot forms in my chest.

"It's different for everyone." His voice is quieter. "We've all had to earn her trust, in one way or another." Furrowing my brow, I take a few steps into the cell. Colby closes the door and locks it. "Why did you make that deal?"

The knot tightens. "Does it matter?"

A silence falls over us, so much so I wonder if he is even still there. I look over my shoulder and see him still standing there, watching me.

"He deserves to be a kid. I didn't want his entire life to be dwindled down to being a pawn." My voice is a whisper.

"Then you made the right move." His eyes locked with mine, his stare piercing through me. "To protect someone you love, that is always the right move."

I open my mouth to say something, but he walks away, up the stairs and out of sight.

Was he trying to comfort me?

WE HAD SAILED out the moment Colby got back from putting the letter I wrote for my apparently royal relative in the post deposit. At least that was what I was told by one of the other crewmates – Hedda. She is not the type of person I would really ever want to talk to. Someone who seems like being cruel is kind of fun. She came down initially to introduce herself, and all she did was mock me.

Her hair is buzzed but you can still see the bright red colour it has. It blends in well with her sun-kissed skin, her cheeks flaky and peeling from the sunburn.

"If I were the captain, I would just tie you to the anchor at our next stop." Hedda's laugh sends a chill down my spine. "I think you would look really pretty if you were waterlogged and stiff."

I take a few steps back as her hands wrap around the bars of my cell. Her pupils are dilated as she stares straight through me. There is sweat beginning to form on the back of my neck under the weight of her gaze. The intent behind her words doesn't just feel like a joke.

"Look at you... you're the kind of person who I like to just tear apart!" I don't even think she realises she's pressing her face against the bars she is clinging to.

My jaw tightens.

What the infernum is wrong with her?

This is the company I am going to have to be around. I'm suddenly feeling a lot less confident in my ability to keep Renna happy enough to keep her away from Ari.

"Hey!" Colby shouts as he steps down into the brig. "Get back to your station, Hedda." The glower pointed at her seems to be enough for her to jump back from the bars.

Hedda sighs and clenches her fists. "I was only having fun. I wasn't touching her."

"Go." His tone is finite and without a moment passing, she runs up the stairs and past him.

Colby's gaze falls on me, his glare has subsided to a more relaxed state. My first instinct makes me want to thank him, but I hate him, so I don't really feel like being polite to a guy I hate.

"You should probably stay away from the others," he states. "Especially if I'm not around."

What a way to make me feel better after I almost wet myself from that psycho, nearly squeezing her way into my cage.

Be afraid of the people who are surrounding you.

"Then maybe you should keep them away from me," I retort, gesturing to the cell I am stuck in.

He smirks and walks up the stairs, shutting and locking the door behind him.

Just thinking about her makes my stomach queasy. I shake my head and try to pull myself back to where I am now, though sitting in the dingy place doesn't really make me feel all that much better.

I haven't had the courage to ask about my father. A part of me doesn't want to know, but looking at the empty cells around me, I have a feeling they don't normally keep people for long. Slapping my cheeks lightly, I sigh.

Just stop thinking about it.

My hands slide down my face so my fingers can fiddle with the opal necklace that belonged to my mother. A smile somehow tugging at my lips. She would be reminding me that a positive attitude can change anything, not sure if that would really apply to this situation, though. Kellen would be saying how I shouldn't have got myself into this position in the first place and take the first opportunity she saw to try and make our way out by force. Not really my style, and it would mean they would target Ari.

Kellen laughs, her head nearly hitting the deck from how fast she sprung back. "You did not!"

"I swear!" I laugh along with her.

"I wish I could have seen Mel's face when you did that." *She shakes her head. "You, little miss goody two-shoes, manipulating Greggers with blackmail? What did you even have on him to make him cower to you so quickly?"*

"He deserved it! Greggers was being way too aggressive with Mehl. His hands were far more immoral than they normally are." I defend myself, looking up at the fluffy-looking clouds passing us by. "I reminded him that my family is really close with the butcher he works for and suggested that if he didn't stop acting out, I would have no choice but to suggest his employer find a new worker."

Kellen sighs, getting herself in check. "You know he is going to come back at you for that."

I turn to see her looking at me. "That's why I have you, right?"

"Yeah, yeah." She sits up and wraps an arm around my shoulders. "I'll always be there to help you end the fights you start."

The door to the brig opens, pulling me out of my memories. My head snaps upwards towards the stairs, a small gasp leaving me.

Colby leans against the railing, his eyes examine me coming out of my daze.

He seriously gives me the creeps.

"Bored?"

I roll my eyes at his question and avert my gaze.

The sound of his boots on the hardwood planks stops in front of my cell. A lump rises in my throat. I'm not sure if it's a good or bad thing that he is here. I have no idea how long it's been since I've been locked up, but based on the number of meals brought down, I'd say it's been at least two full shift cycles. He doesn't seem like he would be down here unless he was supposed to be.

He unlocks the cell door, the twisting mechanics sending a shiver down my spine. "What do you want?"

My eyes slowly turn upwards to meet his stare.

"You've been a good little pet and deserve a treat." I stare at him, unblinking as I try to process the words that just came out of his mouth. A small smirk widening on his normally bored-looking face, likely enjoying my shocked expression. "At least that's what the boss said."

Jerk.

A relief floods through me, but only for a moment as he gestures for me to stand and follow him.

"And what is this *treat?*" I ask, getting up from my spot on the floor.

Colby extends his hand towards the stairs. "After you."

I stare at him for a moment, his smirk now gone. He points to the stairs with his nose, nodding his head in that direction. It is obvious he is being cautious, having me walk up the stairs so he can't be blindsided.

Funny, cause he's the one that does the blinding.

Opening the door, the smell of the sea reaches my nose, the wind a nice breeze. The sun feels warm as it touches my skin.

There are people walking around the deck, managing the ship as we sail to Yral. "Stretch your legs while you can," Colby mutters.

I watch the waves bob up and down, leaning against the taffrail. The wood digs into my elbow, but I almost welcome it. It's grounding, letting me know this isn't a dream I can wake from. A part of me thinks allowing myself that type of illusion is more cruel than just facing what this really is.

My life.

I don't have to look into a mirror to know I have bags under my eyes. They may even still be red from the salt of my tears and rubbing them last night.

Colby leans against the railing. My eyes fall from his gaze, and I turn my attention back onto the passing sea.

The deck creaks and the sound of his boots makes me shiver. "Normally..." he starts. I hear the flick, looking at the small flame being produced by a handheld igniter. My father has one for the flares we keep on the ship.

Dad.

He takes a drag from the tobacco roll he just lit. A cloud of smoke leaves his lips as he breathes out. "Normally, we start putting people to work right away, or kill them off." My eyes stay focused on the slowly burning paper stuck in between his fingers. "I'm not going to put you to work just yet. We can call this an adjustment period."

"Okay," I whisper back.

The politeness in me almost thanks him, again, for going easy on me or something, but I doubt this is what that is. Maybe it's their way to make sure I won't try to run or attack them. Letting me adjust to my surroundings and this way of life.

Silence envelopes us, but I welcome it. He's not the company I would ask for, but like this, his presence isn't revolting. I can hear the footsteps of the few other crew members walking around behind us, but it's faint compared to the splitting of the sea below me as we cut through it.

I wonder what Ari is doing.

Closing my eyes, I can see him. Sitting on the woven rug in the sitting room, playing with his toys. Mom is relaxed in her chair, drinking her tea and watching him with a smile. Dad is at the table, repairing one of his nets – there was always at least one with a hole in it.

"You're smiling." Colby's voice pulls me back.

"Was I?" I ask, not really caring for the answer.

All I'll have is my memories to last me my lifetime. I'll have to try and imagine what Marinus will look like when he reaches my age. What Kellen will look like once she is made head guard, because I believe she could be. I'm sure she will be able to get her job back. She's good at it, and I doubt her boss has the room to really refuse her if they are so short staffed.

I turn to Colby, his eyes spectating my features. "You were. It's the first time I've seen you do that, at least genuinely."

"I could smile more, but you aren't very funny," I state, tilting my head.

He takes another pull from the roll. "This ship really kills one's sense of humour." The smoke puffs out with his words.

Did they all choose this life, or are they thrown into it just like me?

My eyes wander back to the passing sea that is just. Perhaps with time, my heart will harden and I'll be able to play along. Maybe it'll get easier to be here with them, instead of at home with Ari and Kellen.

I slap my hands against my cheeks and shake my head. There is no point in thinking about them. I just need to stop. Stop wondering and start adjusting.

Let go. Just let it all go.

The sound of a deep chuckle sounds off from next to me as he stares out at the sea.

He really sucks.

Hedda comes up behind us. "Co, what is the little sea rat doing out of her cage?"

Colby flicks his roll off the side of the ship, disappearing into the water. "You should really mind your own business."

The woman's brows stitch together before she's huffing. She stares at me for a moment, my body stiffening until she walks off. I slowly relax the further away she gets, heading towards the bow of the ship.

My captor leans his back against the railing, his eyes watching the crew work. "Can I ask you a question?"

Looking over his sharp features, the dull expression he likes to wear, I mutter, "Sure...?" raising a brow towards him.

"With how sombre you've been, have you been thinking about the different ways to kill yourself?" His eyes shift to meet my widened gaze.

What the fuck.

Is that what I should be thinking about?

My shoulders sag, and I blink a few times before answering. "No." Being direct is the only way I can really answer such a hideous question.

Colby smiles and nods his head. "That's good to hear."

"That's what you wanted to know?" I ask him in disbelief.

Are those the thoughts that go through his head, or has that actually happened with people they brought on board to be crew-mates and is an actual concern he has?

The casual way he just asks a question with such a heavy weight to it, as if I should be used to being asked.

It never crossed my mind to do something like that. Ari needs me. Whether it's here to keep them away from him, or there and actually caring for him.

If Ari had died on that cliff, though...

Colby shakes his head. "I needed to get that out of the way. I need to make sure you aren't planning on throwing yourself off the side of the ship."

I face him. "Of course not! I'm the only thing keeping you from turning this ship around and slitting my brother's throat!"

He stands up, holding his hands in the air. "I'd only do it if I was ordered to." Like that is somehow better. "It's not like I want to see the light fade from his eyes."

My stomach lurches, a lump rising in my throat. I quickly put a hand over my mouth to stop it from coming out as the imagery flashes in my mind.

Colby watches me closely. "Can't even stomach the thought?"

My eyes narrow as I slowly travel up to meet his gaze. His face doesn't seem to show an ounce of empathy. Like this is purely out of curiosity. Does he even have emotions?

Inhuman.

"Your problem is that you care too much." He bends down slightly to hover over me. "I can see you are trying to numb yourself, but you are going to have to try harder. Trust me, it won't come so naturally, you'll have to force your own hand."

I lower my hand slightly. "What are you saying?"

Colby rights his posture. "To become numb, you have to confront all the fear that's sitting right behind those eyes of yours."

The lump goes down with a gulp. He's looking at me like he knows. He knows what this feels like.

I don't want to be like him. To look at someone in pain and not react.

"Once you start committing the heinous acts you loathe me for doing, that's when all of this will become easier," he mutters.

My lip trembles slightly, but I don't want to cry. Not in front of him. I bite down on my lip, halting its quiver. I knew what I was getting into, or at least I thought I did, when I made that deal.

Who am I kidding?

I had no idea what this would actually be like, and I still don't. I'm not ready to hurt someone, let alone kill someone. Having the thought and actually following through with it is very different. I don't know how Kellen has been so strong, been able to be so ready to take the life of someone for the sake of someone else. Jumping off that cliff, the only thing I was doing was making sure Ari wasn't alone. There was no plan on how to save him, to save us. All I knew was that if he was going to die, so was I.

Now I'm here, preaching that I'm willing to do what I must to keep him alive, but I don't even think I have what it takes to actually do that.

To become someone like the man standing in front of me, I don't think I'll ever be ready for that, let alone be capable.

Colby waves his hand back and forth. "You still in there?"

I blink a few times, focusing back on him. "Obviously."

"Could have fooled me," he mutters under his breath while taking a step back, his gaze so intently on me. "Listen. I know this is a lot. That's why I'm giving you time to adjust."

"I appreciate the consideration." I roll my eyes and push myself upright from leaning on the railing.

The words he is saying don't match what I am seeing.

"I'm trying to be nice." And he says that with a straight face.

I whip around as the door clicks shut and point my finger in his face, making him lean back. "Being NICE?" Moving my finger to dig into his chest, I say, "You kidnapped my family, threw my brother off a cliff, and now you are taking me to try and embezzle King Felguard's money!"

Colby's face looks unimpressed at my outburst, his eyes dark and face without a crease.

How can anyone be so heartless, look like that after I list off such horrid things.

"Watch your attitude." Colby glares. Some of the crew stop what they are doing to watch the scene I'm causing. "I'm not very patient with those who whine," he growls, his gaze looking from my eyes to my finger.

"How dare you!" I yell. "Diminish this to something as childish as whining."

I raise my fist and swing it towards his face, but he catches my wrist and pulls me close, our noses touching.

"What did I just say?" His breath brushes against my face. The smell of rum and smoke overtaking my senses. "You are acting like a child. No better than your cowering brother. He is at least an actual child."

I want to go home.

He throws my arm back, releasing his grip, making me take a few steps back. "I wouldn't try that again." The tone is the harshest I've heard of him, and it makes the crew instantly continue their work.

My hand cradles my wrist, a soft pulsing from how tight his grip was. His eyes almost look black with how daggered they glare into me.

I should be the one seething, yet here he is, looking ready to kill me. "Life is brutal. Get over it."

I hate him.

Colby starts to walk away, his footsteps echo off the wooden planks. "It shouldn't be," I whisper.

He glances back towards me. Despite his slim form, he looks so imposing. My heart aches seeing such a cold stare. The things he must have seen to make him like this. I want to pity him, for how miserable he must actually be.

But fuck him.

I tentatively take a step forward to follow, and he continues walking on. We walk in silence, down the stairs and back into the brig. Me keeping a distance between us along the way.

"You are going to have to start pulling your weight, eventually. With that little trick you pulled the day we officially met." Raising a brow, he just sighs. "That light, the thing that made you survive the fall. You need to tell me what exactly it was."

Oh, that.

I shake my head. "I don't know what that was."

"You are going to have to do better than I don't know." His eyes feel like they are digging into me.

My brow furrows. "It's the best I have. I didn't even see the miracle you are referring to. I simply woke up on one of the rocks down there."

I really don't know what it was. My mind has been drifting to the description Ari had told Kellen while he was getting bathed, but it doesn't do anything but confuse me.

We just got lucky.

Colby grumbles a few things to himself as he opens the cell door. "You're telling me, that you really have no idea what that was? No inclination towards some magicae ties your family might have?"

"I said no!" I shout, wanting him to be out of my sight, for this to be done.

A part of me is scared to know, and it shouldn't be important. It was a fluke, a one-time thing. Mother would say it was the grace of a goddess that saved us.

He stares at me, frowning. "Mazu."

Shaking my head, I look towards the floor. "It doesn't matter."

Why can't he just leave it alone? I don't want to know, and I couldn't care less about his incessant curiosity.

"Except that it does," he mutters. "That's why she took your deal."

My throat swells shut hearing his words.

Of course it is.

I'm sure they have plenty of people they could use as a body on this ship; she wouldn't need me for that. Colby locks me in as I step past the cell's threshold. I listen to the retreat of his footsteps until the door opens and closes once more.

I collapse to the ground, squeezing my eyes shut as I bury my face into the palms of my hands.

Shit.

CHAPTER EIGHT

The sword is pulled out of Ari's chest. Slowly, her eyes locked with mine. A smile plastered on her face as bile rises inside my throat.

"NO!" I screech.

A hollowness envelopes me, as does the air inside my lungs.

He's okay.

She wouldn't actually kill him.

He's okay.

He's okay

Please, Haldoris, please let him be okay.

He's okay.

Blood drips from her sword, and my eyes won't let me look at him. I can't see him.

Kellen steps into view, bringing her sword down to collide with hers. The boss takes a step back under the weight of Kellen's force.

I try moving my legs, but my head starts to spin.

Get to him.

Just get to him.

I clamber my way, tripping a few times before my hands land on Ari's small frame. His head is faced away from me. A deep, ugly red is staining his shirt.

He's okay.

Gently, I cup his cheek and have him face me.

"Come on, Ari. We have to go," *I whimper.*

His eyes are lazily half-lidded, and don't meet my gaze. I shake him softly. The only sound I can hear is my heartbeat. He doesn't react, shift, blink.

He's just in shock.

I shake my head. "I'll help you up…"

He's okay.

He just needs a moment, and he'll be okay.

I GASP, sitting upright in my cell. Sweat drips down my face. My heart pounds so harshly I feel my body beat along with it.

"It's not real…" I whimper, my hands coming up to cup my face.

Cradling myself, I try to calm down.

Bucket. Bars. Brown boots.

Taking a few deep breaths, my trembling subsides slightly. Nightmares like that are new. One that feels so real I swear I can smell the scent of metal; his blood covering me as I carry him off. I know it would be a tall order to pray to never have one like that again, but I have a feeling I'll start having more.

My bones nearly jump from my body. "Good morning, Princess." Colby's raspy morning voice calls out as the door unlocks and he walks down the steps of the brig.

I just groan and turn my head to face away from him.

It's like my brain and body knew he was about to show up and woke me up in anticipation.

His yawn is audible enough for me to hear it as he reaches the bottom of the stairs. The sound of his boots on the floorboards stops before he unlocks and opens the cell door.

"What?" I hiss at him. My gaze travels up to meet his as he stares down at me.

Colby leans against the metal frame. "Today is going to be a lot of fun."

In the soft lantern glow, I see him smile. Like the words he just uttered are as innocent as the look he is wearing on his face. There is not a single bit of me that wants to know what he thinks is fun.

"Mhmm," I hum, standing up and straightening my clothes out.

He follows after me once I start walking up the stairs, heading to the main deck. The sun is now rising; the sea looking like glass made out of the colours of fire.

"Yral is not as far as you might think," Colby mutters, stretching out his back while looking out at the ocean. "Will you be ready?"

My eyes study him, and he shifts to do the same to me. He is so guarded and numb, it's hard to tell what he actually thinks of me or this situation.

"I'll have to be," I reply.

No matter what I have to do, I'll do it. For Ari.

At least, that's what I keep telling myself. After our conversation yesterday, I'll become like Colby if I have to, but that's not my goal. A shiver runs through me just at the thought of throwing someone, a child, off a cliff and not feeling one way or another about it.

He watches me for a moment longer. "That's the spirit." Rolling my eyes, I turn away from him. "You are finally thinking clearly." Colby's footsteps circle around me, walking into my gaze once more.

"No one on this boat can claim they are thinking clearly. None of this makes sense, this way of life, the things you do to people."

The iciness in his dull, watchful gaze gives me goosebumps. "You say that with such conviction, but you know so little of the world." I furrow my brow as he takes a step closer. "The circumstances that put us into a position where we must do such things to people like you."

I laugh, shaking my head. "Are you saying that no one has a choice in all of this? That we are slaves to fate?"

"Would you say you have a choice in the life you are now leading?" He takes another step closer.

It's not as simple as saying yes or no.

"Then I say it speaks more about you wanting to be on this boat, a part of this crew." He finishes his thought.

There is no sane person who would actually choose that. They are all freaks, messed up in the head for wanting to be involved with Renna, for wanting to be on this damned ship.

"My choice was to spare my brother from not having a choice," I clarify. "It had nothing to do with you, this ship or Renna."

He opens his mouth to say some sort of rebuttal, I think, but Mallin's voice calls from behind me. "Colby, I need you!" There is a touch of frustration in his tone.

I turn around to look at the tall, brooding man. He was introduced as our chef in the very brief passing as I was boarded onto the ship by Colby and Biggie, but the scars that riddle his chocolate complexion would suggest he plays a few roles just as everyone seems to here. Colby sighs and excuses himself as he and Mallin head towards the kitchen.

Watching the two talk, I can see a displeased expression cross Colby's face.

"This is your job." I overhear him scold. Mallin simply nods and disappears back through the kitchen door.

The jerk saunters his way back over, perching his hands on his hips, looking me over for a second, like he is trying to determine something, but closes his eyes and sighs.

I tilt my head. "What, trouble in paradise?"

He rolls his eyes and drops his arms to his side. "Let's focus on why I have you up nice and early instead."

My body goes a bit rigid as he pulls his dagger from the holster that sits on the back of his waist. Instinctually, I take a step back, but all that does is make him chuckle as he watches me.

"Relax." He twirls the dagger around.

Easy for him to say that. He's not the one who just had his entire life ripped out from under him a few days ago by the very person trying to tell him to 'relax.'

"We have a few things we need to go over," he states. My eyes darts from his to the dagger to his on a repeated loop. "First, we need to go over how exactly the meeting with the King, or likely his representative, will go." He takes a step closer. "Second, I'll need to teach you a few skills with something like this"—Colby waves the dagger at me—"to ensure that if something happens, you'll at least be able to try and make your way back to me if we get separated somehow, because if you don't, my first stop will be to see little Marinus."

I grit my teeth. "There is no need to remind me." The words come out more like a growl.

He flips around the dagger for me to take the hilt. "Just need to make sure you know the consequences of your actions, Princess."

My urge to teach him a lesson in consequences is severe, but I slowly grab the hilt and take it in my hand. He's stupid if he thinks I can't at least defend myself, though I guess I haven't been the best at it since him and I have had the unfortunate chance of meeting.

"Third, you're going to tell me about how you survived that fall." His smirk is no longer present.

Perhaps the very thing that saved me and Ari is what's going to get us killed, anyway. I have a feeling if I don't produce results in that last area, my life will literally have no meaning to them.

"Fine," I mutter, looking down at the dagger in my hands.

My finger traces over the blade's edge, remembering when my father gave me a dagger for my fourteenth life celebration.

"To keep those you don't want attention from away."

That's what he said. Looks like I didn't really take those words to heart, and neither did he. My eyes trail up to Colby's once more, nearly letting the question fall from my lips, but I don't. It would be too much to know. He's alive for all I know, and that's what I'm going to focus on. Ari and I are not in this alone.

"Mazu." My head snaps up to see Colby tilting his head as he looks down at me. "Are you imagining different ways to use that thing on me?"

I chuckle a bit. "You bet."

I YAWN as Colby opens the door to my cell. His hair doesn't have that perfectly messy look this morning, but more of a rolled out of bed and put clothes on look.

"Do we have to do it this early?" I mumble, rubbing my face to try and wake myself up.

He nods. "I told you, it's not a good idea to have you roaming about with the rest of the crew yet."

We walk up the stairs, him just behind me. The wind this morning is brisk and causes me to shiver and wrap my hands around my arms.

"You say that like I actually roam around," I say through my chattering teeth.

Colby slinks off his coat and throws it at me, and I can see the goosebumps instantly raise on his arms, but his face doesn't seem to react to the cold like his body is. My eyes look between him and the coat, not expecting the gesture. Everything he does feels like a test, though. He's hot and cold. One moment he does something truly heinous or asks questions that feel so pointed or targeted, and the next he is acting like he's looking out for me.

"Listen, they tend to be rough on newcomers. Right now, they see it as me being the only one giving you that hard time," he states, his tone more serious like this is a secret to be kept between us and us alone.

Okay?

It's not like my time with him is pleasant, but I'll take his word for it that I'd rather not be mingling with the whole crew.

Slipping on his coat, I can smell him. Smoke, rum and his natural musk. There's another scent though, something more floral.

"So to go over what we did yesterday..." he says as he walks towards the stair to the upper deck, pulling me out of my head, and I follow him.

"Sitting with the rep, I'll need to remain calm but have an air of gloom and doom," I reply to his unasked question. "That I will have no problem with. It's the blatant lying that I still don't think will pass."

He takes a seat on one of the steps, leaning back on his elbows and spreading his legs. "Not if you don't believe in what you're saying. Once I'm convinced what you're saying is true, you will be able to lie to just about anyone."

I raise a brow. "What kind of person would I not be able to lie to?"

He pauses for a second. "The kind of person who has done nothing but lie for whatever means necessary. Someone whose career or life is built on those lies."

Colby goes to reach for a pocket that isn't there and sighs before extending his hand to me.

"Yeah?"

"Smokes," he mutters, twitching his hand towards me again.

I feel around the different pockets and touch the familiar shape of an igniter and pull that out, along with a small pouch that was stuffed in there with it. Tossing both over to him, he doesn't hesitate to light one of his tobacco rolls up and take a deep inhale.

"Those smell disgusting, by the way," I mutter.

He smirks as he blows out the smoke. "They taste good, though."

Rolling my eyes, I look out to the ocean, watching the colourful waves and wrap the coat around me as another cold, strong breeze brushes across me.

"Go over the lie again," he instructs, relaxing in his spot as he stares at me.

I uncross my arms. "Oh please dear representative, won't you show me pity and give me a year's worth of living expenses?"

Colby just takes another drag of his roll, not very amused with my jest.

Clearing my throat, I sigh and close my eyes. "Things have just gone from bad to worse. I know most in my position would defer to depositing their younger sibling to an orphanage in order to survive, but I know that would not be my mother's wish. My father has not been pleased with the reaction or lack of help from the Torrin family and has abandoned us with the debts of the healer's payments in the wake of my mother's passing."

"Stop," Colby mutters with the roll between his lips. "If you keep your eyes closed the whole time, the full weight of your words won't be as impactful. Memorising the script isn't enough."

I may be a singer, but putting on an act is not my strong suit. Squeezing my hands together, I nod and try again under his scrutinising gaze.

All to tell a lie.

CHAPTER NINE

Biggie chuckles as his fist connects with my gut, making my legs crumple underneath me. Bile quickly rises in my throat from the impact, but I swallow it back down. Hedda grabs my hair and pulls me back, throwing me to the ground so they can stare over me.

I was sleeping a few minutes ago, and woke up to these monsters descending on me like demons in the night. A part of me feels like I'm just in one of my nightmares. Hedda kicks my side, making me cry out as I immediately cradle that side.

Is this what Kellen had to put up with when facing our bullies?

She never let me stick around. Ordered me to run away whenever things started to get more violent. She was always meant to be a guard, a protector of others. Me, on the other hand, I get myself in situations like this where I make things harder versus just taking them out. Though, if I'm being honest, I couldn't even if I tried.

"Hey!" Colby's voice cuts their gleeful laughter short, instantly turning around.

Wow, I am grateful to hear his voice.

Storming down the brig's staircase, he extends his hand. Biggie and Hedda pause before she offers him the key she must have stolen from his belt at some point.

The moment the key is in his hand, Colby's hand slaps across Hedda's face, making her yelp. Biggie growls at him, but with one second from Colby's pointed glare, Biggie backs off.

"You know better than to mess with the Captain's things." Colby's tone is low; his gaze darkened, my body trembling from the pain coursing through it. "Renna will decide just how brutal your flogging will be once I tell her."

Am I the Captain's thing?

"We kept away from her face!" Biggie tries to argue.

It's funny he thinks that is perhaps a negotiation point for lessening his punishment. Though, I am surprised they would even be punished. The anger spewing from Colby is jarring as it is. It is good to know that flogging is a reasonable punishment on this ship, for something as small as a squabble, or perhaps it's more about them stealing from him?

"Get out of my sight," Colby growls, making them both rush out of my cell.

He walks up to me before crouching down and looking me over. I sit up slowly with a wince, and he sighs.

"So much for your ingenious plan..." I mutter.

Colby cracks a smirk. "Didn't think they were so eager to play with you."

Rolling my eyes, I slide myself so I can rest against the wall. My eyes stick to him as he continues to inspect me, probably making sure that I don't look roughed up for my *incoming meeting. Being beaten will likely raise questions for whoever I meet with.*

"Do you need anything?" His voice is quiet.

Here is that manipulation tactic again.

Trying to soften me around him, making me gain some false confidence in him. It won't work, though. When I look at him, memories of the cliff continuously flash across my mind.

I WAKE UP GASPING, clutching my side as my sudden movement irritates my still bruised body. It's taken a few days for me to ease into the pain and just deal with it. Colby helped me rehearse a few of the dagger manoeuvres in a fight, correcting my stance when facing someone. Nothing fancy, but perhaps enough to get me out of a tight spot. I could have used that when a certain idiot behemoth abducted me.

A sigh leaves me as I lean against the cell wall while I wait for what I know is coming next. Colby has kept me to a tight schedule. Wake up at dawn, train, eat, and go back to the cell.

I've met a few more members of the crew. Colby has had me eat meals with them – since Biggie and Hedda's little late-night visit – to show that I'm not scared of them, even though I really am.

Some are crude, others are rude, and everyone has adopted Colby's nickname for me.

Princess.

Definitely doesn't help with them looking at me as one of them, but a part of me is okay with that. They aren't my kind of people. To be honest, Colby isn't even quite like them either, but I could just not know them well enough.

A shiver runs through me at the thought that getting to know them is something I will have the rest of my life to do.

Especially if I end up coming through on this embezzlement scheme as well as figuring out this power they claim I have.

I was just lucky.

The brig's door opens, Colby's face coming into view by the soft lantern light. "Ready?"

Nodding my head, I stand up and walk out the cell door once he unlocks it. My heart is saddened by how quickly I've adjusted to this. My mind never strays from home, though. Ari, Kellen, Dad. I'd give an arm or a leg just to be at a tavern table with Lip and Mehl, hearing their light bickering or planning out a set list. Rehearsing in Kellen's sitting area to prep for an off-hand show or competition.

"How is your side?" Colby's tone is gruff, yawning as we step onto the main deck.

I poke at it. It still feels a bit tender. "Fine."

He nods and stretches. "We are going to talk about something you have been pushing off for quite a while."

"Are you going to grill me again?" I ask, leaning up against the railing.

"If you don't start showing the potential that made her interested, you're going to miss the days that it was me doing the grilling," he states, his eyes darkening. "Once King Felguard is sending us the money, she's going to expect results."

I try to swallow the lump forming in my throat. "We have gone through this multiple times. I don't know." The sound coming out of my voice is more pleading than anything.

Nothing in me quite understands what happened.

"That's not good enough!" he shouts. "There is something, somewhere, inside you that came out when you were falling from that cliff."

"Because of you," I mumble, crossing my arms.

This is not the kind of conversation I want to be having this early in the morning, or at all.

He steps forwards, invading my space. "Get over it." Colby's voice drops, both in tone and volume.

"Get over it?" I scoff, shoving him away from me.

He takes a step back, looking me over before gesturing with his hands to come at him again.

"You want to hurt me?" I grit my teeth at the question.

A part of me does. I want to throw him off a cliff and see how he fares. "Then do it." His voice is commanding, and that annoying stoic expression sitting on his face makes my blood boil.

This is all just a stupid test to him.

"You want to be angry? Then be angry!" His voice is loud enough that I don't doubt he is waking some of the crew up that is sleeping below us.

I can see some of the moonshift crewmates peek out to watch the commotion, but I'm not falling for any of this. He will not bait me.

A glare forms on his face as I simply frown at him. "It's time to put on the pressure."

He lunges forward and grabs me by my throat, a gasp escaping me. Colby pushes me, my back tilting over the railing, the pain shooting through my spine. It feels like if he pushes any harder, it'll snap.

"Colby," I grunt.

"If you really don't know, then we will need to experiment." He leans in. "Maybe it's a defence mechanism. It can only come out if your life is in mortal danger."

My eyes widen as he draws his knife.

"You... wouldn't."

He presses the dagger against the bit of flesh on my throat not covered by his hand. "But I would."

They need me alive. They need me to speak to the King.

My value goes beyond just the abilities they are curious about. Ones that I'm not even sure actually exist.

I close my eyes. "Fine."

His grip tightens before the pressure of his weight pushing into me lightens.

Colby's footsteps retreat, and I open my eyes to see him staring at me. His face isn't expressive like I thought it would be. It's like he is in a different place all together, or like I am a window he is just looking through.

"Why did you do it?" He sheaths his dagger.

I glare at him, rubbing my throat. "What?"

Colby takes a deep breath, his shoulders relaxing from the tensed position.

Was he bothered by having to force me like that?

Doesn't matter if he is or isn't bothered. He does this all for her, so his precious captain has a new toy to play around with.

"The reason you chose to save your brother." His eyes drift past me for a moment before they lock back onto mine. "If you had just let him die, none of this would be happening. So why. What pushed you over that ledge?"

I take a deep breath and toss my arms up. "Wouldn't you?" My voice is soft. "I would have rather died than watched him die."

His gaze is cast downwards, his dark locks obscure his face. "I see."

We stare at one another in silence, the throbbing around my throat subsiding.

He makes no sense.

The actions he takes, or doesn't take. The questioning and soft moments of reply. Like, what is the point of even asking that question? It doesn't seem like it is earth shattering or even helpful in making sense of how Ari and I survived that fall. All

I know is that I was begging for a way to save my brother, or at least ensure he knew I didn't just let him die.

"Colby! It happened again," Mallin calls out, sticking his head out of the kitchen.

Apparently, supplies have been going missing over the week that we have been travelling. It has been one of the many mysteries aboard this ship. Nothing I care to investigate, and honestly something I can't understand why they are. It's not like we are in the company of high moral individuals. Them taking an extra ration of food doesn't seem all that out of character, so why is it such a big deal?

After a few minutes, Colby joins me once more. He looks at me with a furrowed gaze and hands on his hips.

I know he isn't stupid enough to think it's me, but I can see his mind turning.

"Mazu?" I pull the towel down, uncovering my face. Mother smiles down at me, her hands on her hips. "Running away to the beach, as nice as it is, is not the right response."

Rolling my eyes, I turn to lie on my side. "There is no good response when it comes to him."

She chuckles, her hand caresses my shoulder. "You know, I used to think that."

"Then why did you marry him?" I ask.

Mamma hums, "Because I came to understand him. He was so used to no one listening to him that he began to raise his voice as an attempt to force people to listen."

I sit up, facing her. "He is the one who never listens."

"Have you told him that you feel unheard?" She tilts her head.

No. Of course I haven't.

"The way he reacts is not always right, but all people act a certain way because of the issues they are trying to work through. Does that mean we should just stop trying to connect with them because it's hard?" Her question irks me.

It feels like it is always about him and how I have to be the one to bridge the divide between him and me. I know people have their own issues, but so do I.

"It's not my problem, they should figure it out them-selves." My voice trembles.

He should figure it out himself.

She shakes her head. "They will have to figure it out, but sometimes they just need someone to help them start down that path. Sometimes, it's hard to look at ourselves the way others do. If we don't communicate our issues, how will they know there is one?"

I STARE at the tray in front of me. The food looks and smells good, but a few bites is all I was able to make myself eat before it became my entertainment. Potatoes, peas and dried meats.

The hilarity.

Rolling my eyes, I close my eyes for a moment as Biggie's laugh nearly shakes the galley. Which is really just a small room a handful of us are crammed into when it's our shift to eat. Mallin is at the stove keeping things warm for when the next shift comes in. Colby has made Yelna my spare keeper when he is busy and can't be around me all the time. They are quiet. A short bob and baggy clothes. They haven't done much to be friendly per say, but the moment Hedda or Biggie try to get close, they are quick to draw out their dagger and stab a nearby surface. The silence is welcome. I'd rather eat my meal, or shove it around on the tray, before getting put back down in my new home. I'll honestly miss these days of me being locked away once they trust me enough to sleep with the rest of the crew.

The door swings open; Colby's hurried steps cause everyone's heads to turn and lock onto him. My breath hitches; he is headed straight for me. The glare on his face and heavy breaths send a chill down my spine.

What the infernum did I do?

"Get up!" he yells. I clamber my way up from my seat as he gestures for me to walk out.

"What is go—" He cuts me off by shoving me towards the door to move quicker.

"You're just going to have to see for yourself," Colby growls.

My eyes widen the moment my feet hit the main deck. I hear shuffling and strangled grunts. My heart drops to my stomach.

Kellen?

Her face is pressed firmly into the deck, her hands pinned and bound against her back, and Hedda's knee digging into the centre of her spine.

"Get off her!" I shout at Hedda, taking quick steps towards them, but Colby grabs my arms and pulls me back before slamming me into the wall. "Colby!" I shout at him.

He looks over my face as his viper grip doesn't budge against my protests. Over his shoulder, I see Kellen trying to get up, but Hedda slams her head into the boards. Blood trickling down from the impact.

I whimper for her, confused as to how she's here, why, and what's going to happen next. Nothing is coming to mind. How to get us out of this, how to make sure Kellen won't be stuck here with me. How to ensure she gets off this boat alive.

My lips tremble, and Colby pushes off of me, taking a few steps back. "You're so helpless," he mumbles before turning around. "And you," he crouches down next to Kellen, "are just a fool."

Kellen growls and tries getting up again. Colby stops Hedda from punishing the efforts and instead orders Hedda off of her.

"The Captain doesn't like stowaways," Hedda scolds, but Colby helps Kellen stand, anyway.

Kellen's eyes find mine and she gives me that look of 'I couldn't help myself.' One she has given me after every bar fight or stupid idea she's followed through on.

This one takes the cake.

There is no situation where this ends well. Death, torture, or a form of forcing my hand. Not a single path will have us walking out of this together.

I can't think like that.

"What are you doing here?" My voice is barely a whisper.

Colby holds her steady as he pulls out his knife and pokes it into her back. "I'm interested in the answer myself."

"You think I was just going to be able to let you go?" is all she says in return, her gaze intense on mine.

I shake my head. "You shouldn't have come."

"What was your plan here?" Colby interjects, breaking our eye contact as we both look at him.

She looks at the deck. "It doesn't matter now, does it."

He tightens his jaw. "Definitely not, but I can't help but be curious." Kellen remains quiet, and Colby sighs. "This is how things are going to go." He starts pulling her to the edge of the ship.

I immediately follow, but Hedda gets in my way. "Move!" I shout, shoving her.

She falls, but her grip remains, pulling me down with her.

Kellen turns and tries to lunge towards us, but Colby slams

her against the railing. "Mazu, you are going to either use those powers of yours, or I'm going to kill her."

Hedda shoves my chest with her feet as she pulls them up. My back slams into the hardwood of the deck, air escaping from my lungs, but I rise.

"I-I can't!" The lack of air forming my lungs makes it hard to get out.

"Sorry, Princess, but there are no knights in shining armour allowed on this boat." He grunts and shifts her weight over the railing. All he has to do is let go.

My feet pick me up and I run towards her.

"Mazu!" she screams as his grip releases.

I extend my hands, my mother's necklace glowing as a pulse of energy emanates from me.

Chapter Ten

"But I don't want to go to bed." I pout as Mamma tucks me in.

She chuckles softly, brushing the hair out of my face with her fingers. "How about I tell you a story?"

I nod my head, turning on my side so I can stare at her better as she rests her chin on one of her hands.

"Hundreds of sidereal years ago, the Goddesses of Vitaterrium once communed with their creations. People like us were able to travel to their realms through the doorways and ask for our prayers to come true."

My eyes widen. "They got to meet a goddess?"

She nods. "They would even bestow gifts onto those who they deemed a true follower of their ideals," Mamma explains, pulling the opal necklace she always wears. "My mother used to tell me that this very stone was our gift from Haldoris, the Seasire herself. The one who commands all waters."

"What does it do?" Reaching out towards it, my fingers pet the smooth stone.

She smiles brightly. "That I don't know, but my mother swore that if we ever needed her, the Seasire would be there when we call for her."

"So she'll answer our prayers?" My mother chuckles at my questions as she cups my face.

"Maybe..." Her eyes flicker over my face. "One day, this necklace will be yours, and if the time comes where you need help, just close your eyes and call out to her."

My brow furrows. "Like say her name?"

Her hand grasps mine, pulling it away from the necklace to place on my chest. "Call her from here..."

I COLLAPSE ONTO MY KNEES.

Was that what I did before?

Colby looks at me with wide eyes, Kellen coughs up water as she lays in front of me, soaking wet.

Hedda, somewhere behind me, mutters, "What the infernum?"

"You..." Colby takes a step forward, using his finger to point between the edge of the ship and me. "You just manipulated the water."

I finally release the breath I was holding, my eyes meeting his. The deck is covered in water from the small wave I brought on board to bring Kellen back up.

He was going to kill her.

My gaze hardens as I glare at him. "That's the second time you've thrown someone I love over the edge of something."

Colby raises his hands. "To be fair, it seems the most effective way to get you to do something." His voice is a tad quiet.

"I hate you." The words spit out of my mouth.

Before I can stand, Colby raises his dagger. "I'll blind you if you try." The steel blue eyes I'm staring at darken.

I'm not stupid enough to do what he thinks I'm going to try.

Hedda approaches Kellen and me, pulling her up and away from me. My heart clenches as Kellen stumbles a few times before she can even get a steady footing.

Colby's stare draws my attention back to him, a frown on his face when I was expecting a smile. "Thought you would be more happy about all of this..."

"The boss' happiness is what matters... and she won't care unless you know how to actually use it."

I remember now, what my mother told me all those years ago, the fable she had used to halt my whining.

"How did you do it?" he asks, walking up and looking down at me.

That can't be right.

Colby crouches down, playing with his dagger in his hand. "Mazu." When I shake my head, he sighs, but his tone softens. "You felt it that time. You saw what you did. Tell me the details."

"Leave her alone!" Kellen barks, as Hedda keeps her still.

His eyes don't even shift from me.

My mouth opens, but I don't know what I can say. It felt like I was about to have a panic attack. Desperation. A part of me isn't sure what I witnessed is even real.

Did I really do that?

Magicae is something I've seen a few times in my life, but no one openly practises it unless they have a licence in the Southern Territory. It's illegal otherwise. My family, none of us can do things like that. At least not what I've ever seen, and as far as I'm aware, you have to inherit magicae, right?

Colby stabs his knife into the deck, bringing me back into the moment. "Spit it out."

Say something.

"It..." His eyes widen in anticipation, leaning in to not miss a word. "Was like a jolt."

Raising a brow, he questions, "A jolt?" Colby's voice sounds out the word slowly, like he hadn't heard it before.

I nod my head.

He chuckles a bit, the wide smile looking foreign on his face. "A jolt?" He brings his hand to his face, covering one of his eyes.

Colby stands, offering me a hand, his chest still rumbling with laughter. I take it, and he pulls me up.

"Did you hear that?" He points the dagger at me like it's a finger. Kellen glares at him, and Hedda's furrowed brow is so deep set from the obvious confusion. "The in-depth description she just gave of this unknown magicae ability?"

"You're creeping me out," Hedda mutters. "Stop talking at me like I even know what you're saying."

Colby runs a hand through his hair, his laughing and smile fading slowly as his eyes land back on mine.

A shiver runs through me, my feet feeling suddenly frozen in place on the deck under the weight of his gaze. "I guess we just need to make you feel that, jolt, over and over again until you get a grasp on what the infernum that is even supposed to mean."

I swallow thickly as his gaze doesn't break.

"Let's take them down to the brig. We should be getting to Yral this evening," Colby states, simply gesturing for me to follow Hedda as she roughly handles Kellen down the stairs to where the cells are. "Princess."

KELLEN SITS in the cell across from mine. Her eyes cast downwards. "You remember that time when we were still youngins, we were running through the streets late at night with an empty bottle of port we were planning on using to spin the bottle with our friends?"

"The time when they thought we had drunk said bottle because you had accidentally spilled the remaining of its contents on us when you were getting it down from your father's cabinet?"

She chuckles and nods. "The guards put us in jail until our parents came..."

I smile, remembering the confused looks on our parents' faces when they saw us sitting huddled together in a cell, an actual passed out drunkard sitting in the opposite corner of us. My father had refused to come, but my mom was smiling just as she normally was, even when things weren't great.

"My father laughed so hard, and with your mom smiling next to him, the guards probably thought they might have been proud of us," Kellen says, tilting her head back so it rests against the wall behind her.

Closing my eyes, I sigh, just trying to remember her smile. This wouldn't be the same, though. What would she think of her family split apart like this? Is Father with her now?

"I haven't been able to ask them about my dad," I whisper, my eyes opening to look at her.

Kellen shifts, her head tilting towards me. "Sounds like you."

Raising a brow, I ask, "What does that mean?"

She clicks the toes of her boots together as she stares at me, amused. "You seriously are stupid sometimes."

What a thing to say to someone, especially when she was the one to sneak on a pirate ship, knowing it would likely get her killed.

"And you have a way of really making me feel better," I mutter, crossing my arms over my chest.

Kellen intertwines her fingers and rests them in her lap as she just chuckles to herself, making me pout. "You've always avoided a problem unless it's in your face asking to be dealt with."

I frown. "You do realise what likely happened to him, right?"

That thought has kept me from asking.

"Yeah," she states. "Is it different if they were to actually say it? Would it make you actually confront those pesky emotions?"

She is just egging me on, wanting to push me further and normally I would play along, but right now I am not in the mood. I shouldn't have brought it up.

"Shut up," I mutter.

"He's dead," Kellen says sternly. "What happens if they say those words?"

My eyes shut tight.

Stop it.

I don't want to hear those words.

"How about we talk about the fact you snuck onto a pirate ship and nearly just died?" I shoot back.

"Okay." My eyes open at her compliance. She brings her knees up, placing her arms on top of them. "I thought I made myself pretty clear at the guards' station."

I scoff. "That's not explaining how, Kellen."

Now I get to point the questions at her.

She's quiet for a moment, before a sigh leaves her mouth. "The hit I took didn't knock me out... and I knew if I just got up, that stupid cheap trick with blinding me wouldn't go anywhere, so I waited until I heard your footsteps fade away," Kellen explains matter-of-factly. She plays with her fingers as she continues. "Was as simple as getting up and following you. I told a guard on my way to get reinforcements, but for one reason or another, no one came."

I furrow my brow at that. No one even tried to come help her? Perhaps the idea of 'my friend is getting kidnapped by pirates for an embezzlement plot against a foreign king' didn't sound all that believable. Even if she had put it more simply, maybe it was one of those guards who just didn't care. Like Kellen had mentioned at the station, or more so pointed out to her boss, is that our guards have come to do less and less for their people.

"When I saw that one chick leave, I saw my chance as the crew that was still on deck turned their backs. They had been loading stuff onboard and used it to hide behind until I could make my way down to the hull and find a secluded spot." Her eyes lift from her fingers to find mine.

Damn, she is impressive.

I close my eyes and chuckle softly for a moment. She really is so good at her job, but she's just thrown it all away. I'm not sure if I'm amused even though I'm angry with her because I'm sitting here and admiring her skills, or that I'm laughing so I don't cry from the guilt of dragging her into this.

"Mazu. I know what I'm willing to die for." Her tone settled, like she has made up her mind on how she wants her life to end. "Stop acting like you're the only one allowed to be reckless when it comes to someone you love."

"I'm not worth this. You have a future in Berkin. You have dreams. Why are you throwing that all away? Did you even think what it would do to me to see them kill you? Because that's what they are going to do!" My voice cracks as my eyes start to water, but I look upwards, trying to absorb the tears back in, my jaw clenching.

"You don't have dreams? You don't have a future? Do you

know what it felt like to let them take you away?" Kellen's tone stays even. "I played dead so I could follow you, and hope for a chance for both of us to get away."

"I didn't ask you to, Ke—"

"And you will never have to." She cuts me off. "Did Ari ask you to kill yourself so he wouldn't be alone?"

My gaze shifts down so I can meet her glare.

I'm really not worth this. I have nothing to offer her. The only value I have is whatever these criminals are putting on me, and even that comes with the stipulation of me controlling this ability. I can only hope that if I do end up useless to them, they continue to leave Ari alone.

"If they end up killing me," Kellen's soft voice cuts through my thoughts, "I need you to know... to hear this loud and clear..."

"No," I shake my head, "they aren't going to kill you. I'll make another deal. I'll make sure you survive this, Kellen."

Her brow furrows; the words she was trying to force me to hear are seemingly pushed to the back of her mind. "Deal? You made a deal?"

"To take Ari out of the equation... I agreed to become a member of their crew," I state. The confidence in that sentence wears thin as the anger rises in her.

Kellen stands and walks up to her door, slamming her hands on the bars. "You sold yourself?"

The door to the hull opens, and Colby comes down a few steps, observing the tension in the room before walking over to my cell. Kellen's fingers grip onto the bars, her knuckles turning white. He unlocks my door, gesturing for me to head up the stairs.

"You girls getting along?" His voice is hushed as I pass in front of him.

"Peachy," I mutter as I walk up the stairs.

Colby follows close behind me, leaving Kellen alone.

Did he tell the boss about what happened earlier? Or was she spectating it?

He leads me to the Captain's Quarters, knocking before he opens the door. A trill of smoke swirls around her as she sits in her chair smoking. It's like a fog has settled in this room, and the pungent smell makes my eyes water.

She smiles brightly. "My little gem." She hums, standing up, setting her roll down on a silver ashtray that looks like it is screwed into the wooden desk.

I bite the inside of my cheek as she walks around the desk to sit on the front edge. Colby nudges me forwards, making me realise I had frozen in the middle of the doorway.

"You are showing me some promise with what you did today." She chuckles.

Staring at her seems like the only thing to do. I was hoping to have something better to offer her in exchange for Kellen's life. I didn't think I would be coming face to face with her right now.

"Colby has been doing his best to get things going, but he's been telling me you have been a little resistant." Her smile turns into a forced frown. "So, I want you to tell me what it really was like to control the ocean."

"It wasn't the ocean..." I mutter under my breath.

The boss leans in, cupping her ear, prompting me to say it again, but Colby pushes me closer so she is only a metre in front of me, if that, before I do.

"If you saw... then you know it wasn't the ocean, but a small wave." I force a smile as I repeat myself.

Her brow quirks up as she examines my expression. "A 'small' wave to wash a human back onto my boat." She leans back on her arms, tilting her head. "I see what you mean, love. My gem is resistant to these abilities of hers... and to us."

Colby clears his throat. "I'll keep working with her."

"No... I think I'll play with her a bit... have a heart to heart." Her eyes harden and are pointed at me as she responds to Colby.

He steps forwards, allowing me to take in his scowl. "Once we finish our business in Yral, we will head back to base. I'll be able to have more room and time to properly train her. I will get you results, Renna."

What is happening?

Is he doing this for me, or is this more about his pride to impress the boss? Either way, everything is telling me I really don't want to be left alone in a room with her.

She stands up and walks up to Colby, looking over his face, her hands cupping his cheeks. "Interesting..." she mutters. Renna stares at him for a while. His shoulders are stiff and he keeps his arms glued to his side. "Fine... I'll let you play with her a little longer."

"I won't fail you," he mutters, a smile spreading across her face as she hears him say that.

The dynamic they have, the way she looks at him. It makes me feel queasy.

Renna rubs his cheek with her thumb before dropping her hands. "Take her to her cage then... I want you back in here, though. I'm feeling a tad neglected."

"Of course."

CHAPTER ELEVEN

Colby's expression haunts me as I sit down in my cell. That far away expression in his gaze I've seen once before when we talked about what it means to be on this ship. He's not a person I care for, but it doesn't sit right with me.

She almost seemed jealous.

"Mazu. Stop ignoring me." Kellen groans, her head banging against the bars of her cell lightly.

I just curl up more, laying on the floor as I avoid the conversation she wants to have. It won't matter what I say. Taking a deal was a stupid thing in her eyes. She wants to know everything I said, what the parameters are of this deal.

"You won't make it in this life, Mazu. You have a hard time even with stomaching violence. Do you think you'll be able to actually carry through with an order?" I cover my ears to try and block her out. "They will destroy you."

Probably.

I sit up, making her eyes widen as I lock onto her. "Just because violence is not my immediate response to something does not mean I will allow you or anyone to belittle and walk over me."

We stare at each other for a moment. Silence enveloping us as we settle our differences on the matter.

"I won't let you do this alone," Kellen states.

My heart lurches at the implication. "Don't."

"I told you, I know what I'm willing to die for. That should tell you that I know what I'm willing to sacrifice, too." Her words are definite.

There is no fighting her on this. We are both too stubborn, and I know that no matter what I say, the only way she is getting off this ship alive, and willingly, is if I am getting off with her.

I'll have to try.

A shift in the ship makes us both tumble to our sides. Loud shouts and heavy footsteps from above us let us know we are docking. My heart sinks in my throat.

Kellen sits up and grips onto the bars to stabilise herself as the ship continues to bounce. "What are you going to do?"

I take a shaky breath. "I'm going to smile."

The door opens, and Colby heads down and unlocks me from my cell.

"The boss is going to have you and me stay in the city proper," he states. My eyes linger on him a bit. There's a redness around his neck, along with a bite mark.

I've seen Mehl and Lip with those kinds of markings before. Kellen would tease them about it all the time, but I just never really cared to hear those details of their love life.

Colby gestures for me to move. "Go."

Nodding my head, I wave to Kellen and give her a forced smile. She just stares as I head up and out of the hull. The night air is brisker than what I'm used to, but feels amazing as my nerves are heating me up. Renna is standing in the centre of the deck, talking to the crew, but she turns at the sound of our approaching footsteps.

"My little gem," she coos, smiling at me, her platinum hair flowing around in the wind. "You're going to do a good job for us, right?"

My forced smile doesn't falter. "Of course."

Her eyes widen a bit, but so does her smile. "Lovely."

Colby walks ahead of me. "We will be off then." He takes Renna's hand in his, bringing it up to his lips to leave a brushed kiss against her knuckles.

"Keep her close, Colby. I'd hate to have to punish you for losing her." Renna's grip on Colby's hand tightens as her words turn harsh.

He nods, and she drops his hold on him. We walk off; the crew turning back to their boss as we head down the ramp. The tall spiralled towers of the castle are visible in the moonlight. Its light blue pointed roofs and sandstone bricks are more dreamy in the hazy glow than I remember when I came with Father on one of his rare trips out this way. The ocean sparkles as it crashes against the beach. The sight of something I've grown so accustomed to brings me comfort as we head into the city. Like I'm not all that far from home, despite being in a different country with a stranger who has turned my life upside down. A few lamps keep the alley ways dimly lit as we make our way through. The bright colours I remember, muted in the night.

Is this where their nobility live? Everything looks so new and expensive.

Colby is slightly ahead of me, my eyes wandering to his neck every once in a while, but I look away. The way he looks at Renna doesn't reflect the same type of soft gaze Mehl and Lip have for one another; and the way Renna looks at him is more like a cat would look at a mouse. It makes me wonder just how willing of a participant he is in all of that, but I am most definitely not going to ask about it. I despise the guy and knowing more about what goes on behind closed doors is not any of my business. He's the one choosing to work for her anyhow. I can only hope that Renna doesn't have a habit of expecting things from all of her crew.

He turns inward towards a building. "We're here."

The Seashore Slumber.

We walk into the Inn. Everything on the inside feels still. The fire in the hearth is low, cushioned furniture sitting around it for guests to relax in. The front desk lining the furthest wall is empty, but Colby walks up to the desk, tapping the bell that jingles.

A very tall but lean man saunters in, dark circles under his eyes but a warm smile plastered on his face. "Hello there. Are you looking to check in?"

"Whatever room you have available, please," Colby says, his voice is quiet, the atmosphere seeming to impact him just as much as it is impacting me as I take very careful and quiet footsteps towards them.

The man nods and opens a ledger, reviewing it for a moment before grabbing a key from a hook on the wall behind him. "Will you be settling the bill after your stay?"

Colby simply nods, and the man starts walking towards the stairs. "Very well. Please, follow me and we will settle you into your home away from home."

My brow raises as Colby looks back at me.

I think we just had the same thought.

A small smirk on both our faces after hearing the man's sentence.

Home away from home?

Cheesy.

The man unlocks the nearest door as we step onto the first floor landing. "Please, enjoy your stay, and don't hesitate to let me know what I can do to make your stay more comfortable."

He hands the key to Colby before we walk in, closing the door behind us. I take a few steps further, admiring the large room. Well, it could be considered two rooms, a small frame with curtains on either side of it to partition the bedroom from the lounge we are currently standing in. Two chairs facing a rounded coffee table are off to one side, while the other has a proper dining table. Walking into the bedroom, a large canopy sits in its centre, its back facing us, as it points towards a window that shows the expansive and glimmering city of Yral.

"You're quiet," Colby mutters as he takes off his coat and lays it against the back of one of the lounge chairs.

I turn to look at him. "Just taking all this in..."

"Princesses shouldn't be so surprised by luxury," Colby states, stepping into the bedroom.

He smirks and looks at me with a quirked brow. I don't understand how he can be so casual after what he did just yesterday to me, to my best friend. Does he think I've got over it or that I shouldn't hold it against him?

Rolling my eyes, I say, "Well, just because you call me princess, doesn't make me one. I'm pretty sure this is the nicest room I have ever been in..."

Colby stares out the window for a moment before looking back at me. "That's sad."

I really do hate this man.

Kicking off my shoes, I sit on the edge of the bed. My eyes widen at how soft it is, how fluffy the comforter is. My hands run over the fabric for a moment before I lay back.

This is what it must feel like to lie on a cloud.

My eyes close for a moment as I imagine it. High in the sky, away from all of this, nothing but light blue and white surrounding me.

I open my eyes as the bed shifts. I tilt my head to the side and see Colby lying on the bed, an arm behind his head as he leans against the pillows on that side, his eyes meeting mine.

My body jolts up and I turn to face him.

"You know, you shouldn't let your guard down like that," he mutters with a smile.

"What is this?" I grumble, pointing at him on the bed.

"I'm getting comfortable." His eyes locked on with mine.

My brow furrows. "You expect me to lie in bed with you?"

"You want to sleep on the floor?" Colby asks. "Because you can if you want to. I'll be sleeping right here if you need me."

Why must he ruin everything good in this life?

"First, I'll never need you," I state. "Second, why didn't you ask for a room with two beds?"

He closes his eyes. "I'm actually very useful." Colby's voice is softer. "I saved you from being under the boss' grip, didn't I?"

So that was about being kind.

My eyes bore into his, mainly because he didn't even answer the second question.

He doesn't shift or even open his eyes as I stay silent. Though I have a thousand questions running through my mind at what that even means. Is this supposed to be a moment where I thank him? Not that I would. He has endangered the people I love, literally tried to kill them. Has berated and imprisoned me and is part of the reason I am even here at all.

"Just lay down." He sighs, eyes still closed.

I sit still for a moment before I shift, crawling under the covers.

At least he is laying on top of them.

"Did she hurt you?" I whisper, my eyes closing as my head sinks into the pillow.

Even if I hate him, I can't help but feel bad. There are moments where it is like he is just trying to survive, that all of this is for something else and not because he wants to do it, but he is also on that boat. He does terrible things and doesn't seem to feel remorseful even in the slightest.

A silence hangs in the air before he answers. "Do you care?" His lids slowly open, and he turns his head to me. "Because you really shouldn't. Just focus on yourself."

"Then why did you save me from Renna?" I ask back. "Doesn't seem you follow your own advice."

Colby twitches at my comment. "Touché," he whispers. "She didn't do anything I'm not used to at this point."

"What? She normally chokes out her crew?" I ask, knowing I am trying to pry without actually saying it out loud.

His eyes widen a bit before a genuine laugh escapes him. He covers his mouth with the hand that was resting on his chest. The shake of his laughter shifts the bed along with him.

I chuckle a little, too.

"You are not cut out for this world..." He sighs as he calms himself down from his laughter.

His eyes go distant, not quite looking at me or anything in this room, his smile faltering.

"I do what I have to..." Colby's voice is barely a whisper.

I feel so sorry for him.

WE HEAD TO THE LIBRARY. The place where the letter stated we would be meeting with the representative from Felguard. Colby moves along with the crowd of the city. It is way more dense than what I'm used to in Berkin. This is the type of crowd we pull for festivals or holidays, but this is just their day to day, apparently.

He occasionally looks over his shoulder to make sure I am

still there and keeping up. I eventually grip onto the back of his coat as the crowd gets thicker, and threatens to pull us apart. If it wasn't for Kellen back on the ship, I would use the crowd to my advantage. Colby probably knows that which is why he is being more relaxed, despite the perfect opportunity for escape being right here.

We wander up to a tall tower. The staircase on the outside of the building causes me to raise a brow in confusion, though. Small doorways are set at every floor that leads inward with no windows in sight.

Colby guides us through the ground floor doorway. My eyes examine the floor to ceiling bookcases that make up the walls of this building. Books floating around and into people's hands or back to their places on the shelves.

Colby tugs on my wrist, gesturing for me to follow him to the circular desk in the centre of this place. Three keepers working in the middle of it.

An orcish woman looks up as we approach and smiles a toothy grin. "Hello scholars, how can I assist you today?"

"We are looking for any correspondence that may have arrived for a Mazu Hali," Colby states, leaning against the desk.

The woman shifts over to another part of the desk, flitting through a stack of letters. "Hali... Hali... Ah." She pulls out a sealed letter before walking back over.

"Can we have proof of self?" she asks.

Colby looks back at me, and I nod.

I present my wrist to her before she pulls up a small crystal that hangs from a silver chain. "Mazu Hali, Berkin Resident, Limoria."

The crystal glows a pale green colour. "Perfect. Thank you." She hands me the letter.

My hands shake as I open it, wondering if my disbelief will

come true, that my family has no ties with the crown of Felguard.

Dearest Cousin,

My heart is burdened to hear of your swift losses. I will have a member of my guard, Shaw, greet you. Please meet her at the barracks near the edge of the city.

I look forward to meeting you soon, Mazu, and hope you've arrived in Yral safe and well.

Best Regards,
King Kage Felguard

I hand the letter over to Colby to read before I face the keeper who helped us. "Thank you."

She smiles and nods her head. "My pleasure."

Colby folds the letter and hands it back before walking us out to where I'm guessing the barracks is.

"The wording was weird." I look up at him as he speaks. "He said he would see you soon, but is sending a rep."

"Maybe he sees his representatives as an extension of himself?" King Felguard lives in another world than us. I'm sure the way he sees the world is much different.

Colby just hums, clearly pondering, as we continue to make our way out. "Just stay close to me, and I swear to whatever goddess, if you say anything about what we are doing..."

"I got it," I spit at him. "What happens if this Shaw asks about who you are?"

He looks down at me. "I'm the friend you are staying with while you are here."

Nodding my head, we continue to make our way through.

Simple enough.

CHAPTER TWELVE

THE LARGE BUILDING we walk into is full of guards, but the most relaxed guards I have ever seen. They don't even wear armour. All decorated in silver and light layers. With how wealthy this place is, you think they would be more worried about being attacked or something.

One of the guards walks up to us, a large framed man. "Hello. What is your business here?" His tone is serious, but he has a slight smile on his face.

Colby steps forwards. "We're here to meet a representative from the Felguard Country."

The guard looks us over, his smile faltering for a moment as disbelief nearly overrides his welcoming atmosphere. I am now very aware of how rough we must look. It's not like cleanliness was the top priority on the ship. We're at least bathed, but our clothes probably look wrinkled, as they are the ones we slept in.

'*Gives us a pathetic appearance,*' Colby had said.

I shake my head as I recall our talk when we woke up, but I

snap back into the moment as Colby and the guard move towards a sitting area.

"We will notify the rep." The guard saunters off.

I take a seat, Colby standing at the side of my chair.

"Put on that stupid smile, and beg," Colby whispers, lowering himself to make sure no one but me can hear him.

A young girl walks up to us, her face completely void of any expression. Not stoic, but void of feeling, it seems.

What?

"Hello. I'm Shaw. Do you have the letter?" she asks, holding out her hand.

Well, isn't she one to just get right down to business. My eyes dart to Colby for a fleeting moment before I reach into my pocket and pull out the one we picked up from the library. I smile at her before handing it off.

She glances at the seal and nods before looking at Colby. "Who are you?"

Colby puts on a stupid smile of his own. "A friend she is staying with while she's here."

Sure, he gets the easy one liner.

Shaw stares at us for a moment before accepting the answer. "Please stand." I do as she instructs, my brow furrowing, a tad confused. Colby is just watching slightly from behind me. "We will be leaving to meet with the King."

"What? He's here?" I ask, looking at Colby, who has the same confused look on his face.

Shaw grabs my arm lightly. "Please excuse my touch."

Within a blink of an eye, my head spins for a moment. A large imposing door is suddenly in front of me. My heart is in my throat as the young girl releases my wrist from her grasp.

I look down at her with wide eyes.

Did she just teleport us?

This was not what any of us were expecting. We thought

he would have a representative waiting for us. Most countries have at least one rep inside the other countries' capitals, but having me teleport to him was never even on the table.

Colby definitely didn't prepare me for this during our morning training sessions.

How in the infernum am I going to do this? Kellen, myself and Ari are all depending on me to do this right. To ensure that the funds are going to be provided. What is Colby going to tell Renna? This could be a serious problem. I haven't even earned their trust yet.

The girl knocks on the door a few times before opening the door slowly and walking in, leaving it open for me to follow her.

It's happening now?

Glancing around quickly, it definitely looks like I am in a castle, or at least somewhere where they casually have a golden vase with precious jewels sitting on an ornate foyer table.

"Your Majesty. Mazu Hali, as requested," the girl says, before turning and leaving us alone in this grand space.

Just breathe, Mazu.

The only part I know about the new king's ruling is that he is new, young, and the son of the former Tyrant King. I'm not sure how, but based on what I've heard, he's highly respected by most of the leaders of Limoria. I am more familiar with his father and lineage. Those who have ruled over the largest country in our realm since the Ancestry War that divided our Limoria into multiple countries. His father was always written about in the papers. The Tyrant King. The Felguard Country was in a rapid decline. People fleeing their homes to escape the harsh tax and internal conflicts. Enslaving magicae users as a way of protecting the country, but nothing in the papers or rumours ever really told us who he was protecting them from.

Lying to this man, whether or not he is a relative, doesn't seem like the best move, but what else am I supposed to do?

I avoid looking directly at him, taking in the mass amounts of books, but my eyes focus on one of the many paintings in this room. It's a painting of the Yral library. The view of the ocean just past it. It's not painted with the normal light shades of blue and white, but gold and silver, making the tower more striking.

"It was a gift from the council of Yral when I made my first visit," the King states, making me turn to him finally.

His slicked back raven hair and unshaven face make his emerald eyes pop, just like the white tower resting against a golden sea.

"Well, that's nice of them," I mutter and take a step inward, forcing a soft smile onto my face.

Being given such a gift for just simply showing up... must be nice to have such a luxury.

He gives me a brief smile in return before gesturing to the seats resting on the side of us. I follow his lead and sit in one of the lush chairs, fiddling with my hands.

"When I heard of my aunt's passing, I felt it was only right to bring you to the castle," he says, clearing his throat for a moment. "I am not unfamiliar with loss, and in tough times we often need support."

I stare into him. Those eyes have dark circles under them. They are red, even. They almost look like Ari's eyes after he's cried for a while. Like my eyes the day my mother died. He shifts himself, forcing me to blink a few times as I realise I had been looking at him for too long.

He didn't even know her.

He doesn't know me.

He doesn't know of anything that's been happening.

The King's brow furrows slightly. "I don't mean to generalise your loss. My mother and I simply want to extend an invitation for you to move to Draco, where she and the rest of our family, on that side, live. I'm sure it would bring some semblance of support for you and your brother."

"Your mother, what?" I ask, frowning.

He's already come up with a plan without even speaking with me?

He takes in an audible breath. "I want to provide you with the funds to make such a trek, and perhaps assist in finding you a place to stay and the furnishings necessary."

My body goes rigid. He's willing to provide all of this. To build a new life for my brother and me. My anger starts to boil at how easily he is willing to throw money our way.

Why didn't he save her?

If she was alive, if she was here. None of this would have happened. She would have known what to do. I would have been the one thrown from the cliff instead, and maybe Ari wouldn't have had to experience that. My family would still be a family if she were here.

Don't lash out, Mazu.

Curling my hand into a fist, I smile at him. "I appreciate the offer, Your Majesty, but Berkin has always been our home. With wanting to honour my mother's choice to move us there, that is where I intend to stay."

King Felguard's eyes dart around my face, almost like he is reading a book. My back stiffens under his gaze as it lingers.

"I completely understand, and please, call me Kage." His smile falters for a split second. "Though, I am curious what it is you were wanting from me then, besides my 'highly valuable time', as you had put it in your letter."

All I need to do is say it exactly how Colby and I practised it.

"As you know... things have just gone from bad to worse." My eyes squint. "I know most in my position would defer to depositing their younger sibling to an orphanage in order to survive, but I know that would not be my mother's wish, just as it would disgrace her leaving Berkin." Kage leans to one side, resting his cheek against his hand. "My father has not been pleased with the reaction or lack of help from the Torrin family and has abandoned us with the debts of the healer's payments in the wake of my mother's passing."

He smiles, making me halt in finishing my speech. He looks me over in my entirety this time. The King gestures with his hand for me to continue, though.

"I-It would help us, greatly, to have some type of stipend until I can find more steady work..." My nails dig into my palm, his eyes observing the movement.

"I could just pay off the debts, no?" he asks, sitting upright. "All I would need is the bills to get past my council, but I have no doubts they would approve of those."

No, that wouldn't actually work, since those bills don't exist and not what Renna had asked for. It is seriously getting to me, though, just how easy it would have been for him to help my mother.

He leans forward, a smirk on his features, those red-rimmed eyes wide as he continues to take me in. It feels like I am an ant under a spyglass.

"Mazu?" Kage asks, his voice lower in tone than it was before.

I clear my throat. "I could try and find them... but I have worked out a deal—"

"I'm sure you have." He interrupts me. "With the **Lardo in Aumento,** correct?" My body freezes as I look down at him.

Is that the name of Renna's crew?

He crosses his arms over his torso and tilts his head. "Your father had already sent me a letter of your mother's passing. So when you wrote to inform me of the same thing, I sent Shaw to Berkin to check in on things. Apparently, you tried filing a missing person's report on your father, along with that battery charges, and breaking and entering against some assailants you stated were trying to get you to embezzle." He leans back in his chair. "I was shocked you didn't include that in your letter. Unless, for some reason, you wouldn't want to draw attention to that... like in case they had already got to you."

I stare at him, my lips parted, utterly dumbfounded. He knew I was lying from the minute I started talking.

I failed. I failed before I even got here.

The air in my lungs exhales in the realisation. He took it upon himself to investigate and screw everything up. They're going to kill Ari.

"If you knew... why did you bring me?" I turn fully towards him.

The King follows me with his gaze. "To save you." His words are a matter-of-fact but lack any warmth you'd expect from a saviour.

Although his words I'm sure are meant to bring me comfort, my panic only rises. I reach out and grab onto his suit jacket. His eyes widen but don't flinch.

"You don't understand!" My voice is shrill. "They will kill them."

Kage raises a brow and pulls my hand off of him. "Them?"

I retract my hand completely, bringing it to my chest and gripping onto my own shirt.

"My brother and Kellen," I mutter, trying to force back tears. "They are waiting on me." My eyes bore into his. "Their lives will be in danger if I just disappear. I think they are already freaking out thanks to suddenly being teleported."

A part of me wishes I could have seen Colby's face after we vanished right in front of him. I wonder if he is sitting there waiting or if he immediately ran to inform Renna.

"I have no intention of letting you go back," he states, opening his eyes to look at me. "I do apologise for your friend, but you should know I—"

"You said you understand loss, right?" His eyes twitch as I cut him off. I stand up, as if it gives me some sort of dominance over this situation. "Then you know I can't accept that answer!"

He blinks a few times, the smirk he had been wearing completely gone. "Before you so rudely cut me off, I was going to tell you that I have your brother. Here. Right now. Safe." My heart lurches, tears almost immediately wanting to spill over. "Does that change things? Your friend might not make it, but you and your brother are safe."

Ari's here?

My first instinct is to run through these halls and scream for my brother, to see his face, hold him in my arms and confirm that he is actually safe, that his life is no longer on the line, but then there's Kellen. His life may be spared in this conflict, but now they have her to hang over me, just as they at first had him.

How did Shaw even get Ari to come with her? Did Mrs Relch really just let some random person take him?

"So?" He raises a brow, gesturing with his hands to give me an answer.

"No. It doesn't..." I mutter. "Kellen's life means more than I can really explain."

He straightens his posture, making my legs falter in the strong stance I am trying to put on. Not that I think he would actually do anything to hurt me physically, being a king and all, but his hardened gaze makes me believe he is more than capable of forcing me to his will.

"You would still risk your own life, going back to save this, Kellen?" His voice is quieter.

"Yes."

Kage sighs, standing up and walking over to the desk that sits in this room. He waves me over, and it takes concentration for me to actually walk over to him.

His finger taps on a document before looking back at me as I approach. "How much do you know about the group you are travelling with?"

"You make it sound like I'm buddies with them... I don't know anything, really. The name you said kinda sounded familiar. I think my father told me about them at one point," I state, my eyes drifting to the paper he is touching.

The King picks it up and hands it to me. "Nothing has been confirmed as of yet... but we believe that the Lardo in Aumento are working with or for a much more dangerous group called the Domi Nostrae."

Domi, what now?

"Okay? So that means..." I trail off, hoping for him to finish the sentence.

He walks around the desk and takes a seat at the large cushioned chair. "If you want to go back..." His Majesty pauses, his brow pinches together tightly. "I need you to find proof of this, and stop any of the activities that are happening, or if it proves too dangerous or you find yourself in over your head, retreat and inform me."

A spark lights in me, hearing him say that. I can't leave Kellen there. Everything in me is telling me to stay, but my heart feels like it'll be ripped out of my chest if I do.

I nod my head. "You'll have Shaw send me back?"

"This is not sanctioned. If you die, I'll call it a tragedy," he states. "If you don't get away, I'll have to get involved to pull you out. Which, if that happens, I'll ensure you work for me for the rest of your life to pay this country back."

That sounds horrifying.

He leans forwards. "At worst, I'll reveal you're a spy, so they will terminate you and save me the trouble."

Why does it sound like he has done that kind of thing before?

"You should know, this is a one-time thing, Mazu." His voice is tense. "Me putting my trust in you like this. Had it not been for recent events..." His eyes glaze over for a moment. "I wouldn't even consider it, but I can see that Kellen means something to you."

My hands intertwine in front of me. "I don't plan on getting kidnapped and forced to embezzle and join a criminal organisation again. This is a one-time thing," I confirm.

He nods, clearing his throat and dissipating any fog from his gaze. "So you know, I'm turning this into something that can be covered up. Maybe something will turn out of this with you cutting one of the threads the Domi Nostrae have, giving this more value to me letting you go, but I'm not betting on you." My brow furrows to interject his rude statement, but he raises his other hand to halt my sentence. "I'm allowing this, because I recognise the look in your eyes... It's one I've worn. I'd rather give you a leash than you run off and do something stupid."

The urge to roll my eyes is strong, but he just compared us, which I'm not sure how to take. "Maybe being rebels runs in the family."

Runs in the family.

My hand comes up and rests on my mother's necklace.

"I'm sure it does," he says, staring into me. "We won't have much time to get you ready, but I'll give you the funds they are likely going to be expecting you to secure. Did they give you an amount?"

"Enough to live off of for a while." He nods at my words and takes a key off of his belt, unlocking one of the drawers and pulling out a pouch.

As he counts the coins inside, I chew on my cheek.

Should I ask him?

"Do... Do you know if magicae runs in our family?" My voice is soft.

His eyes flicker up at me before he continues to count. "No. Though we come from a long line of worshipers who believed that goddesses could gift their essence to those of strong faith."

Mother's story.

"Your mother. Did she ever tell you stories?" I ask.

Kage tightens the string on the pouch to re-close it, tossing it onto the desk and nearer to me. "Stories?"

I grip onto the necklace, his eyes watching my movement before leaning back in his chair.

"The ones about Haldoris?" Maybe I shouldn't be asking.

He sighs. "It's easier if you just ask the question you're really wanting to know the answer to."

Is he like a mind reader or something because at this point, he just sees through everything.

Compared to him, I feel like a petulant child. I know he isn't that much older than I am, but the way he speaks, thinks, how he holds himself, even in his looks. The gap feels much larger as he sits there, staring at me.

"There are moments. Moments where I have been able to do things I shouldn't be able to do," I whisper.

"Like?" he asks.

With his father's obsession with magicae, I would think he would hold more interest, but he doesn't seem fazed or particularly interested.

I shift on my feet, feeling crazy for even talking about this. "Like... control water? I've only done it when it's been a life or death situation," I explain. "They have seen it, and want to utilise it... but I'm not sure how to control it."

He points at my chest. "Let me see it."

My grip tightens, but I slowly remove the necklace before handing it to him. "It was my mother's, and hers before that, and so on."

The King examines it for a moment, holding it up to the light of an oil lamp on his desk. I watch him in silence. He stands and walks over to a wall of books, glancing over the titles before he pulls one down and returns to his seat.

"It's okay if you don't kno—" He holds up a finger before flipping through the pages.

Leaning up against the desk, I try to peer at the book he is looking at but it is in a language I've never even seen before.

He can read that?

"There's likely an inscription or ritual, if this is a goddess-bestowed gift," he mumbles. "But if you've used it, you must have done it somehow."

I furrow my brows. "I never did a ritual."

"When was the first time you were able to access the power?" He offers me the necklace back.

"When I jumped off a cliff to be with Ari after he was thrown off..." I state as I put the necklace back on.

The King's eyes widen. "So that part was true in the reports?" His finger points back to the necklace. "And that necklace saved you?"

I nod. "That's what everyone thinks happened... but I blacked out. I kinda remember the vision I had, but it's fuzzy."

"What did you see?" Kage asks.

"I was floating... and there was a woman singing in the background." My eyes close as I try to remember more clearly, but it feels almost a million miles away.

He sighs and runs a hand through his hair. "You play

music, or sing, or something, correct?" he asks, closing his eyes for a moment.

He knows about that?

"Sing," I mutter, opening my eyes to meet his.

"Magicae is not as complicated as people think it is..." he says, standing once more. He looks down at me, that smirk returning to his face. "Sing."

CHAPTER THIRTEEN

COLBY LEANS BACK in the chair, his leg bouncing as he watches the guards go about their business. I walk up behind him, his head turning as he hears my footsteps approach.

"You're back?" Colby stands and faces me properly.

I pat the satchel I'm now wearing. "And I got what we needed."

He pauses, looking me over, though I'm not sure what exactly he is looking for. My brow raises as he continues to just stare. My heart beats faster, hoping he can't really tell just by looking at me that I'm now in kahoots with the King.

"Did anything happen while you were there?" He finally snaps back, meeting my gaze. "You look okay."

Time to lie, just like Colby taught you.

"Do you care?" I ask, throwing his words back at him from last night. He tilts his head at me and scowls, but I flash him a smile instead. "Just kidding. I'm fine and nothing happened. I shed a few tears, and he complied..."

Colby's gaze hardens. "Is that so..."

I nod my head. "To be specific, he said that he wasn't going to let someone in his family go into poverty." My voice is steady as I force my eyes to remain on his, versus looking away like my body is telling me to do.

He stares at me for another moment before his eyes soften, just ever so slightly. "Then let's go."

Nodding my head, I gesture for him to lead the way. He grabs at the satchel, pulling it off me and throwing it over his shoulder before heading out.

We start our trek an awful lot like we did on our way to the Library; me trying to not get separated from my captor. He grabs my wrist as he looks back and sees me getting slowed down by the crowd. I'm used to tourists, living in Berkin, but this is a whole other level.

"Don't go getting lost now, Princess," Colby teases.

Kage puts a book and other things in the satchel with money, making me look at him a tad confused. "What's all that for?"

He glances up at me before putting in a few sheets of paper. "Things to make all this more believable. Walking away with nothing but a pouch seems strange when you just met with family, royal or not."

I nod my head, taking his word for it. For someone of royal blood, he sure seems well equipped to counteract or know how to deal with lowly pirates.

"You've done this before?" I ask as he hands me the satchel.

He quirks a brow. "Not this in particular, no, but I've dealt with delicate matters such as this."

That just makes me think of a dozen other questions. Like what a delicate situation is supposed to mean exactly. Though there are more pressing questions, or maybe ones I am more curious about.

"So..." I ask, kicking my shoe at the carpet. "Are Ari and I going to be invited to your royal wedding? Cause, I'll need a dress for something that—"

"No," he states firmly, his hand gripping onto the desk. "The book I gave you is on the Torrin family history, something that might be believable to get you more familiar with the family who is now 'financially' responsible for your life."

Pushed my luck on that one, I guess, but the way he shut it down felt awfully cold for how receptive he's been to me. He's not cuddly by any means, but he didn't even flinch at declining the idea of his 'family' being at his wedding.

"Shaw will take you back," he mutters, running his hand through his hair and looking over some documents on his desk.

I furrow my brow. "No goodbye?" I chuckle.

He looks up just enough for our gazes to meet. "I'll be in contact. Just reply inwardly when you hear it."

I furrow my brow. "What?"

Kage waves me off, and so I take a few steps back, watching him return to whatever it is he is doing before walking out of the room.

Shaw is leaning against the wall. "You shouldn't have asked." Her voice is quiet.

"Asked what?"

"About the wedding."

Colby and I board the ship; the satchel from Kage still on Colby's shoulder. The crew watch us, all of their eyes going to the bag as we make our way to the Captain's Quarters.

He knocks three times, waiting for an acknowledgement before opening the door and walking in. "She did it."

Renna slides off her bed, stands and walks towards us. "Oh?" Her smile makes me sick.

"I told you I would," I point out.

She chuckles. "That you did, little gem. I knew you would shine brightly for me." Her hand rises and reaches for me, but Colby slings the satchel from his shoulder and presents it to her. Her eyes flicker to it and her smile widens as she takes it in her hands. "I love presents..."

"I know." Colby hums towards her as she opens it.

Renna glides over to her desk and pulls out the contents. A book, paper, ink, a seal and wax, but most importantly, the pouch of coins. She shakes it a few times to hear the clinking before undoing the string, pouring the coins onto her desk, a decent pile, enough for me and Ari to live off of modestly for a year.

"A little stingy..." She pouts, counting them. "But this will do for now... we will call on him again. Tell him you bought a house or something that caused the funds to dwindle quickly..."

Yeah, he's not going to go for that.

There's my time limit. It's not really a number of shifts or mooncycles, but it tells me I have until the money runs out.

"Tell the crew once we've finished restocking, we can head home." Her orders for Colby. "You have been a very good little pet... and I'll trust you'll behave as long as your friend is on board."

I nod my head.

Renna has no shame in using people. She is acting like my friend is currency.

She tilts her head. "What was her name? Kellen? She's cute, has the same stoic look about her that Colby does."

My gaze hardens, my fists curling at my side. Does she think I'll behave if she starts treating Kellen like her own personal doll? She can toy with me, but I'll—

"Would you like me to notify you before we take off?"

Colby asks, drawing our attention away from the current conversation.

Her eyes narrow at him. "Sure."

That's the second time he's saved me, and I think she is starting to notice.

"You better start listening, Mazu... I don't need another deckhand, and I have no problem using you to earn money. I'm sure there are plenty of people who wouldn't mind spending some time with you." The words turn my stomach, bile slowly rising in my throat at the thought.

"Come on," Colby whispers, taking a step back and opening the door for me to head out through.

Chapter Fourteen

Never have I been more glad to have asked a question in my life.

"Focus." Colby sighs as he sits on the deck's stairs, watching me extend my hands over the rail. "I can tell your mind is wandering again."

Knowing what I do now about this necklace, thanks to Kage, I have a shot at trying to fulfil the 'use' Renna has for me. Not that I want to give her anything she wants, but this means I'm able to stay outside that cell and near the person who has the keys for Kellen's.

My hands drop, and I grip onto the railing. "It's not that easy to keep your mind clear for shifts at a time."

"Then take a break," he mutters. "Take some food down for her. Eat. Then get back here."

"It's almost dark, can we—"

"No." His tone is stern. "Do you understand what's going to happen? Making small little waves isn't going to be enough to impress her."

Hedda laughs from above us as she leans over from the gun deck. I glare up at her, but she wiggles her brows before walking off.

Colby sighs. "Go."

A part of me is grateful he is putting the effort into helping me, but at the same time, I don't get why he is. It doesn't take a genius to realise he isn't in love with his boss. His words from Yral, sharing that bed, confirmed something for me. Colby is most definitely following orders, but not because he enjoys following through with them.

I wander into the kitchen, grabbing today's dinner rations for myself and Kellen before heading down into the hold.

Kellen sits up as she hears my footsteps come down the stairs. "Hey."

"Hi," I reply, sliding her food under the small gap on the floor.

Sitting down myself, I lean against the cell that is still my bedroom. Captain Renna lets me run around all day, but doesn't trust me to be left alone to roam about the ship at night.

Fair.

"How's the training going?" Kellen asks as she takes a bite of her food.

Things have been tense since I got back. She wasn't exactly happy to hear that I had been safe, teleported thousands of kilometres away from danger and surrounded by one of the largest armies in our realm, only for me to come back to save her.

Again, fair. I would have been mad at her had the roles been reversed.

"Slow... Colby doesn't think I'll have it developed enough by the time we get to their base," I inform her, tearing into my bread roll.

She looks up from her plate. "Can you see where we are, if we're getting close?"

I shake my head. "We're in the middle of the ocean for as far as I can see."

Kellen hums before she starts eating again. "Are you getting close with him?"

A laugh escapes my lips as I dip my bread chunk into the meat sauce spilled over the mashed potatoes. "Yeah, no. I don't care if he is helping me out or doing all of this to keep himself out of trouble, but he is still the man who tried to kill the two most important people in my life."

That's not technically a lie. I don't care for Colby, but I am curious. Something about him just doesn't add up. He's not like Biggie, Hedda, not even Renna.

My eyes flicker to the soft smile on her lips. "What, are you jealous I'm making a new best friend?" I tease.

Her smile falters slightly before she shakes her head. "Not at all. I already know I'm irreplaceable. You proved that by being a complete and utter idiot, again."

I glare. "Rude."

She chuckles and we continue to eat, enjoying each other's company like we always have. Though, I have to admit that I miss our spot on the pier. Our feet dangling off the edge, drinking whatever foul liquid Kellen was able to scrounge up for us that night. I miss our friends too. Lip and Mehl, I wonder what they think is happening right now. If they have filed a report or if they think we ran off without telling them.

"I still can't believe you chose not to see Ari..." Kellen says as she finishes her food.

"The way I see it, is that it wouldn't have been fair to him. Give him the false hope of an extremely brief reunion for me to leave with more lies... and... if I..." My voice trails off as I push around the last bite of food with my fork.

Kellen moves to the edge of her cell and extends her hand to me. "I know."

I smile and rest my hand on top of hers, our eyes flickering between each other. I lean my forehead against the bars of her cell door and she does the same. Her eyelashes are long, her chocolate eyes easing the stress that's been tensing my shoulders; her complexion looks washed out from her being down here for nearly half a mooncycle now.

"Mazu. You can do this," Kellen whispers.

Maybe I can.

"I'll give it my best." My smile falters as I pull away.

She slides her tray out for me so I can take it back to the kitchen. I pile them on top of one another before standing up.

"Have fun," she says as I start up the stairs.

"See you tonight," I mutter.

After the trays are dropped off, I go back to the side of the ship. The sun casts an orange glow across the still blanket of water we are tearing through. The normally blue sky is filled with pinks and reds, the white of the clouds adopting some of that colour.

♫

There was a fair maiden with eyes bright and true,
She sailed on the ocean, her heart feeling new.
She'd watch the horizon, where the sea meets the sky,
And wonder about love, with a soft, wistful sigh.

Oh, the waves they did whisper, the wind gently crooned,
But the maiden was puzzled, her heart lightly tuned.
For she felt a warm flutter, a feeling so rare,
But love's true meaning seemed to elude her stare.

Her thoughts were a whirlpool, her emotions a tide,
She longed for the answers the sea would provide.

She'd watch as the sun set, painting the sky,
And dream of the day she'd understand why.

Oh, the waves they did whisper, the wind gently crooned,
But the maiden was puzzled, her heart lightly tuned.
For she felt a warm flutter, a feeling so rare,
But love's true meaning seemed to elude her stare.

One day on the deck, under the moon's silver light,
She met another maiden, whose smile was so bright.
Their eyes met in silence, a bond did ignite,
And suddenly, everything felt just right.

Oh, the waves they did whisper, the wind gently crooned,
Now the maiden's heart sang, no longer marooned.
For in that sweet moment, she began to see,
That love's true meaning was simply to be.

♫

I finish the song meant only for the ocean and myself to hear, but I hear a round of applause from behind me.

Colby's eyes gaze at me softly, his hands falling to his sides. "Wow."

My cheeks burn from embarrassment as I didn't realise he had even come up behind me. I turn back to face the sea.

"Did you write that?" he asks, walking up to the railing, leaning over so I can't hide my face from him.

Jerk.

Shaking my head, I say, "No... my mother did."

"Love is simply to be." He repeats the last line. "Do you think that's true? Love could be that simple?"

I shrug my shoulders. "Maybe for some. I don't think I've

ever been in love, or even had a crush on someone before"—my eyes glance his way—"so I'm the last person you should be asking."

He smirks. "Such a liar..."

"What?" I ask.

There is a pause between us, his eyes widen, blinking a few times.

"Wait, you really mean that?" he asks, surprised. "I had that figured out all wrong then..." Colby mutters to himself as he looks up, calculating something in his mind.

Is he insinuating something?

"Here, I thought I had you falling for my charms." He sighs, a small smirk on his lips as he starts to light one of his tobacco rolls.

I roll my eyes and extend my hands out towards the ocean, ready to move on from this conversation.

Sing.

The King's words ring in my head, and I whistle a few notes, the ocean responding, a rounded pillar of water coming out of the sea before breaking like a wave and returning to where it came from.

"Think the whistling showed better results for you," Colby states as he stares at where the water had popped up.

Nodding my head, I say, "Thought I'd switch it up..."

Hold on.

My head whips to look at him, his eyes looking first before he faces me. "What. You didn't realise that I picked up on your not-so-subtle humming you do every time you try to make it work?"

"Why didn't you say anything?" I ask, tossing my hands up, a tad upset my ruse is up.

He rests his chin on his hand, making him look up at me versus how he normally is looking down. "To be honest, I didn't notice it right away, but once you were regularly at least shifting the ocean every time you changed a note, that's when it clicked." A cheeky look comes to his eye. "Now that I know you can sing, though, you should just go all out and see what happens."

I scoff and take a deep breath to calm my irritation.

"Don't worry. I won't tell the boss you were holding back on us," he leans in and whispers.

A nervous shiver runs down my spine.

KELLEN'S HANDS are bound behind her back, a rope tethered to the cuffs and in the hands of Hedda. I stand beside her as the strange mass just ahead of us comes into view. I cup my hands around my eyes to shield the sun to help me see better.

It looks like buildings.

"I know that geography was not my strong suit in school... but there's no island out this way, is there?" I ask, looking at Kellen, whose face is turned up towards the sun, her eyes closed.

She reluctantly turns her chin downwards and looks at me. "There could be. Small islands aren't on the maps."

"It's a marsh," Colby says. "A bunch of tiny overwatered islands..." A sigh leaving his lips.

"Not a fan?" I ask, looking at him.

He shakes his head. "Of the place, no. Of what's here, more than you could imagine."

Kellen quirks a brow. "And what's here?"

Colby smiles. "The only thing that keeps me sane."

"That is incredibly vague," I point out.

"Yeah, I know." His smile drops, his hand dipping into his

pockets as we wait to get closer to the dock. "The place is called **Liberta**. A neutral breeding ground for all pirates, but our boss is the queen of it all."

Kellen scoffs, making Colby and I glance at her but turns back forwards.

I help the crew dock the boat, mainly because Renna was ordering everyone to do so; Hedda handing Kellen reins to help.

The ramp gets slid down, allowing us to start off-boarding. Apparently, while me and Colby were gone, the rest of the crew were busy doing their own work in collecting more for their trove. A large chest is carried down and taken to a place I heard Renna refer to as the Fool's Room.

Since when is having money being a fool?

Looking around, it really is a marsh with buildings practically floating out here. There are foundations for some of the buildings, then there are ones where they have support beams coming out from those with a solid base to suspend it in the air. It's all rather dull. The only pop of colour against the muddy shades the buildings are made of are the garments being strung out to dry from people's windows.

"Pretty, right?" Renna comes up behind me.

It's not an aesthetic place, but I can see the appeal. The canals that run in between the builds, bridges connecting the different islands, small gondolas that help people move around quickly.

The potential is there.

Colby walks up after helping unload things. "What's next, boss?"

"We have a meeting, but I don't want to leave our little gem here to wander around and get into things she shouldn't." She tilts her head in thought. "Can you be a good pet and sit still if you come with me?"

Her verbiage makes my eye twitch, but I nod.

Colby gave me advice as he was helping me train. *'Always do what the boss says.'* Not the first time he's mentioned something along that vein, but he really meant it as an instruction this time. In this place, she doesn't hold back from what he told me. She's brutal, and it can even unnerve him at times.

Hedda takes Kellen again, apparently showing her to the brig they have here. My eyes linger on her, mouthing a 'see you later' and earning a forced smile from her.

I have to trust they will keep their word in letting her live to keep me in check.

"Come along." Renna hums as she gets into one of the gondolas.

We follow in after her; Colby takes his station at the dolfin and starts us down our path through the canal. I watch as the burgeoning village passes by, people walking the narrow streets. Renna sits back, a content smile on her lips. There's a light in her eyes as she looks at everything.

This is her home.

I wonder how she would feel having it all ripped away from her, like how she ripped mine away from me.

CHAPTER FIFTEEN

WHEN WE GET to where this meeting is being held, Colby helps us out of the gondola. "Best behaviour," he whispers to me, his eyes piercing into me as he does.

I flash him a smile and follow after Renna. A sign is nailed in just above the door frame.

The Council.

It's void of personality, but there's a desk sitting off to the side when we enter. The weathered-looking gnome sitting up the moment their eyes land on Renna.

They bow their head. "La Regina..."

"Do you mind being a dear and sending word to the others that we have arrived?" Her voice is soft, fingers gliding over the wood of the desk as she stares down at them.

"Of course... right away," they say hastily before jumping down from their seat and scurrying out of the place.

Colby takes a step forward. "It'll probably be a shift before things get started, do you mind if I take care of some things?"

Renna chuckles. "You really can't wait, huh?"

He just stares at her, his shoulders tense.

"Go." She rolls her eyes. "Take her with you." Colby's eyes furrow as he glances back over his shoulder to me. "Or don't and stay."

I look between them, not entirely sure what is happening, but Colby turns, waving me to come with.

Our feet pound against the planked streets, some sections feeling like if someone stepped too heavily, they would fall right through. His pace is fast and I have to jog just to keep up.

"Where are we going?" I ask, but he doesn't answer me.

His eyes are glued forwards, shoulders tense, and I swear his pace picks up just a little more.

Did he forget I'm here or something?

After a while, he slows down and approaches a door to a long building, knocking on the door in a pattern of sorts. He then takes the keys off his belt to unlock the door. A large man stands up from a stool right in the doorway. He glares at Colby and me as we step in.

"You're back." The man states the obvious.

"Great chatting," Colby says before he races up the stairs, taking two at a time.

As we head up, there are doors that line the walls, all with padlocks keeping them shut, and two letters nailed on each of them, but they are all varied.

Is this a storage place or something?

He runs down the hall and unlocks the door with 'CL' nailed onto it. The moment the door swings open, he's inside, and I tentatively follow in, closing the door behind me. He is apparently very eager for whatever he needs to grab.

There's a small living room, a single wooden chair facing a coffee table, with a rug sitting underneath it. A small kitchenette, which is made up of a water basin and burner.

So this is his place of residence?

There's another door that's open, and I'm guessing it's where Colby ran into. Soft murmurs come from the room and I quietly approach, peeking my head in to see what he needed so badly that we nearly were running.

"You okay?" a soft voice asks, their hands cradling around him, one on his head while the other slowly strokes his back.

Colby's face is buried in their neck, arms wrapped around their waist, holding them close. "I am now..." he mumbles against their skin, the grip around them tightening. One of his hands comes up and entangles his fingers in their hair. "I can breathe now."

Woah.

My mouth falls open a bit, seeing the shared moment between them. Colby's face lifts from their neck to capture their lips in a heated kiss. The sounds of their passion make my face feel heated.

I take a step back, but the floorboard creaks, causing both of their heads to snap towards me.

Colby stands more upright, but he doesn't remove himself from their form. "Mazu, what the infernum are you doing in here?"

"I'm so sorry... I... I was just following after you still and... I —" The words tumble out, my cheeks likely turning a bright pink from the embarrassment of watching something so intimate.

They are really pretty together, though.

Over Colby's shoulder, they stare at me with wide eyes. Their hands shifting to rest on his back, gripping onto his clothing as if not sure how to react to my presence.

Colby's gaze hardens. "Didn't think to sit in the damn living room?"

The thought may have crossed my mind had he told me literally anything about why we were coming here.

I point with my thumbs towards said room. "Right. I'll go do that..."

"And shut the door," he grumbles.

Taking a step back, their grip loosens and they stand up a bit straighter. "Wait! No. Who is that?" they ask, staring between the two of us.

"Fen, this is Mazu, Mazu, this is Fen. Door? Thanks."

They laugh lightly, untangling themselves from Colby slightly so they can face me properly, but Colby's hands drop, one wrapping around their wrist lightly.

"This is a first," Fen states, looking back at Colby. "You bringing a friend home."

Not the term I would use. Reluctant and forced colleagues, maybe.

"I was kind of forced to..." He sighs.

And he didn't correct them.

"Oh, come on now..." They chuckle. "Forgive him. We don't normally interact with others when together." Their seafoam green eyes are striking now that I'm really looking at them. "I'm Fen Wistra." They extend a hand to me.

My eyes glance at it, but Colby grabs their hand before I can really consider shaking it.

What, does he think I'll throw them off a cliff?

Their long fawn blonde locks are a striking contrast to Colby's raven colour. Where he wears dark shades, they wear light. It's like looking at the sun and moon at the same time.

"I'm Mazu Hali. Nice to meet you," I state, returning their polite introduction. "I can give you two some time," I mutter with a smile.

"Great," Colby agrees coldly.

"No, please stay," Fen counters. "It's been a long while since I've talked to someone new."

Colby frowns and squeezes their hands, but one look from

their eyes and he rolls his, loosening his grip, and sits on the bed. His hand drops to cradle the back of their knee as they stand somewhat in front of him. It's like he almost can't bear the thought of not being connected to them in some way.

Fen shakes their head. "Did I say I was sorry about him?"

You have no idea what you're saying sorry for.

This scene in front of me is strange. I don't even recognise Colby. The expression he's wearing is light, his eyes wide and bright as he admires them, but the moment his eyes meet mine, his stoic expression returns, but it feels less harsh and cold than it was.

"Being here can get pretty boring. I'd love to hear about what you two have been doing." Fen's smile falters as they sit down on the bed next to Colby.

Stepping further into the room, my eyes lock with Colby. He raises a brow at me, and I'm not sure if I should take it as a curious expression or a warning.

Does he actually tell them things?

"Mazu and I got off to a rocky start, but I've been helping her train and getting her accustomed to the demands of being a part of the Lardo in Aumento," Colby says simply. Fen's posture stiffens, and Colby instantly runs his hand gently up and down the back of their thigh to soothe them. "She's got roped into it, so you don't need to be afraid..."

I feel so sorry for them, seeing that flash of fear run through them.

What exactly is this place?

Their shoulders relax and the soft smile on their face returns. "Wrong foot?" Fen arches their brow. "What did you do?"

He laughs awkwardly. "I think it's maybe been more docile than a lot of other things I've done..."

Docile?

Hearing his light-hearted laugh sends a surge through me, and all I want to do is wipe that smile from his face.

I take in a deep breath. "He threw my baby brother off a cliff, where I then proceeded to jump off to try and be there with him in his last moments, but we survived—"

"Mazu!" He tries to interrupt.

"—Colby then abducted and threatened me. Forced me to embezzle from a foreign government, tried to kill my best friend and is now keeping her captive to keep me in check." I gasp from the vomit of words.

He takes a step forward, but Fen grips onto him.

"Keep your mouth shut!" he shouts at me before turning to Fen. "I am not keeping her captive. Renna is." Like that makes the difference. "Everyone lived. It sounds bad, but it's all okay..."

All okay.

Nothing about this is okay. My entire life has been uprooted, and this is somehow all okay? My family dispersed, and this is all okay? Kellen is being used as bait, and this is all okay?

Fen's eyes are wide and mouth slightly agape as they practically ignore Colby's defence; their gaze locked on me. Their eyes watering. "I'm so sorry..." Their words are quiet as they shake their head. "I... I'm so sorry, Mazu."

I furrow my brows, not sure why they are apologising.

"Hey..." Colby brings his arms around them, shushing them.

"I've caused you both so much pain." They gasp as their body begins to shake, a sob building up. "You need to just forget about me. You're destroying yourself, Colby..." they say to him.

"No." His voice is stern. "Look. I'm sitting right here in front of you." They cover their mouth, muffled wails coming out as Colby clings to them. "I'm earning you that freedom, Fen."

Freedom?

An unsettling feeling sits in my stomach as I watch this. This place isn't a place where they stay. It's a prison for them. They were locked in here.

Will they put Kellen in here?

They take a few ragged breaths, their hand falling to their lap. "I've dragged her into this same mess, Colby. I signed her up for this!" Their voice breaks, taking a moment to try and collect themselves. "I'm not worth the damage done...."

Colby kisses their head. "I did this..."

"For me!" My heart sinks hearing the pain in their words.

My eyes take in Colby, his face twisted into a mess of emotions. It's almost overwhelming to see him wear such a look openly. Mr Stoic isn't actually that at all.

He's just a really good liar.

"Stop this, Fen," he pleads. "I'm the one being selfish in all of this. All I'm asking is you to bear with it... Please."

"You won't recognise yourself when this is over..." My heart lurches for them. "I can see it already... and now I know why you come back darker than before. Why you can't laugh or smile the way you used to..."

"And that's all mine to bear." His voice softens. "I swear, I'll get us through this and let you be the selfish one."

Colby swipes the tears away with his thumb as he cups their face. His lips tenderly brushing against theirs.

I walk out of the room, closing the door behind me. This moment is most definitely for them and doesn't need to be witnessed by me.

My heart is pounding.

None of this excuses him, but I see it. Just like Kellen said, she knows what she's willing to do, to sacrifice. My feet carry me to the wooden chair and I fall back into it. I lean my elbows on my knees, resting my forehead against my hands.

What am I willing to do to keep Kellen safe?

I look up, my eyes falling on the door. There is only a keyhole on this side. My guess is that they don't get a key to leave here.

CHAPTER SIXTEEN

My back is thrown against the outside wall of the building we were just inside of, a gasp escaping me as Colby stands in front of me, his arms crossed over his chest.

Saw this coming.

"What is wrong with you?" he growls. "Can't read a room?"

I shove him back. "If you have a problem with Fen knowing, then maybe you shouldn't do such terrible things!"

He grabs the collar of my shirt before slamming me into the wall once more; the pain radiating through my back this time.

"I do it FOR them!" he yells back. "And I know you're not stupid enough that you didn't already put that together."

My hand curls into a ball. I shouldn't have done it, forced the truth on them like that, but I couldn't take it, seeing him so at ease.

Colby's body is shaking, his eyes flickering between mine. "Just wait... you'll see how it feels to become a person the one you love won't even recognise."

Dropping his grip, he takes a few steps back, along with

some breaths. His eyes are watering, but he turns his back to me.

Way to go, Mazu.

"Renna is going to be expecting us," Colby states, rolling his shoulders back and taking one last deep breath. "Move."

Colby and I walk in silence to where the meeting is going to take place. Though, I have a lot of questions for him. Like how he ended up working for Renna. How long he's been working for her. What he meant by earning Fen's freedom. What he was like before joining the crew. But, the look on his face tells me to keep quiet, that shove being the lightest of punishments.

'You're destroying yourself,' is what Fen had said. Makes me think that's what Colby was talking about when he was getting me up to speed with how the ship worked. Why he said I did the right thing.

I don't want to become like him.

There's a respect I have for him now, though, not that I agree with what he has done. I can't blame him for getting agitated with me. I'm not even sure why I even blurted it out.

Yeah, I do.

Though I didn't hurt just him, I hurt Fen, too. Revenge was what I wanted. For him to feel ashamed or guilty. They offered an apology so readily and the thought of it being them begging for forgiveness consumed me. I don't even think I really comprehended that in the moment, but thinking about it, it's what I wanted.

For Colby to hurt.

My brow furrows, my heart contracting. Neither of them really deserves that. The moment I saw Fen, a part of me knew instantly the causation of everything that moves the Colby that exists in the Lardo in Aumento. It's them. The same reason why I jumped off that cliff, sold myself, chose to come back.

Love.

We arrive back at the council building, and once we're inside, the gnome from before quickly escorts us to a meeting room. Renna is sitting at the head of the table, laughing at something the man on her right must have said before taking a drink out of the goblet in her hand. Her eyes land on us and points at the two most immediate seats on her left.

"Do us a favour and keep your mouth shut," Colby commands as he sits right next to Renna.

I take the other seat, my posture rigid as the crowd suddenly turns their gaze at us newcomers. "Don't mind them. They're my faithful little dogs," Renna explains, putting her glass down on the large rectangular table in front of us.

"We're glad to have La Regina back with us..." the brunette-haired dwarf sitting at the other head of the table states.

I do a double take as I register his features. If he wasn't a pirate, I'd be beyond tempted to talk to him. While growing up, we learned a lot of the dwarves that once were the founding council members of Limoria before it progressed to a monarchy and the land was divided up, well before the true king eventually took over, but we all know how that ended. They created the majority of our societal systems. The Ancestry War drove them to the Northern Territory, where they have primarily stayed as a collective, but I guess even they have their rouges.

Colby elbows me, and I glare at him. "I'm happy to have returned home." Renna smiles.

"We have been working towards making this a full-fledged city. The funds coming in from our benefactors have been fundamental to the construction and development," he says, rolling out a scroll, a blueprint of this floating private haven.

The boss leans forward and takes a look. "See, I told you getting a little political would work in our favour."

Political?

169

"Have we been able to secure the location of the doorway?" Renna asks, taking another drink.

I lean back in my chair, a headache forming. At this point, I'm not sure if I can think about all of this at once, my mind still asking a hundred questions from our visit at Fen's, and now they are talking about stuff that's far beyond what I even care to listen to. I just want to sit with Kellen and figure this all out, to get us away from all of this.

I wonder why Colby has just accepted this. I plan on getting Kellen and me out. I can't stand the thought of my life being this, not that my cousin, the King, would actually let that happen per his threats. Does he think there is no other option? Has he ever tried?

So many questions. My brain hurts.

"I'll let the Domi Nostrae know," the man on Renna's right mutters, writing something down.

Wait, what did I just miss?

Everyone begins to stand, and I'm slow to follow, earning a pointed stare from Colby. I stare back, irritated that he is holding it against me as much as he is.

He's never once apologised.

Renna walks to the side with a lanky woman, their tones hushed. Her gaze meets mine, and I immediately look to a grumpy Colby as he leans against the doorframe as we wait for the boss.

"Hey," I start, his eyes shifting to glance over my face for a moment before looking back at the blank wall. "I'm sorry if I hurt Fen. Not that you have cared to express the same remorse for hurting those I love..." His jaw clenches. "I don't like you. You're an absolute arse and the day I'm free of you will be a happy one." My tone is quiet but harsh.

He turns his head to actually face me, and if looks could kill, this one might do the trick. "You really don't learn, do you."

My mouth hangs open a bit in shock, expecting something else to come from him. "What you did was petty, but what I've done is necessary."

I furrow my brows. "Maybe what I did was too."

A scoff leaves his lips. "We both know that's a lie."

My intentions were definitely not pure or kind, but they could be. If Colby is willing to kill, bite, and tear through people, then would he be willing to risk everything to get them out of this?

"Is it?" My head tilts. "Because I think they needed to hear what it is you are really doing for them."

Colby clicks his tongue against his teeth. "What, so they can be tormented by the imagery you painted for them?"

Shaking my head, I say, "So maybe it'll push you to fight this."

"What?" His eyes widen. "What are you on about?"

This is stupid. So stupid.

King Felguard would probably have denied my request had he thought this is what I would be doing, but to be honest, I can't believe what I'm about to do.

"I can get them out. Fen, Kellen, us," I whisper slowly.

He stares at me for a moment before looking towards Renna. Colby shifts his posture to block our lips from her view.

"Are you serious?" The tone in his voice makes me feel like I'm making the right choice.

Telling him is fine. He can fill me in with what the Domi Nostrae is doing or wanting and we can use that to get the King on board to help them too.

Right?

My mouth opens, but it shuts as Renna's smile peers at me as she peeks her head around Colby's frame. "Oh, please don't stop talking on my account. Chatting about anything interesting?"

The little amount of food I ate this morning turns in my stomach.

"Our Mazu was just wanting to show you some of her progress," Colby says, looking down at Renna as he meets her gaze.

He couldn't have said something else?

Renna's smile widens, and she steps closer to me, looking me over. "My little gem wants praise?" Her chuckle sends a shiver down my spine.

That feels like the thing I would least want from her. Praise from her would probably mean I just lost a piece of myself, and that's the last thing I am trying to do.

I DON'T LIKE how eager she is. She sits on a barrel, crossing her leg over the other. Perfect posture as her hands rest on top of her knee.

"Come on now... don't be shy." The sweetness in her voice is sickening, her eyes looking like that of a siren, appraising my every move.

My eyes shift to Colby, who leans against the wall of the boss' storage house for things not as shiny and or precious. He nods towards the water and I turn to face it.

♪

There once was a girl with eyes like the sea,
Her heart belonged to the ocean, so free.
With salt in her hair and wind in her sail,
She'd dance on the waves, a true seafaring tale.

Oh, the sea, the sea, the call of her heart,
It pulled her away, it tore her apart.
But she'd never leave, no, she'd always stay,
Forever in love with the sea's endless sway.

She'd sing with the gulls and swim with the fish,
Her laughter would echo a mermaid's wish.
She'd chart her course by the stars up above,
Guided by dreams and a heart full of love.

Oh, the sea, the sea, the call of her heart,
It pulled her away, it tore her apart.
But she'd never leave, no, she'd always stay,
Forever in love with the sea's endless sway.

Through storms and through calm, she'd brave the unknown,
In search of adventure, in search of her own.
For the sea was her home, her truest friend,
And she'd follow its song, wherever it'd bend.

Oh, the sea, the sea, the call of her heart,
It pulled her away, it tore her apart.
But she'd never leave, no, she'd always stay,
Forever in love with the sea's endless sway.

So here's to the girl with the sea in her eyes,
May she always find solace 'neath starlit skies.
For the ocean's her love, her joy, and her pride,
Forever in her heart, with the tide by her side.

♫

The ocean waters dance around me as I sing, waves ebbing

and flowing with the tune, sharp peaks poking out and rolling burbles depending on the pitch and tone. As my song ends, the water falls, soaking the wooden deck we're on.

My eyes look at Renna, whose expression has me take a step back.

She's mad.

Renna uncrosses her legs, jumping down from her temporary throne and struts to me. "I have a question for you." Her tone is sharp. "Did I not ask for you to be more useful?"

I nod.

"Right. IF I wanted you to put on a pretty show, I would just have you strip down and have people pay for it." I clench my fist tightly at her words.

Disgusting.

She closes the distance, and I bite the inside of my cheek. "You want to be of better use? I need you to be able to overwhelm someone. Drown them. Whip them. Hurt them. I need a weapon, and if you can deliver, I'll ensure you and your friend make up for wasting my time."

My heart lurches, looking to Colby.

Help me.

He pushes himself off the wall, but Renna raises her hand, slapping me across the face. My head turns from the impact. I cup my cheek and look back towards her.

"I'm disappointed you couldn't come through, Colby." She sighs. "Now I'm going to have to be rougher than I would have been..."

My feet stumble backwards, but she reaches out. Her hand grips onto my hair, pulling it to make me fall down onto my knees.

"You know what the problem is? You haven't really had a taste of violence." She looks over her shoulder and nods towards me, beckoning Colby.

His pupils contract, hesitating for a split second, but he clenches his jaw and walks up to me. Her hand releases my curls, and I drop my head before I look up at him.

"Don't..." My eyes lock on with his.

"Then do something, Mazu." His tone is harsh as he grabs my collar and pulls back his fist.

Fuck.

I'd think this man was absolutely a monster, had he not mouthed the word 'please' before his fist connected to my face. I cry out, bringing my hands up to my nose. My eyes water and I feel blood running down. He shoves me to the ground, raising his foot and bringing it down on my rib cage, the air extracted from my lungs. My eyes lock with his. His brow pinches together.

"DO IT!" he yells. The volume startles both me and Renna. "Or are you really just that pathetic?"

He kicks me again, earning a whimper and groan from my lips.

Colby's doing this for her. This is part of what he is willing to do for love.

A melody leaves me. Water coming up from the floorboards. I can feel the ocean just beyond them as we sit on this floating village.

Again, and again, and again, his foot collides with a portion of my body until I create the form. A tendril of water solidifies and wraps around his throat, pulling him back and throwing him against the wall.

It's time I show them mine.

Colby grunts at the impact, falling to the ground.

Renna claps and smiles brightly. "Yes! That's it!" She takes a step towards me. "Hold on to that feeling. The desperation and anger."

My blood drips down my chin, dropping into the thin layer

of water I've flooded the floor with. I try and wipe it off with my sleeve as it's soaked through; it acting like a washcloth.

A part of me wants to rip her limb from limb. "You want a taste?" I ask Renna, making her halt her approach towards me.

"Oh, come on now... I'm here to help guide you. Just like I've done with Colby." She points at him as he slowly stands back up, rubbing his throat. "He wasn't always so useful... He's always had one really great use, but I helped show him his true potential. Someone who shapes the world as it should be."

"And what kind of world is that?" I ask, sitting up, a hiss leaving my lips from the pain radiating in my chest.

Renna smiles. "One where only the strongest get to be on top."

CHAPTER SEVENTEEN

THE MOMENT KELLEN's eyes meet mine, she stands and runs to the edge of her cell.

"What the infernum happened?" Her voice stern, her knuckles turning white from how harsh she is gripping onto the bars as she examines me up and down.

Colby walks in behind me, his fist still bloodied from where he had hit me. "Renna was feeling a bit aggressive."

Kellen daggers him with her eyes, making me chuckle a little. Just seeing her is helping ease the pain in my body.

"I'm fine..." I mutter, walking up to the bars and placing a hand on hers.

She shakes her head. "I'm so sick of you lying to me, of you lying to yourself. You're not fine." Her voice trembles, making my eyes widen. "None of this is fine."

My heart sinks as her composure wavers. I grip onto her hand tighter, my eyes darting, never having seen her like this before.

Looking back at Colby, I narrow my gaze. "Unlock the cell."

He furrows his brow. "You know I can't—"

"Now!" I yell, reaching out and grabbing his collar. "Open it."

Colby rips my hand off of him before he takes his keys out and places it into the keyhole. He pauses for a moment, sighing, before proceeding with unlocking it. The moment he opens the door, I rush towards Kellen, my arms wrapping around her shaking form.

She never cries.

Kellen buries her face into my neck. I wince as her hands grip me tightly, the bruising on my body already sensitive to any touch. Closing my eyes, I try to absorb as much of this moment as I can. Colby is breaking the rules here and might not let this happen again.

I took for granted how tough she has always been. Kellen has always just been there, ready to pick up the pieces, even if I never really let her. Her company was always enough to push me to pick them up myself, maybe allowing her to pick up one or two that had wandered too far from my vision.

She means everything to me.

A sharp inhale of breath comes from Kellen, and I pull back slightly, thinking I must have squeezed her too tight.

"Who?" she whispers.

What?

"You said 'she means everything'..." Kellen pulls away, the tears still running down her cheeks.

I bring my hand up to wipe them away, but she turns her head. Did I really just say that out loud? She takes another step back, but I step forward to close the distance.

"You." I can't have her thinking anything else.

Kellen and I both know that I've never been the best when

it comes to verbally expressing how much I care for someone but, she needs to know that it means I'd be willing to cross lines I wouldn't normally cross just to ensure her life, happiness and health.

"You... I meant to say, you mean the world to me. I didn't realise I had said it out loud..." My voice is a whisper, but the hurt in her eyes fades as her gaze softens. "There is little I wouldn't do for you... but I won't become a monster. I'll get us out of this in a way that you'll recognise me at the end."

I'm sure Colby is feeling me jab him with those words, but it's thanks to him that I know what I want to do, what I have to do, and most importantly, what I am willing to do.

"You can do this, Mazu..." Her voice is soft.

She allows me to wipe away her tears this time as she stares so intently at me.

"Kel... I'm so scared..." I mutter. "Of losing you..."

Kellen's eyes flick between mine, searching them for something, but they eventually drop, glancing at my lips. "Why is that?"

I shake my head. "I-I'm not sure how I can explain it... The connection we have... It's changed."

A chuckle slips from her lips. "No... I don't think it has. Not for me." I look at her with a furrowed brow. "I've always loved you, Mazu..."

My eyes go wide and my breath hitches.

Is that what this is?

"I want more with you..." She steps forwards and closes the distance between us.

Biting the inside of my cheek, my eyes bore into hers, tears still spilling down.

She loves me.

That makes me think of my parents. My mother loved my father. She stuck with him, even when he was cold or distant.

Even when he hurt her by forgetting the important things, leaving us more often than not when she got sick. I don't want that for Kellen; I don't want that for myself.

"I don't know if I can give you what you want," I whisper honestly. "And I'm terrified of what 'more' would mean."

Kellen shakes her head, her nose brushing against mine. "You don't have to have it all figured out right now. We can take our time."

Everything in me wants to just agree, to close what little distance there is between us, but I can't cross that line without being certain. "Love feels dangerous to me. It makes me question everything – what it means, what it should be. I want you so much, but the thought of risking what we do have, or hurting you, terrifies me..."

"Mazu..." Her gaze hardens. "I am not weak... and neither are you! If you want this, want me, we will make something that works for us... don't compare it to anything else."

I instinctively lean in, nearly touching our lips. "I want to be with you, but I also don't want to hold you back. For you to feel you're settling for something less."

"You are all I have wanted and waited for," she states. "There is no world where I would be settling for you. You are everything."

I hiss as she cups my face, but she shushes my complaints as her lips press against mine. A ragged breath escapes me as she pulls back enough for the air to pass through before I grasp the back of her neck to pull her back in.

Don't stop.

Her hands travel down to wrap around my waist as our lips move against one another, firmly, desperately. She hums against my lips as I tangle one of my hands in her hair.

"Please, stop," Colby groans from behind me.

My cheeks redden as we slowly part. "Sorry," I mumble,

not sure if I meant that for Colby or Kellen for getting carried away.

I just needed to have this moment, because I don't know how any of this is going to turn out.

Kellen chuckles but as I tuck her hair behind her ear, my eyes taking in every inch of her face, her gaze hardens and her smile drops.

"Mazu..." Her tone warns. "There is no sacrificing yourself, you got it?"

She really knows me well.

A soft smile is all I can manage as an answer before I pull away from her completely and walk out, Colby relocking the cell door.

"I'll do what I can to keep her out of trouble," he offers, and Kellen's eyes widen. "At least until you can take over."

Kellen really laughs this time, like we used to laugh back in Berkin. "Good... She can be stubborn and stupid."

Rude.

"So. Are you going to finish what you were telling me before?" I look up at Colby as we sit at the edge of the dock.

My feet dangle into the water as he sits cross-legged. I feel more confident than I did before in my ability to trust that he won't just turn me over, but I have to be careful. Colby won't hesitate to throw me under the bridge if we get caught, if it means sparing Fen from any pain. Either it means I have to lie to him, or keep the entire truth to myself.

Nodding my head, I say, "Yeah..." He raises a brow, sitting back on his hands as he looks at me, waiting for me to continue. "When I met with the King of Felguard... he knew everything.

Why I was really there, who I had been taken by. He even has Ari safe and sound in Fosa."

"What?" Colby sits back up. "He knew, and he sent you back?"

"I asked him to allow me to come back, for Kellen," I explain. "But it'll be our ticket out because he warned me that I wouldn't have long to get her out. He'd come after me."

Colby does not need to know that the King also said he would have me killed if I couldn't get away.

He looks out to the water. "So, because you are his cousin, he's willing to get involved in all of this?"

I shake my head. "No... it's only if the Domi Nostrae are involved will he be able to."

"You're kidding," he mumbles.

Shaking my head earns me a groan from his lips, his hand palming his face, his eyes peeking at me through his fingers. I stand up and stretch, looking around to make sure there is still no one around.

"You were in the same meeting as me, Mazu. Messing with the Domi Nostrae doesn't seem like the brightest idea," he states.

My gaze glances down, watching him play with a string on his trench coat. "I wasn't really paying attention..." I admit. "But he doesn't need us to mess with them. Simply inform him of what they are doing."

"First, you really are an idiot." I scoff at his insult as he holds up one finger. "Second, you make that sound like it's going to be easy." He holds up a second finger. "Third, please tell me you have more to this plan before you thought to bring it up to me, who, by the way, is a pirate tasked with ensuring you don't escape."

I whistle a little tune, my mother's necklace glowing softly as the water responds to my call.

Raising a brow, I mutter. "Are you saying you're going to tell on me?"

Colby smiles, shaking his head. "Easy there, killer... I'll help you out, but know that this is for—"

"Fen. That's why I am asking for your help. I want to help them, too." My words make his smile falter.

He stares at me for a long moment; the wind jostling our hair and clothes as our eyes connect. "You do?"

I nod my head, giving him a smirk before I walk off. He quickly stands and falls into step next to me.

"So, what did they say the Domi Nostrae wanted?" My voice is hushed.

The sun begins to set, the warmth of the day slowly fading along with it. I shiver for a moment as another breeze hits our backs.

"There's apparently one of the goddesses' doorways in the strait between Berkin and the Lonely Isle," he states, my jaw dropping as he continues. "Our ship and crew have been tasked with locating it and reporting back. We have pinpointed where it could be."

My heart flutters hearing that we will be back in Berkin, or at least close, sometime soon. Though, a new realisation hits me.

"Kellen and Fen will be stuck here, though." I look up at Colby, who nods solemnly. "We could try and sneak them onboard, like what Kellen did when we left Berkin."

He sighs. "They will check to make sure their collaterals are in place before we leave."

"Which means that there is an opening from that moment and the moment we leave. They have to inform Renna before we head out," I say, knowing it is easier said than done.

Colby doesn't glance towards me as we continue our stroll back to the quarters they are providing us during our stay. He already has a room he's come back to quite a few times, but they have prepared one for me. Hedda had told me to not get my hopes up for anything as comfy as what I had at home.

"You are asking for a miracle," he states.

"I think we will need one no matter what..." I reply honestly.

Even if we do get them back to the ship, ensuring they go unnoticed, and getting them off and somewhere safe, won't be a walk in a park either. I would suggest we just steal a boat and head out on our own, but with how many people there are around the ship docks guarding them, that might be even harder.

Colby cracks his neck, rubbing it out with a pained look on his face. "Let's sleep on it," he mutters.

"What's wrong?" I ask, his eyes darting to mine as I do.

He straightens back out. "Just sore from how tense I was."

I roll my eyes. "You're gonna complain?" I point a finger to my face. "Look what you did to me."

A chuckle escapes his lips. "Yeah... I'm sorry. I just knew if I held back, Renna would have called me on it and made the situation worse for all of us."

My body freezes as I hear his words, his head turning back as he notices me stop.

"You... apologised," I mumble to myself.

He tilts his head, the smile from his chuckle still resting on his face. "I did... and I am sorry, for all of it. Everything I did, Mazu, I really hated doing it."

Colby quickly faces forwards and starts walking again, his shoulder slightly shaking as he does.

I hope one day I'll fully be able to forgive you.

CHAPTER EIGHTEEN

THE ROOM IS AWFUL. Hedda wasn't kidding. Opening the door pushes the thin mattress, causing a slight resistance. The only thing that really fits in here is a bedroll laid out on the floor.

"At least it's yours, and you aren't having to use a random bedroll every night that someone else would have slept on the night before," Colby says, patting my shoulder before heading off to his room.

This is a boarding house, and it is by far way worse than what I thought one would be like. I'd rather be staying with Fen in that drabby place than here. At least they have better accommodations for those they are forcing to live here full time. I lay down on the bed and stare up at the ceiling.

We will be heading back soon.

Colby and I will need to be prepared once Renna gives us the orders to start boarding. There has to be a way for us to get both of them out, on this ship, and hidden for long enough. If they are discovered, I don't think Renna will be as kind as to allow the stow away to live in the ship's brig again. Maybe that is the better option for them.

Stop it. Focus on what you need to.

Renna is likely going to be taking up my time during the

day moving forwards, and as horrible as that is, it could give Colby a chance to set in motion what we need him to. I won't have much access to anything, and people won't trust me since they've never seen my face before. He should be able to get to Fen and get them out of that place. It's sneaking them on board that might be harder. We will get them a change of clothes, put them in a crate, and have them loaded onto the ship. Kellen knows how to lock pick, but distracting the guards will be the hard part. I could cause a fight, with Hedda or someone, and draw their attention away from their posts. Kellen then could meet up with Colby and Fen and get in the crate too. It'll have to be a big crate, and we will need a reason for what's in it, but it will have to come from someone else's mouth. Otherwise, Renna could have suspicions. I don't know how she would, but she could.

I sigh and close my eyes. This could completely fail, and make things worse for all of us, but if I leave this place without Kellen, I'll never see her again and I can't let that happen.

"Come on, Mazu..." Mother holds my hand as we walk into the school.

It's big, new, and I don't like it.

Shaking my head, I tug on her hand, trying to pull her back out of the building. Mamma is stronger, though, and drags me in with her. There are rooms on either side as we walk down the hall. A door with a window at the end of the hall is the one we walk through.

A man smiles down at me from his desk as we walk in. "Hey there, you little youngin. Are you getting dropped off at school?"

Nodding my head, I mutter, "I'm smart."

He chuckles. "Well, of course! Not many youngin's actually get to go to this school. So you are really smart."

The man and my mom talk for a while but the conversation is boring. I look around the room, wooden chairs aligning the wall; a young girl with roughed up knees and a messy bun is sitting in one of them. Her arms are crossed, and she looks bored as she stares at the floor.

I let go of my mother's hand. "Hi there," I mutter as I stand in front of her chair.

She looks up and stares at me for a moment. "Yeah?"

"I'm Mazu..." I clench my hands on the hem of my shorts. "This is my new school."

"I'm Kellen," she introduces herself, looking down at me. "The older kids are jerks and—"

The man stands up from the desk. "Miss Varon. You know better than to use that kind of language, especially in front of one of your younger classmates." He turns back to my mother. "I am so sorry, ma'am."

My mother waves her hand dismissively. "Her father has said worse. Please don't apologise."

Looking back to Kellen, I chuckle, and she smiles at me.

"I'll make sure they don't bother you..." she says. "I get in trouble for it anyway, so you shouldn't get in trouble too."

Nodding my head, I exclaim, "I'll protect you too!"

She bonks my head lightly with her fist and scowls. "I just said not to get in trouble..."

"Let's go, Princess," Colby states as he pounds on my door, and I sit up slowly, rubbing the sleep from my eyes.

My mind wanders to the dream: how long it has been since I've thought about that moment. A smile spreads across my face as I bring a hand to my lips, the tiredness leaving me quickly when I remember hers against mine. I would have never thought the words 'I love you' would have come from her.

I wonder what Mother would think.

There were times where she would clean Kellen up from the fights she got in. Always scolding Kellen for it, asking where her normally stoic persona disappeared to in those moments. It would end in a thank you from my mom though, for Kellen looking out for me and our friends.

She has always been like that, the first to jump in or show up. Home wasn't always the best place. Her father neglected her at best and her mother left them before she could ever form a memory. I always figured she would rather have been getting us out of trouble than sitting at home, but her risking everything she has built up outside of that old house to be here with me tells me she is just trying to be better than her parents. Show the love she has always wanted. For someone to just show up for her.

We are going to get out of this.

I groan as I get up. The bruises definitely settled in from yesterday and sleeping on the floor didn't ease the soreness.

Opening the door, Colby is leaning on the end of the hallway. "Morning, Princess."

"Morning, jerk," I say with a smile, but it makes him quirk a brow.

He pushes himself off the wall and starts us for the exit. "Pleasant as always, I see." Rolling my eyes, I jap him in the ribs lightly, making him chuckle. "Oh... I see, you're sore."

"That's an understatement," I grumble.

Colby opens the door for me as we head out onto the street. "Hate to tell you, but you'll feel worse tonight."

Right, my playdate with Renna. She wants to give me a 'taste for violence.' A lovely way to say that she will just keep breaking me until I want to do the breaking.

I glance around, making sure there is enough distance between us and Hedda, who is walking to the mess building just ahead of us, along with any of these other pirates.

"You need to get a crate ready for both of them," I whisper, pulling Colby's gaze down to meet mine as we walk.

"Really? That's your plan?" Colby asks, making my eyebrow twitch. "How are we supposed to get them in there?"

"You are going to be doing the majority of the work here since I will be indisposed most of the day," I continue. "Fen will be the easy one to get out, as long as Renna thinks you're at the ship while they do the check in to make sure their prisoners are still that."

Colby shakes his head. "If it was simple, I would have done it."

"Except you were alone, and didn't have someone else distracting Renna," I explain, and his expression softens slightly. "Kellen will need something to get herself out of that cell, and then a diversion so she can sneak out to where the crate will be."

"There are too many variables in this..." he mutters.

I nod my head in agreement. It's not a perfect plan, and any number of things could go wrong while trying this, but we have to at least try.

I SWALLOW the lump in my throat as I step into the building Colby directed me to before we parted ways. The beginning of our plans taking shape.

There is nothing inside the building except a single stool sitting next to a large wooden box. I jump as I feel her come up from behind me.

"Good morning, my little gem..." A shiver runs through me and I immediately take a few steps away so I can turn and face Renna. "I'm happy you came so willingly. A part of me was worried Colby would have to force you through that door, but I don't even see him."

My stomach starts to lurch as she bites her lip, closing the distance once again. "I-I knew that regardless, I would have to be here, so..."

She chuckles. "Yes, you seem to catch on pretty quickly. I would hate to have to ruin your friend's pretty face if you decided to try and fight my order." Renna looks me over for a moment, her smile fading a bit. "Where is he? With that pathetic little thing?"

I swallow, not quite sure how I am supposed to answer that. Colby and I never really discussed the frequency in which he is with Fen. Would it be strange if he wasn't with them?

Nodding my head causes Renna's eyes to roll. "Some habits are very hard to break."

She's jealous.

"He will understand soon; only the strongest will make it out." Her words are cold and her eyes harden.

There is more to that sentence, and I think Fen is in more danger than what Colby even understands.

Renna walks past me and opens the lid to the box, her smile returning to her face. "This world is going to change, Mazu."

I tentatively take a few steps to her. "What do you mean?"

"Do you know how I came to power? How I reign over the council of the most vile and morally dark groups in our realm?" Her voice sounds too sweet for words like that. "Because, I'm the worst amongst them."

My heart sinks, my feet freezing in place. "I am willing to do anything and everything to make my dream a reality. My one true love. I'll do what it takes to see it through, Mazu."

Her smile and eyes widen as she looks back at me.

I should run.

"A world where money means nothing compared to your

strength and power. I'm going to make sure that world exists, and you're going to be a part of that."

Clenching my jaw is the only thing I can really do. My body is shaking and despite everything in me wanting to run, I can't. I'm glued here to the floor. I know I have to be here, give Colby the time to do what we need him to, but I don't want to spend a second longer with her. With that smile. With those eyes.

She looks like a monster.

Renna walks up with a dagger in hand. "Come here," she coos, curling a finger to beckon me forwards.

My feet stay firmly planted, and a pout appears on her lips. She comes to me, tilting her head, using the dagger to move my face side to side.

"Don't be so scared…" she whispers. "I promise, I'm not doing anything that I couldn't handle…"

Furrowing my brows, I stare at her, but my eyes widen and I gasp as the dagger tears away at my skin. Looking downwards, red is dripping down my fingers, a cut laid across my forearm.

Renna flips the dagger around, handing it to me. "Now… I want you to do that again, and again, until you stop reacting to the pain."

"You, you want me to—"

"Yes, and I'm not asking twice." Her voice makes me flinch. "We need to toughen you up."

I just need to bear this.

CHAPTER NINETEEN

My arms twitch from the abuse they took. I had to move onto my thighs when I ran out of 'canvas' as Renna put it. The healers they have here are not the warm and welcoming kind I am used to. Though they do their job, wrapping my cleaned wounds with bandages.

"You should be fine. All the cuts are shallow, so they will heal quickly. Just change out the bandages every morning," he states, handing me a roll to do just as he says. "I'll bill your captain so you can leave now."

I nod and stand up, my head foggy from my day with the evil incarnate. My feet carry me towards the jail where they are keeping Kellen. I just need to see her and I'll be okay.

"Mazu?" Colby's voice calls out. Turning my head, I see him walking to me, his eyes raking me over. "What did she do to you?"

A pathetic laugh leaves me as I shake my head. "She had me do this to myself."

His eyes widen, teeth grinding against each other as he examines me again.

I wonder if he had to go through this.

Renna mentioned having to put him through a training that helped mould him into a dog that bites. Though the look on his face suggests she personalises her training sessions to her students.

"Are you okay?" His voice is soft.

Shrugging my shoulders, I just face towards the direction I was walking. "Can I see her?"

Colby sighs. "It's best you don't, Mazu... Better if you create distance with what we're planning."

Nodding my head is all I can do, the disappointment settling deep into me. I'll just have to bear it, because all that matters is getting her and Fen out of here. Saving them from being pawns in that insane woman's plans. A part of me knows I am being selfish now. As risky as this plan is, I'd rather we all die than be a part of whatever this world-changing event is.

"We should get some food." Colby cuts through my thoughts.

I look up at him. "Yeah. Okay."

As we walk to the mess hall, the only conversations being had are by those we walk past. Some talking about the scores they've had recently, others about things they've come across in their adventures, one where she was talking about some massive creature that nearly capsized their ship.

Renna wants a world where money means less than the power of an individual. I think she's wrong in saying that is what she actually wants. She wants a world where those who have the strongest under their command are the ones at the top. I don't think she is actually all that physically powerful. I think it's her will that is strong. A shiver runs through me just imagining what she did to get to the position she is in now. What inhuman feats she accomplished to look at a person and see nothing more than a tool.

"Mazu... Mazu," Colby says, my eyes blinking a few times as he waves his hand in front of my face. "You probably don't even know how we got here."

I take a look around and see the mess hall. "Sorry, I must have zoned out."

He raises a brow and tilts his head as he looks down at me. "I'd say."

We walk into the mess, and Hedda bursts out laughing at something someone else said; a pain jolts through my brain at the sound of it. Her cackle. I glare at her, but turn my head as her eyes meet mine.

Gotta build our fight up somehow.

"I was able to get some of the things done, but I'll need at least one or two more days to ensure things are with our best foot forward," Colby whispers.

Nodding my head, we get our food and sit down. He leaves me be, which I am thankful for. There are questions I want to ask, but I don't think I can handle any social aspects at the moment. The only thing I want to do is see Kellen, but since I can't do that, sleep seems like the best next thing.

Renna really is evil.

Every time I bend my arms to take a bite, I wince. When I rest my arms on the table, I wince. Colby accidentally bumping me in the arm, I wince. To think, I have to go back there tomorrow.

"You'll make it out. You're stronger than I am, and I survived," Colby mutters as he takes his last bite. "Though, I'm sure she will push you harder because of that."

I chuckle. "That was almost supportive."

"I try."

As we stand, Colby takes my plate to put it with the rest of the dirty ones. My eyes drift over the crowd, taking in the diverse and motley bunch I am surrounded by.

My hearts stop as they land on a very familiar face.

Father?

I blink a few times, trying to see if the pain is just causing me to see things, but it's him. A surge of relief runs through me, before I think about why he is here. Did he take a similar deal as mine? Does he even know we are alive? Is this something forced against his will to be a part of this life?

My legs carry me to him, and I can hear Colby calling after me, but I don't care to wait.

"Dad!" My voice shrieks, causing more than a dozen heads to turn towards me.

As my father looks up from his plate, his body stills. I rush to him, my arms wrapping around his seated form. The pain pulses through me, but I don't care. His body is rigid, not even moving to comfort me as involuntary tears fall from my eyes.

He's alive.

I feel hands lightly grasp my shoulders. "Let's move this outside," Colby whispers in my ear, but I don't shift. "Hugstari. Move outside. Now." My father stands on his command, breaking my contact with him to move towards the exit.

Maybe I should have asked and saved myself the turmoil, as it seems like Colby knew my father was going to be here or that he was at least alive.

Colby keeps his grasp gentle but persistent as he walks us out of the mess hall. "Over there." He points out an alley between the two wooden buildings.

Our steps clatter against the wooden planks of the deck, and the moment Colby releases his grasp, I rush back to my father's side. He opens his arms, but I try to ignore the hesitancy. He was never an affectionate person, but I wouldn't think he would care in the moment of our reunion.

"Mazu..." He sighs, patting my head. "You're too old to be crying in public like this."

A scolding, it really is him.

I pull back and wipe my tears, putting on a smile. "I know... It's just that, I thought you were dead..." My words are hushed.

He rubs his face with his hand before pinching the bridge of his nose. "I could say the same about you... when you jumped off that cliff."

"Dad, you don't have to worry. I have a—" Colby places his hand over my mouth, grasping it firmly. I shove him off me, looking back at him with a glare. "What was that for?"

Colby casts his eyes to the ground. "Mazu... your father is choosing to be here."

I scoff. Of course he thinks that. Like he thinks I'm choosing to be here, but there's not a choice when it comes to – wait. Why would he choose to be here if he thought Ari and I were dead?

My eyes shift from the ravenette to where my father is hiding his face from me.

"Dad?" The word is hardly a whisper.

He doesn't move, like he has suddenly turned to stone. I shake my head, my throat feeling like it's closing up.

"Dad!" I croak out.

"I never wanted him!" His words burst out like that is supposed to make me understand or mean something to me. "I only ever wanted her, Mazu... your mother was the one person to love me. To see through the rough skin and choose to stay even when I didn't deserve her."

My hands curl into fists, my mouth opens, but nothing comes out.

What is that supposed to mean?

"Do... do you mean Ari?" My eyes examine his face, begging for that not to be true.

"She wanted to have you, and I was okay with that. I could handle having one, but when we found out she was pregnant again... the thoughts that ran through my head made me feel like I was going mad. Wren's health was already declining, and I knew that the little monster inside her was going to weaken her even more."

A monster? The only monster here is him.

"How dare you..."

I've never seen my father look so small, so weak, so pathetic. He was this imposing figure. Someone who scared me. Someone I saw as dedicated to his craft, but now I know it wasn't a dedication but an avoidance.

"Mazu. You have to know that I died the moment your mother did... I thought you would have a better life... one where you wouldn't be burdened by caring for your brother, or a father who could never love you the way you needed me to." His words are genuine. The tears in his eyes, the way his arms flail around, his hunched over posture as he begs me to understand. "When you jumped off that cliff... I thought maybe that was the even better choice. So you wouldn't have to be alone."

It wasn't Renna, or the connection we had to the King of Felguard. No unforeseen fate was at fault for the mess my life had turned into, the trauma Ari had to go through, or the current torture I'm going through, but my father's fault.

He sold us out.

My fist connects with his face, forcing him to turn his gaze from mine. His hand comes up to caress his cheeks as he looks back to me, but the moment his shocked gaze locks with mine, my knee finds his crotch.

It's all his fault.

A hum begins to purr on my lips as water rushes over the top of the boardwalk towards us. His eyes are sewn shut from the pain. He doesn't even notice what's happening until I shape the liquid to create an inescapable dome around his head.

His eyes widen, his hands coming up to try and rip the water away, but his fingers simply pass through it.

"Mazu!" Colby shouts, grabbing my shoulder. "Let it go."

Ripping my shoulder out of his grasp, I don't dare tear my sight away from watching the traitor struggle to breathe, collapsing onto his knees.

I want him to die.

CHAPTER TWENTY

"DID YOU KNOW?" My voice is quiet.

I stare out at the ocean, Colby having forcibly dragged us away from my father before I ended up killing him.

"Yeah. I did," Colby mutters from behind me.

Of course he did.

My jaw clenches, nodding my head before I whip around and face him. He is holding his chin, where I had elbowed him when he first began pulling me away. The steel blue colour of his eyes are trained on me, obviously waiting for my reaction.

We aren't friends. He doesn't owe me anything. In fact, he could have used this info to torment me, but he didn't. Even though I know that, even though I should be thankful for the fact he didn't let me do something as regrettable as murdering my father, I raise my fist and swing at him.

He takes a quick step back before I can actually connect with that pretty boy face of his.

Colby raises his hands. "Mazu, I know you're angry..."

"That is an understatement!" I shout, stepping closer, but

he takes another step back, matching me pace for pace. "My father – that man..."

The betrayal eating away at what feels like the rest of my heart.

I could have killed him.

She's winning, wearing me down. All week she has been showing me how I have no control. Forcing me to use my own hands to cover me in scars. Forcing violence into the forefront of my mind.

"I know, but you never asked. I would have told you the truth, but I figured either you already knew or you weren't ready to talk about it." His words are soft, hushed, and his damned piercing eyes are locked intently on my movements.

Just one hit...

Colby narrows his gaze. "If I held up a mirror right now, I don't think you would know who you were looking at."

The words hit me, halting my stalk towards him. My hands tremble and my eyes cast downwards.

"You don't know me, what I can or can't do," I whisper.

I can hear him come closer, stepping tentatively. "You're right, I didn't know you before, but I know the stances you took. This lashing out does not align with the person who would have rather helped than hurt. Who had a chance, more than once, to bash me over the head, but refrained, because like you said in the cell, you want to walk out of this being able to still see you."

Bringing my hands up to my face, I let them shield me from the world. He's right. I don't want to be reacting this way; I don't really understand why I am. Before, I would have just turned an eye, or used my tongue as the method of lashing someone, but to attack my father...

"Mazu, I'm not going to let you become like me... that's

why I pulled you away. I want you to be able to face a mirror one day and not be ashamed of what you see staring back."

My knees give out and I sob, his words meaning more to me than I think I could actually articulate to him.

None of this is real. I just want to be home, in my bed, waking up from the worst nightmare in history.

I can't do this. I'm not strong enough.

No more.

No more.

Haldoris, Seasire, my goddess of the sea, please grant my wish.

My eyes burst open as Colby's body collides with mine, a spray of water washing over us, before we are surrounded by water. The pain in my arms makes me gasp, but the ocean is the only thing to breathe in.

What did I do?

Colby wraps his arms around my waist and starts trying to swim us back to the surface. At least, that's what I think he is doing.

My throat and lungs burn, my eyes sting, and my abdomen is convulsing.

I'm drowning.

As our heads emerge, I start to sputter up water, coughing over Colby's shoulder. He has one arm holding us above the water as it grips onto the deck, while the other is still firmly around me to help me not go back under.

"Keep coughing," he mutters against my hair.

My stomach turns from the water exiting my body, wanting to empty the contents in it as well.

My arms are circled around his shoulders, and as I start to calm down, I hold on to him tighter, my body shaking as I wail in his arms.

He doesn't move, and we sit there, half in and out of the

water. The ocean rocks us with the small waves moved by the breeze.

"I thought you told me you wouldn't try to kill yourself..." His voice gruff. "You'll make it out of this, Mazu. I swear."

That wasn't me trying.

MY BILE HITS the floor as her foot connects with my stomach again. "I'm impressed. You were able to take a few more hits than I was expecting you to." Renna smiles, taking a few steps back to watch over me.

The feeling of the wood under my shaking hands is what's grounding me in this moment, my vision blurring as I try to get my breathing out of control. A string of saliva dripping from my lips.

Just keep taking it, Mazu.

Feeling the pain is the only thing that helps keep my mind from the images of what I had done to my father. The blood coming out of his mouth before I created a water prison around his head.

"Don't let your mind wander too far. We're not done yet, my precious little gem." She coos, crouching down to my height. "You are going to be what completes my crown."

Lifting my head, my eyes meet her. Her gaze is soft as she stares at me, a gentle smile resting on her lips. She disgusts me, how she can admire what I look like right now after she had beaten me senseless and to the brink of unconsciousness. My abdominal muscles are twitching from the abuse.

My body shakes as I try to grapple with what I just did. I don't even remember singing, whistling, or making a single note with my vocal chords.

"Do I need to lock you in your room?" Colby asks.

I can tell he is joking. That exasperated tone is one he's used often, but I'm sure there is some sincerity in him asking that question.

Shaking my head, I say, "No." My voice is hoarse from the salt water that had forced its way into my lungs.

He sighs, combing his fingers through his wet hair, his hair staying slicked back. Colby strips out of his coat, laying it on the deck to dry out, along with his shirt.

Despite his kindness in saving my life versus just putting it in jeopardy, I can't help but roll my eyes.

Of course he's fit.

Not that I'm interested in touching a single inch of him, but I can't lie. He looks good.

I chuckle a bit, leaning down to press my forehead against the planks. My mind must be so broken, desperate for any distraction that I'd rather think about Colby than what is really going on.

"You're seriously laughing..." He scoffs.

Turning my head to the side, I stare up at him as he looks down at me. Maybe it would be easier just to give up and stop trying to hold some sort of moral ground. It's getting me nowhere, only puts me through turmoil.

Looking at people like Renna, these moments of heartbreak would probably mean nothing to her. The only thing that matters is her own selfish desires, regardless of the cost or consequence.

As long as she gets what she wants.

"Colby, you don't need to worry about me," I state as I sit upright. "I'm going to do what I need to, to make sure that Renna loses."

His brow furrows, and he crouches in front of me to be more at eye level. "What the infernum is that supposed to mean?"

My lips seal shut. The only way this plan of ours is going to work, the only way Kellen and Fen make it home safe is if we play by the rules presented in front of us.

The man I've reluctantly come to know leans away from me for a moment, his eyes scanning over my face.

"Kellen wants you at the end of all of this, Mazu. Not some justifiable corrupted version of who you are." His words are stern, like how I would scold Marinus when he wouldn't play nicely with other kids in the play area in Berkin's town centre.

I smile at him, forced through the tears I feel slip down my cheeks. "But I don't think that's the version of me that can save her."

Colby is filling Fen and Kellen in with what our plan is. As stupid and reckless as this plan is, I know if we don't try at least something, my cousin might not give me another chance. If he takes me back to the Felguard Country, they won't hesitate to rid themselves of Kellen.

Just push through.

"You know... I might actually want to be here if you gave me a better reason than threatening me." I spit on the ground, clearing my mouth from the taste of vomit on my tongue.

Renna chuckles and nods her head. "You want a pep talk?"

A sigh escapes me, my eyes still struggling to focus to see clearly. "Something to that effect."

"Unfortunately for you, Mazu, I don't care if you are on board or not," she tilts her head, "because you are going to do what I say, regardless."

My gaze narrows at her.

She really is just a cruel person. To stare down at me the way she is, knowing how much control she has over me.

The way she smiles makes my blood boil the longer I have to look at it. "Don't be so upset, my gem. I promise, once you lose whatever hope you have, you will be much happier."

"Easy to say when you're the one holding the leash," I mutter, standing up with a wince.

"And I've earned the right to," she states.

Does she really believe that what she is doing is okay? That she is entitled to do as she pleases with those she sees as pawns?

"The only way to have control over your fate is to take control of everyone else's." Her explanation is easy enough to understand, but it's beyond appalling.

I stare at her, not quite sure what I can say. Saying something defiant, or pointing out the flaws of that little philosophy of hers, might feel like the right thing to do, but I don't see the point of it. There is nothing – no words – that would change her mind or the situation I am in.

She laughs. Something about my expression turns the normally docile look on her face into one that more so matches her twisted mind.

"Oh my little gem, there is so much potential... I can't wait until I break you."

My jaw clenches as she steps up, tossing her dagger towards me. The bandages on my arm protecting me from the sight of the last time I held that dagger just a day ago.

Renna gestures towards it. "Go on, I want you to do it until you can't feel it anymore."

I swallow the lump in my throat before leaning down, my hand gripping onto the leathered hilt.

Just keep taking it, Mazu.

CHAPTER
TWENTY-ONE

My HEART BEATS out of my chest as I squeeze her hand tightly. My forehead pressed against the bars that separate us. Tomorrow is the day we risk everything.

"Are you sure?" Kellen's voice is hardly a whisper.

A sigh escapes my lips, and I shake my head.

Of course not.

There are so many things that could go wrong, and if they do... a shiver runs down my spine even at the thought.

My eyes open to meet hers, already watching me intently. "We can do this," I state, needing her to believe in my confidence.

Putting all my trust in Colby could be the biggest mistake of my life. If things turn from bad to worse, he likely won't have a problem throwing me under the bus to protect Fen.

Kellen blinks, her eyes remaining closed a few brief moments longer than necessary. Her gaze doesn't meet mine. Instead, they focus on my wrapped arms, then my bruised face and swollen nose.

Her thumb rubs over my knuckles. "I hate that you won't tell me what she is doing to you..."

I smile, bringing my hand up and through the bars to brush a strand behind her ear. She's doing what she always does, trying to take care of me.

"As long as we get out of here, it doesn't matter, because she will be behind us," I whisper back.

Kellen scoffs. "You really think it'll be that simple? These moments will leave their mark, Mazu."

Nodding my head, I pull back a bit. I know she is right. The pain I am feeling physically is hardly the problem; it'll be the scars left behind. Deep and rooted, these memories will be.

Keep smiling.

As long as I can keep our hopes up, we will get through this alive. We have to.

Colby walks down the steps, drawing my attention to him as he leans against the entryway. "Time to go."

Kellen grips onto my hand tightly. "Don't do anything I would do."

A chuckle escapes my lips. "Of course not."

I take a few steps away from her, our fingers brushing against each other as we slowly detach what little contact we were able to have. She gives me a smile before I turn and face my coup d'état partner.

We head back up; the sun turning to twilight. "Did you tell her?" His voice is soft as our footsteps echo across the planks of wood.

Like he is one to talk.

"There's no point," I mutter.

He doesn't say anything, and I'm grateful for him just letting us leave it there. I don't want Kellen knowing that Renna has been forcing me to torture myself as a method of numbing my mind. She's now begun having me watch her torture others, even kill other people.

The screams rattle my bones, my eyes glued shut. All they had done was steal double their ration, and she is beating them with a hammer. The cracking of their skull is something I will never forget.

"Look, Mazu." Renna's words come out rugged. "Look!"

I swallow harshly before peeking with one eye and I gag at the scene in front of me, my hand coming up to stop myself from releasing the contents of my breakfast.

She smiles. "The beautiful thing is, that I'm not just teaching him a lesson, but everyone."

My jaw clenches at her twisted idea of beauty.

Renna tilts her head, taking a few steps towards me. "Hit him," she orders, raising the hammer up with her bloodied hand.

A tremor runs through my body as my fingers grip around the slick handle.

My stomach flips at the flash of memory. Watching the light fade from that guy's eyes was more than I could take. I'm even more thankful Colby didn't let me witness me doing that to my father.

It doesn't matter how much hatred I feel for him at this moment; he is still my father and crossing that line is one you don't come back from.

"Tomorrow morning is when we head out, and you still haven't told me how we are getting in contact with you know who to help us get out fast once we dock at Berkin," Colby says.

Honestly, I'm not even sure how either. Kage just told me to wait until he reaches out, that I'd be able to respond when he ends up contacting me.

"Right now, what we need to focus on is getting off this marsh with both of them." My reply is short and earns a glare from him.

Colby shakes his head, but we keep on walking towards our rooms. He has been spending every moment he can with Fen, but even here, Renna has called on him and demanded his presence a few times.

I wonder if he has ever refused her, told her he didn't want to, but maybe he does. It's not something we have really talked about further since that night we spent at the Inn.

Does Fen know?

Opening the door, I hold it open for Colby to walk through before we head down the hall where our quarters reside.

"You'll have to perform perfectly tomorrow," he bends down and whispers in my ear.

I nod my head as Colby rights his posture. "I'm aware."

He walks off and I head into the small room they've 'gifted' me. There is nothing to do but lie down, and so I do, the bedroll offering little comfort.

Am I really the same person I was back in Berkin? No, I know I'm not. Though I am not entirely different, I am now taking risks. Higher stakes than deciding to change the set song before getting on stage, that's for sure. Kellen has always been a go big or go home type of person. I had always admired her for it, but when I would tell her, she would explain that the only reason she could be like that was because she had nothing else to lose.

I still have things to lose, but I no longer have a choice but to jump at this chance. Kellen is only hesitant because of the consequences it would have on me. She should be more worried about her very life being at stake. They won't hesitate to just kill her. Renna still thinks she can retrieve Ari whenever she wants.

My mind doesn't really want to imagine losing Kellen, but it would be the biggest mistake Renna ever makes. Marinus is safe, with a royal family that will look after him if anything were to happen to me. I wouldn't hold back, and I think I'd become the very thing she has envisioned me becoming. A monster. I wouldn't be one she controls though.

The goal is to get Kellen out of here, reunite with Ari, and put these last few horrible moonshift cycles behind us.

"Mazu, my name is Samir. I am reaching out to you on behalf of the King of Felguard."

At the speed of which I sit up, my eyes flash white for a moment.

Who the infernum was that?

I slowly open my door, but don't see anyone outside.

"Have you been able to discern the nature of the connection the Lardo in Aumento has with the Domi Nostrae? You can respond by having the intention of handing me the words like you would someone a letter, but in your mind." Her voice sounds young.

This is what Kage meant by him getting in contact with me. Of course, he would have access to someone who had magicae that could connect to people telepathically.

"Uh, well, yes." Wait. What if this is a trap? "But, I'm not telling you." I try to recover in case this is actually Renna testing me.

Did Colby tell her?

There's a moment of silence from the voice inside my head, and I put my feet up against the door, bracing myself against the wall. If this is Renna, they are going to storm in here.

"King Felguard said to mention the Yral Library painting you were admiring while you were here." My body relaxes, and I let out the breath I was holding.

Thank the goddesses.

I close my eyes and imagine the words. "Yes, they are being funded by the Domi Nostrae in exchange for them finding the precise location of the doorway just off of the Southern Territory's shores."

With communication like this, Shaw, who can teleport, his Elven bride, and Limoria's largest army, it's no wonder why the leaders of our realm were quick to recognise him despite the way he came into power and at a young age.

There is another pause, my palms sweating in anticipation. This is where the King will tell me whether I'm worth the trouble of getting a quick exit from him via Shaw.

"Have you located it or is that still in process? What is your current location?" she asks.

"In process," I state back. "And we are at a remote marshland a half mooncycle out from the mainland of Yral. We will be sailing out for Berkin tomorrow morning."

A big part of ensuring Fen and Kellen's safety is getting them as far away from Renna's grasp as possible. The likelihood of one of us getting caught lying, hiding, or doing something that will lead to the discovery of our jailbreak attempt is high. The only foolproof shot is having back up from the largest and most powerful country in all of Limoria.

"We will be in contact with the council of the Southern Territory. Just ensure you arrive at Berkin, the King will have us watch out for you."

She says that like it's going to be an easy feat.

My head rests against the wall. "Wish me luck."

CHAPTER
TWENTY-TWO

HEDDA WATCHES me intently as I help load up the cargo for the ship. She is sitting on the large crate Colby had filled with ammunition and weapons, but there is a false bottom. It looks like it's full, but there is a piece of wood that will conceal Kellen and Fen.

I didn't bother to ask how he was able to acquire the materials, mainly because it doesn't matter at this point. My eyes look towards the jail where Kellen will be attempting her escape as soon as she hears the signal.

"No slacking," Hedda hisses.

I roll my eyes before picking up a sack of potatoes and carrying it up the gangplank. Renna told us we both needed to help onboard the rations supplies, but here I am doing it on my own. It makes me feel a bit better at picking a fight with Hedda. I just need to wait until Renna gets back from doing her checks.

Colby said it was strange that she would check in on the hostages herself, but it could be because Kellen is new.

The sack hits the deck with a thud. Biggie is currently in the fight of his life with some rope for the rigging.

One would think Renna would hold a standard of intelligence with her crew.

With how much time I've spent out on the sea throughout my life, I think the moments on this ship will be the ones that will forever be burned inside my mind. Perhaps I should be grateful for that. Have these memories overwrite the ones I have with my father. Get rid of the happy or cherished thoughts and only leave the ones of hate. It would be easier that way. To loathe him for what he did to his family – to my family.

I head back down and am about to grab another sack when Renna steps out of the jail.

Show time.

My eyes glare towards Hedda, making her smirk and raise a brow.

"Have something to say, Princess?" she asks.

This is going to be easier to start than to finish. I'm just hoping Renna will find our squabble annoying and have us pulled apart.

"Yeah, I do," I hiss, stepping towards her.

Hedda's eyes dilate, hopping off of the crate. "Thank the goddesses." A chuckle follows after her praise, obviously looking forward to having a reason to fight.

She cracks her neck as I get up close in her personal bubble. "I'm so sick of your stares, your predatory attitude."

"I could say the same thing about your spoiled arse." Her grin is wide, her eyes sizing me up.

My hands clench into fists as she shoves my chest, forcing me to take a step back.

"Always taking up the attention of the Captain, of Colby." She shoves me again, and I nearly trip over my own feet from the force. "Getting special treatment just so you could foster your little magicae trick." She swings at me with a grunt, and I lean back to avoid it.

Didn't think she actually hated me, but apparently she is seriously not a big fan.

"You wanna fight?" She growls. "Then fight!" She lunges at me, taking me down to the ground.

I groan as my back hits the dock, but it's silenced as her fist connects with my face.

My mouth already pools with blood from the force. She is not holding anything back. I go to shove her off, but she pins my arms down and spits at me. The fluid hits my cheek and I glare up at her, tempted to give her a mouth full of my blood, but I know it would just come right back down.

"What's this?" Renna's voice reaches our ears, her heeled leather boots at my eye level. "Playing nicely, I see."

I roll my eyes as Hedda sits back and releases me from her grasp. The nearest guards by the jail, a gracious term for the thugs being paid to not let prisoners escape, are making their way over towards us.

At least it's working.

My hand comes up to nurse my jaw as I glare towards Renna, who is smiling down at us.

"She instigated it!" Hedda whines.

Our captain glances between us. "Is that so?"

A lump in my throat rises. "Only because she was just sitting around, and I'm getting sick of her taunting," I argue back.

Hopefully Renna will buy that and not look into it more deeply.

She crouches down, her pupils are pinpricks despite the light. "I'm so proud of you, my gem." Renna pats my head, her smirk widening. "Now finish it."

"What?" Hedda and I say in unison.

Renna yanks me up, pulling out the dagger she has forced me to run across my own skin a near hundred times. "Finish it. You want those stares to stop? Then make them." Her words are said plain and simple, like the action should be that way too.

Just kill her.

That's what Renna wants. For me to cross the line I can't come back from.

Hedda shakes her head in disbelief, taking a few steps back, but Renna grabs her arm.

"I-I—" I mutter out, which makes the Captain's smile falter. "That's not what I wanted."

"Mazu, don't back out now." Her tone lowers. "Commit!" she commands.

Hedda breaks away from Renna's grasp and starts running down the dock. I sigh with relief, but Renna orders the guards to restrain her.

Crap.

She shouts and fights against their grapple, as they drag Hedda back towards us. Her feet kicking in the air.

This is not what I wanted. It was just supposed to be a fight. A few punches, praying that Hedda didn't accidentally kill me. Renna putting a dagger in my hand and encouraging the violence on my end is something I should have considered. It's what she has been training me on since we arrived.

I stand up slowly, my hands gripping around the hilt of the blade. The guards force Hedda to her knees right in front of me. Renna's gaze bores into me, while the woman who has been nothing but crude to me can't bring her eyes up to meet mine.

Despite the pure dislike I have for Hedda, I don't want to kill her. I don't want to kill anyone.

My breath trembles as I exhale. "She's a part of the crew," I state, trying to deter her.

Renna chuckles. "So you consider her your crew? Does that mean you finally recognise me as your captain? That you are one of us?"

I suppose I do.

Not quite one of them, but in this with them. That seems like the better way to phrase it. We're all just Renna's victims. Doesn't matter how good or bad any of us are.

"Do as your captain says, Mazu," Renna purrs. "Kill her."

I grit my teeth and shake my head. Of course it wouldn't matter. She just wants to win. Break me like she said she was going to. Mould me into a gem for her crown.

"Close your eyes if you need to." She leans in and whispers, "I can guide you."

Renna's hand wraps around mine, raising the dagger, tilting Hedda's chin up. Her lips are sewn shut, but her eyes are sharper than the blade as she glares at me. I hope she can see the guilt in my eyes, because that's all I feel at this moment.

My chin quivers, but I clear my throat. "Just drive it forward and it'll be over," Renna says sweetly, using her other hand to brush some of my hair out of my face.

I'm going to fall into shambles.

The things this woman has done to me. Kellen always said I was good at pushing my emotions aside, ignoring what I have to in order to keep moving forward; but I won't be able to avoid this. It will ruin me.

Bandages are still covering my arms, those scars already holding a weight I know will haunt me once what happens settles in.

"Now, Mazu," Renna hisses into my ear.

I close my eyes. Her grip on mine tightens.

"Am I missing something here?" Colby's voice calls out. My eyes shoot open and land on his form jogging towards us.

My shoulders relax a bit, Renna dropping my hand and facing her favourite toy.

She takes a step towards him. "You're just in time to watch a transformation." Her hands showcase Hedda kneeling in front of me, preparing to kill her.

Colby furrows his brow. "That's a shame it couldn't be someone more useless, like Biggie, maybe."

Renna looks back over at Hedda, her sweet look faltering a bit. "I suppose."

"Right before a long trek too, but hey, I'm always in for a show." He shrugs his shoulders before crossing his arms in front of his chest.

His gaze meets mine, sending me a wink, trying to reassure me, I presume. There is no way Renna isn't seeing right through his words, but he's apparently set on keeping his word – making sure I walk out of this still intact.

I couldn't be more thankful.

Our captain squares up to him, looking over his features intently. Colby stares back at her with a simple smile and a steady gaze.

"You'll have to pay up." Renna smirks, dragging a nail down his jawline.

He doesn't flinch. "I know."

I STAYED down by Colby a while after Renna and Hedda took their leave.

"As grateful as I am, shouldn't you be with Fen and Kellen?" My voice hushed.

He doesn't turn to look at me, likely trying to seem disinterested as Renna is close by. "Kellen got out, and they are set," he whispers back.

A wave of relief hits me hearing that she at least made it out. Even if she didn't get on our ship, she's resourceful enough to make it home on her own. Though, as the second part of his sentence registers, I furrow my brow.

What is that supposed to mean?

"Um, the crate they are supposed to get into is literally right next to us," I hiss.

He smirks, finally looking at me, but despite his smile, I see a crease in his forehead. "You thought I would let you just plan the whole thing? Fen is at stake too, and you have been keeping the communication with your cousin under wraps." My jaw clenches. "I needed skin in the game. They are safe, and we will have them on the boat."

I can't blame him for wanting to have some say, but it bothers me that right now, I have no idea where Kellen is or what's happening with her.

"You're lucky I trust you." The words barely escape me.

"Or what?" He scoffs. "You'd kill me? I just saw what that looks like, and I think I'm in the clear."

Colby makes his way up the gangplank, leaving me on that note. I would be upset about his comment, but he's probably a tad disheartened he will be spending additional time with Renna on this trip.

Once Fen is safe, he will be free. Then he and I will be even for the saves.

CHAPTER
TWENTY-THREE

THINGS HAVE BEEN smooth so far. Colby and I are each taking portions of our rations to sneak to our stowaways. We try to keep it as randomised as we can to not stir up any suspicion about why we are always disappearing.

Avoiding a pattern is key.

It's a calm evening, but there's something in the air – a static in the stillness that makes the hairs on the back of my neck rise. The wind had shifted from this morning; it is nipper than what it should be. I stand on the deck, squinting toward the horizon, an ominous shade of grey, and I feel it deep in my bones – a storm is coming.

I glance around, watching the crew work, but even they seem a little more tense, a little more alert. Vince, the first mate, stands at the wheel, his face tight with concentration as he stares out at the water.

"Storm's brewing!" the lookout up in the crow's nest calls from above.

Rogers was his name, I think.

A murmur ripples through the crew. "All hands on deck! Get the sails! We don't want to be caught with them fully unfurled!" Vince shouts the orders out.

Renna steps out from her room, looking around, likely having heard the commotion. Her eyes lock with mine, a smile playing on her lips.

I may not have experienced a storm this far out at sea before, but I doubt it's a thing to take lightly. Even the storms near the shore are rough when on a boat.

Breaking away from our locked gaze, I jump into action, racing to the mainmast to help secure the sails. The wind picks up, and the sails snap, the sound cutting through the rushed pounding of the crew's feet on the deck.

"Grab those ropes!" Colby commands, pointing towards the mainsails' rigging. "We need to bring this up fast."

Nodding, I reach up, grabbing the rope and heaving with all my strength to pull the sail in – the ropes biting into my hands as I put my whole body weight into it.

Why couldn't this have happened when we didn't have two people hiding below deck?

The wind picks up a bit more, my hair whirling around me as those grey clouds seem to catch up to us. I see Hedda working with Biggie on the aft rigging. They're struggling to keep the lines taut against the growing wind. Every time a gust comes, the sails tug hard, pulling against their efforts.

The ship creaks as it fights against the growing pressure of the wind and the waves that seem to be gaining some height.

The first crack of thunder snaps through the sky, sharper than a whip. My stomach clenches at the sound. I feel a pulse from my necklace, pulling me away from the rigging and towards the taffrail.

Something out there.

I grip the railing tighter, staring out at the horizon. The

darkness now stretches out endlessly, but there's no comfort in it tonight. The stars are gone, swallowed whole by the wall of clouds rolling toward us like an advancing army.

Raindrops start to fall, splashing against my cheeks. It's frigid and stings like knives against my skin.

"Mazu!" Colby calls out, but my eyes are glued to the sea.

I don't even know what I'm looking for, or why, but the heat on my chest from the opal my mother gifted me is telling me that we are not alone.

The waves are rising; the ship climbing each crest like a beast fighting to stay upright. Every groan of the wood feels like a warning. Every crash of water against the hull feels like a dare.

"Hold on!" someone shouts over the wind.

The Jacob's ladder rocks back and forth with the ship, wild against the storm's fury. Rogers is heading down as it's grown too hazardous for him to remain up there, though he is now hanging on for dear life. His grip slips, and my heart lurches. I watch in horror as he loses his grip and falls.

"Damn it!" someone screams before he hits the railing with a sickening crack.

He's gone, his broken body slipping into the sea before I can react.

Another wave hits, slamming into the starboard side with the force of a cannon. I'm thrown against the railing, the breath knocked from my lungs.

I instantly hold on for dear life, as I don't want to get thrown overboard.

The ship isn't just battling the elements—it's battling the sea itself, as if the ocean's wrath has focused entirely on us.

"Mazu!" I turn, rain blinding me for a moment before I see Colby.

He's gripping a rope with one hand, the other waving me

over. His hair is plastered to his face, his expression sharp with urgency.

"You need to use your powers!" he yells.

"What?" I shout back, the word ripped from my throat by the wind.

The ship groans again. This time, it's a deeper sound, something unnatural. The whole structure shudders as the storm's full force hits us. The ship lurches, then rights itself, but the deck is slick with water.

"Hold on!" Vance screams. "We're riding it out – just stay on your feet!"

My eyes dart towards him, Renna close by and holding herself against one of the mizzenmast.

"The water!" Colby says, drawing my attention back to him. "We need you to stop it, or slow it, or – infernum, I don't know, do something!"

I freeze, my mind spinning.

Can I even try to fight against the will of the ocean?

"I don't think I can!" My honesty brings a frown to his face.

"You can!" His voice is iron, cutting through the storm. "You have to try." Colby's gaze turns towards the entrance to the hull.

Right.

The deck tilts sharply, and I hit my knees hard, splinters biting into my skin. Pain flashes through me, but it's nothing compared to the dread curling in my chest.

The necklace hums faintly against my skin once more.

I grip it tightly, trying to focus on the chaotic whirl of water around us. "Fine," I mutter under my breath. "Let's see what you can do."

Haldoris, be with me.

The melody comes unbidden, rising in my throat like a

prayer I barely understand. It's raw and uneven, the notes trembling against the roar of the storm.

> There once was a ship that sailed the tide,
> Her crew had nowhere left to hide.
> The storm arose, the winds did cry,
> And tore the heavens down.

> The sea, she screams and takes her due,
> The waves will break and drown the few.
> But we will fight, we'll see it through,
> And bring this vessel 'round.

The ocean pushes back immediately. The power is wild, untamed. It's different from when I've called to it before. Like I'm fighting against the sea itself.

"Come on," I whisper, my voice cracking.

I sing the song to grow louder, my voice cutting through the chaos. The necklace burns against my skin, the magicae surging outward like a second heartbeat.

♫

> The clouds did churn, the sky turned black,
> The storm, it sought to pull us back.
> Her teeth were sharp, her grip was cold,
> And still, we pulled the line

> The sea, she screams and takes her due,
> The waves will break and drown the few.
> But we will fight, we'll see it through,
> And bring this vessel 'round.

The captain called, "Now lash that sail,
Or pray to your goddesses to no avail.
For in her depths, she'll write your tale,
And drag your soul below!"

The sea, she screams and takes her due,
The waves will break and drown the few.
But we will fight, we'll see it through,
And bring this vessel 'round.

Oh, many men have met their end,
Where sea and shadow both descend.
But those who fight may yet defend,
Their lives from death's cold hand.

The sea, she screams and takes her due,
The waves will break and drown the few.
But we will fight, we'll see it through,
And bring this vessel 'round.

So hoist the line, and haul the brace,
Defy the storm's unholy face.
For though she claims all in her race,
Tonight, we will not bow.

♪

A few of the waves break, the ship easing in its rocking, as I force the sea to calm, just slightly.

I turn to look back towards Colby, but my eyes widen as a massive wave towers above the ship like a wall, but it hesitates, the crest frozen mid-air. My chest tightens as I will it back versus crashing over top of us.

The sea, she screams and takes her due,
The waves will break and drown the few.
But we will fight, we'll see it through,
And bring this vessel 'round.

"Now!" I shout towards Vince, my voice hoarse. "Take us through!"

The ship lunges forward, slicing through the narrow gap I've created. The wave crashes behind us with a deafening roar, spraying the deck with freezing water.

Cheers erupt from the crew, but I don't have the energy to celebrate. My legs give out, and I collapse onto the deck, gasping for air.

Colby is there in an instant, his hand gripping my shoulder. "You okay?"

I nod weakly, though I'm not sure it's true. My vision swims, the edges darkening.

"We're not done yet," he says grimly, and I know he's right.

The storm is relentless, the next wave already building in the distance.

Keep going.

I force myself to my feet, every step a battle against the tilting deck. "One more time," I say, though my voice is barely audible.

Colby looks at me, his eyes shadowed. "Mazu—"

"I can do it," I cut him off, though the words feel like a lie. "You said I had to try, right?"

He gives me a tight smile, helping me maintain my balance as I start to sing once more. Though the melody and words are the same, this time, the song is different. It's darker, heavier, like I'm dragging it from the depths of my soul. The necklace responds, the magicae spilling outward and into jagged waves.

The ocean slows, but it doesn't stop.

I close my eyes, pleading with the magicae Haldoris has gifted my bloodline, my voice raw and desperate. It tears through me, wild and unforgiving. Almost like she is mad I am fighting against the ocean.

The wave splits, the ship sliding through the opening.

I collapse again, my vision dimming. I can feel Colby's arms around me, his voice calling my name, but it's distant, muffled.

"What the infernum is that?" I hear someone shout, making me glance to the side.

A face standing out from amongst the waves we pass.

Colby hugs me tighter. "It's a **waterform**!"

That's the last thing I hear before everything goes dark.

I see the ship, the crew, Colby holding my unconscious frame with his eyes wide with fear as he stares towards where I am watching this all from.

That can't be right.

My form feels cold, unstable, almost like I could fall apart at any second.

Colby shakes my physical body on the ship. I can't hear anything, but I can see him shouting down at me.

Am I dead?

None of this makes sense. I try moving, the sensation odd, as it feels like I'm shifting more than taking a step or floating.

I feel a sharp pain in my head, and I fall, no longer looking over the ship but falling down into the ocean. Being under the waves, I feel whole, that before I was just a fraction of what I truly am.

My vision begins to fade as I sink deeper, and as the light leaves me completely, I can hear Colby's voice once more.

"Mazu."

CHAPTER
TWENTY-FOUR

I OPEN MY EYES, a soft light shining in through a window. Blinking a few times, my blurry surroundings come into focus. I'm swaying slightly in the rope-strung bed. My body aches as I start to shift and try to sit up. There's an apothecary cabinet in the corner; that sterile smell used to be around the house when we were taking care of Mother.

Must be in the infirmary.

I rub the back of my neck to alleviate some of the soreness. My mind drifts back to what I had seen before I had lost consciousness. It must have just been a dream, like the one I had when I jumped off the cliff.

Looking over my body, I see someone must have changed the bandages on my arms, but I'm in the same clothes as I was.

Thank goodness.

Regardless if it would have been for my health or not, I would not want anyone on this crew dressing me.

I jolt up, wincing as I do, as the door opens. Colby's

piercing blue eyes stare into mine. A smile spreads across his lips as he walks in and closes the door behind him.

"Well, if it isn't the sleeping princess," he says, looking me over for a moment. "How are you feeling?"

A chuckle escapes me. "Like I'm made of brick."

Colby nods his head, leaning against the wall. "You were on and off asleep for a good chunk of the trip. You don't remember anything?"

Excuse me?

Not being able to recall being awake sends a shiver through me. I could have said or done anything and now I have no memory of it.

Blinking a few times, I finally register what he just said properly. "No... How far off are we?"

Was he able to feed Kellen while I was out? How are they holding up? Have they been found?

Holding up his hands, Colby gestures for me to calm down, my panic must be written all over my face.

"We will be coming up on Berkin in the next day or so," he explains. "You have no idea how happy I am to see you up. I was worried I'd have to leave you behind."

I wouldn't have blamed him if he did try to make a run for it, but Kellen wouldn't have taken off. Too stubborn, though I'm one to talk.

"Did we miss the chance for you to message the King?" Colby asks, but I shake my head.

Regardless, if he did try to reach out, the lady I was talking to in my mind said they would be keeping an eye out.

Or at least I hope things haven't changed.

Colby sighs in relief, running a hand through his raven locks. My eyes focus on a cut that was hidden behind his hair. It looks like it is still in its healing stage.

My finger points to it, and he tilts his head, confused for a moment, before he lowers his hand. "Oh, that? Don't worry about it."

"Was that from the storm?" I ask.

He stares at me, the smile he had been wearing slowly fading. "Renna was a tad upset you hadn't woken up yet. She's needing your assistance once we arrive."

The muscles in my body tense up instantly. "For what?"

"All she said was that she needed you to wake up before she met with the Domi Nostrae." His voice softens, the weight of his words feeling immense.

Trying to predict her intentions seems pointless.

When it comes to that woman, all I know is that she will do whatever she can to get what she wants.

Perhaps it is best to get it over with. Go see what our captain is commanding of us now, but I want to be a tad more selfish than that.

"Can I go see Kellen?" I ask, getting out of the hammock, Colby rushing over to help as I nearly trip and land on my face.

"For someone who nearly commanded the sea, you sure seem pretty pathetic right now," he teases, earning a smack from me. "Sadly, no. If any of the crew sees you, they will draw attention."

I groan, rolling my eyes. Of course I am being denied.

Lazily, I gesture with my hand for Colby to lead the way. Not that I had the energy or emotional bandwidth to deal with Renna right now, I had that lovely thing called *no choice* forcing me to.

Once we are out of harm's way, my breakdown will be a monstrous one.

Just gotta keep it together a little longer.

We exit the small corridor, Colby walking by my side versus just ahead or behind me. I look at him, earning a quirked brow.

"How are you holding up?" My voice is hushed.

His eyes drift off for a moment. "As best as I can be I guess." The honesty from him makes my heart hurt for him. "Stressed, feeling like crap, and ready for this all to be over."

My gaze doesn't tear away from him, even when he doesn't bother to look me in the eye.

"We're going to get through this, Colby." He forces a smile, nodding his head to my words.

It'll all be okay.

Once we arrive at Renna's quarters, I open the door, seeing her laid out on her rope-strung bed – it swaying slightly in time with the ship.

She sits up on her elbows and smiles wide. "I'll forgive you for not knocking this time, my little gem." Renna slides off her bed and struts her way to us as Colby closes the door behind us. "I'm so happy to see you awake. Just in time for me to fill you in with what I'm needing from you."

A lump rises in my throat, but I try to clear it. "What would that be?"

Renna laughs as she examines me. "Don't look so nervous. You should be used to this now. Right?" Her tone turns from playful into something sharper.

I nod my head.

"That little book you gave me," she says, walking to her desk and holding up the Torrin family book. "As fond as the family was of magicae, they never possessed the ability, and asking your father, I know his side and your mother's side of the family didn't either." Renna explains as she flips through a few of the pages. "So, when I talked to my friends we will be meeting up with, they were quite eager to meet you."

My jaw clenches, not liking where this is going. The book snaps closed, and she tosses it at me, where I catch it, hissing a bit from the sudden movement.

"You're the big fish, apparently." Her gaze hardens on me. "They no longer want just the doorway, but you as well."

That sounds like the worst-case scenario right there.

"The Domi Nostrae are now changing the terms of our agreement. Either they have you, or I walk away with nothing. My funding gone." Renna leans against the desk. "With that in mind, you're going to be a very good gem, and do whatever it is they want. Otherwise, I kill the girl and your brother."

She would go back on her word just like that. It doesn't surprise me, but how pathetic that her entire empire relies on ruthless blackmail and its follow through. Everything she has built would be nothing without the love people have for those they cherish.

"You said—"

"It doesn't matter what I said, Mazu. What matters is that I have the power." Renna smiles sweetly at me. "You'll do what they ask, and I'll be happy to throw Colby into a few rounds of punishment as well, if that helps motivate you."

My gaze shifts to Colby, who is outright glaring at her, which I am surprised by. He's always been good about keeping up appearances for her, but I think something changed when I was out of it.

THE SHIP ROCKS GENTLY as we glide into Berkin's harbour, the wooden hull creaking. I can just make out the docks, lanterns flickering in the fog of this damp morning air.

I wish I could say I was overjoyed to see my hometown, but I'm terrified of this next part. Of trying to ensure Kellen and Fen's safety, as well as escaping before Renna or the Domi

Nostrae can get their hands on me. My home will be my battlefield.

This is it.

Colby leans close, his voice a low whisper in my ear. "We've got one shot, Mazu. Renna will have half the crew on deck to watch over things. If we don't time this right..."

I nod, my stomach knotting. He doesn't need to finish his sentence. Everything is riding on this, and there are no second chances.

"Stand by!" Vince calls out, pulling my attention back.

We share one last look; all we can do now is follow through. I keep my head down and try to look busy, hauling coiled ropes with aching arms as the ship drifts into its berth. The rest of the crew are at their stations, them being less rowdy than normal as we pull in.

As the inspectors come aboard, that'll be our shot.

The gangplank is lowered, Renna stepping out of her quarters to do as captains must: represent their ship. She looks over at her crew first, her eyes locking with mine for a split second before counting the rest of them.

With everyone in their place, she waits for the inspectors to come onboard. I take a few steps back. Though I halt as Hedda spots me heading towards the haul.

She isn't where she's supposed to be.

This is it. I'm heading to the hull, which I'm not supposed to be doing. All she has to do is call out and I will miss my shot to get them out.

A smile touches her lips, my fists tightening, and I get ready to sing – but Hedda simply looks away, whistling her own tune.

I don't question it and head down the steps, towards the back, behind the barrels, tapping on them a few times, before pulling back the tarp.

Kellen is gripping onto the dagger we had got her, pointing

it up to jab, but the moment she registers it's me, she drops it and wraps her arms around my frame.

"Thank the goddesses..." she whispers, her hold on me tightening just a tad more.

"I'm okay." My arms wrap around for a brief moment.

We both pull away, knowing our time together will have to wait until all of this is over.

Colby had mentioned that he had to fight Kellen a few times, on her wanting to sneak away to see me while I was in and out of it for a while. I feel bad I made her worry when she should have been more focused on herself.

Fen crawls out behind Kellen, their eyes searching for Colby, but he isn't here.

"We need to move," I state, gesturing for them both to follow me.

They scurry out and catch up to match my steps. As we head up and out of the hull, I peek my head out. Hedda is no longer where she had once spotted me. Renna is in the middle of a conversation with the inspectors – them asking her about what is on board before they fact check her – while the rest of the crew are talking amongst themselves.

My eyes land on Colby, who nods his head towards me before leaning back on the taffrail, enough so to have him slip. Everyone's eyes dart towards him as he catches himself with his feet, Biggie reacting and grabbing his coat to help pull him back.

I gesture for Kellen and Fen to run, to head towards the bow of the ship. Following behind, I send one last glance towards the group of distracted pirates, but my breath gets caught in my throat as my gaze meets Renna's.

CHAPTER
TWENTY-SIX

I BREAK the gaze and run after where Kellen and Fen headed.

Damn it.

"Just jump!" I call out. They look back for a second, but do as I say, throwing themselves over the railing.

While humming a quiet tune, I vault over it myself, commanding the water to catch all of us versus making a loud splash. My melody helps drift us under the docks and towards the beach that they are connected to. We pass by other ships, sounds of crews waking up for the day or loading up to head out.

Renna saw.

Without a doubt, I could see her normally sickly sweet smile had been wiped clean from her face, and instead was replaced with a cold stare. The wish of death was clear in her eyes, with her lips in a firm line.

I need to get them both out of this city.

She won't hesitate to end their lives if she gets ahold of them again, and I have no idea how Colby is going to get away.

Renna could tell; that's why she looked the opposite way. He won't just be let off the hook, or punished. I doubt her infatuation with his looks will be enough to spare him this time.

As we reach the shore, Fen and Kellen turn towards me as I remain kneeled on the sand. "She saw," I whisper.

Kellen pats her head, like she's trying to get water off. "What? Who?"

"Renna. She saw," I say louder, my eyes locking on with Fen's.

They look back towards the ship, a hand covering their mouth. "No..."

I rise to my feet; the sand glueing itself to my soaked clothes. "I'll go back for him."

"Yeah, no," Kellen interjects, looking between Fen and me. "I'm sorry, but we're getting out of here. We can't risk going back!"

Fen's eyes start to water, their legs shaking. "Please, I'm begging you."

Kellen shakes her head and sighs, grabbing my hand. "Colby will find a way. He seems like he's the resourceful type."

I want to agree with Kellen, sweep her away to the Felguard Country, live a life in Fosa, creating music or simply just being together.

"I can't leave him behind, Kellen." My tone firm. "I need you to take Fen and find your boss. Tell him what's going on, tell Cray, too."

She scoffs and squeezes my hand tighter. "No way am I letting you go back to the psycho!"

Pulling my hand out of her grip, I take a step closer, my eyes darting between the two of hers. "Listen, if I can get Renna cornered, we won't have to run from her. We could put an end to her."

"That's a big if," Kellen argues, crossing her arms over her chest.

She looks at me though, that one where she knows she won't win this fight and is helpless as she is being forced to watch this happen.

Like when I got that really bad haircut a few years ago. I was so adamant that she just had to let it happen.

"I'll get them to show up. We will fight her together." Her words resolute.

A smile spreads across my face, and one appears on hers. Our split second is interrupted as Fen pulls us into a group hug.

"Thank you..." Their voice is soft.

I pat their back and nod. "We won't leave him behind."

Fen nods their head, taking a step back and releasing us. Kellen leans in and kisses my cheek before running off, Fen close behind them.

We tried to make it out without a fight, but I guess Renna isn't going to let that happen.

Whatever it takes.

ALL I NEED to do is stall. Simple enough. Just keep Renna's attention long enough that she won't kill Colby and or force me to do awful things.

So easy.

I chew on my cheek as I walk back down the docks. The inspectors smile at me, but those fade slightly as they notice my dripping garments as they pass by. She had to keep up appearances while they were still aboard the ship, but now that they're gone.

My feet move faster, jogging the remaining distance.

Hedda is leaning against the railing next to the gangplank. "So close." She chuckles, throwing her dagger down at the dock in front of me. "You're going to need that."

My jaw clenches. "So what. You're being nice now?" I bend down and pull the blade out of its embedded spot.

Hedda straightens up. "You could of killed me, but you didn't."

I just nod, not needing to share more words than that. We probably both know this is as close to a friendship as we will ever have. Keeping the part where she only almost got killed because I was using her for myself seems like the best option.

She watches me head back onto the ship. The rest of the crew turns and watches me, my grip on the dagger tightening. Some are sitting, others drawing their weapons.

Renna wasted no time letting the crew know exactly what to do if I step back on this ship. If the Domi Nostrae are making me the bargaining chip, it'll be: capture by any means necessary.

"Look who came back! Have a fun little swim, gem?" Renna asks as she steps into view from the upper deck. Vince is dragging Colby up behind her. "You really almost had me. I thought I was finally getting through to you."

Her fingers glide over the railing as she makes her way down the stairs. The wind picks up her golden hair, showcasing the length. She really does look regal, at least when you separate the appalling actions she does.

"But I knew you would come back." Her smile is wide as she gestures to Colby, who is held up by Vince. His gaze turned downwards and hands bound behind his back. "So, we can make a deal."

I scoff and click my tongue as her boots hit the main deck. "A deal? Last time I made one with you, you had no intention of sticking to it."

"Neither were you." She points out. "Running off like that when you swore to remain on my crew."

Renna steps in front of me. It takes more than I wish to admit to not step back. Her copper eyes look me up and down, as if she is trying to find something different with me.

"Tell me, Mazu," she whispers. "How was it? Fighting the ocean's will?" Renna reaches out, her finger flicking the opal stone strung on my neck.

I smack her hand away, making her smile falter. "Just tell me what this deal is already."

She turns her head, gesturing to Vince with a nod. He throws Colby down the stairs, my friend tumbles, grunting with every step he hits until he lands on the main deck. I rush over to him, but Renna grabs my arm and pulls me back.

"Your obedience," she states. "I'll let him live, but only if you bend your knee."

My gaze shifts to hers. "And what, you lock him away, like you did Kellen and Fen?"

Colby shifts, groaning as he looks up to me. "You shouldn't have come back."

He can say that all he wants, but he should have known if it wasn't me, it would have been Fen. This time, though, I doubt Renna would have thought it worth the trouble of keeping either of them around.

What matters is that the people we cherish are safe.

"No, he is too familiar with how things work. It would be one escape attempt after the next and I'd be too tempted to kill him," Renna says, resting a hand on her hip. "I'll simply let him go, but only once the Domi Nostrae have you in their possession. Then they will tame you like one of their beasts." She chuckles, maybe at the thought of me being put in a literal cage or at the idea of me no longer being her problem.

A low rumble of thunder in the distance draws my eyes

towards the sea. The Domi Nostrae are already here in Berkin, and if the King of Felguard is concerned about them, I know that I should be terrified to be in their grasp.

"How long do I have to make the decision?" I ask quietly.

"Mazu, don't," Colby pleads, struggling to get up. "Remember, I'm the one who threw Ari off that cliff, that tried to kill Kellen." I smile at him. "Just run."

Renna burst out laughing. "Oh, how sad! The once cool demeanour you had is now replaced with this pathetic soft-hearted crap."

I raise the dagger to Renna, but she doesn't even flinch. "Answer my question."

She rolls her eyes, using two of her fingers to push the blade away. "You have about a sunshift. They know we arrived and are already on their way to collect you, but I'll be honest. You will either do this willingly, or I'll slit his throat and force you into their hands."

CHAPTER
TWENTY-SIX

"Giving up already?" Mamma's voice rings out from the kitchen. "You almost had it that last time."

I lay back on my bed, my throat sore from the strain of trying to sing those soprano parts over and over again.

A soft knock sounds on my door. My head turns to see my mother walking into the room. There is a smile on her face, like always. She is carrying a tray, steam rising from the teacups.

"I'm not giving up," I correct her, crossing my arms over my chest as she sets the tray down on my dresser. "My throat hurts."

Mother hands me one of the cups as she joins me on my bed. Once her hand is free, she uses it to push hair out of my face.

Her eyes look me over. "That's my girl."

I relax my shoulders and smile before taking a sip of my chamomile tea. The only time I can sing in the house is whenever Father is out of it. Says it's too noisy, but Mamma never *minds it. She helps me practise sometimes, though she says her voice isn't as pretty as mine. I disagree with her.*

She drinks from her own cup, and we sit there in silence for a moment, the sun coming in faintly from the window. The cup warms my hands, the translucent brown colour matching the shade of the caramels Father brought home the other day.

"Mazu..." Mother's voice breaks through the stillness. "Promise me if things ever get hard, like a note you can't reach, you'll always continue to try."

I nod my head. "I'll work on my scale, I swear!"

She chuckles, shaking her head. "I mean in other things too, Mazu. Don't lose hope, even when you think what you're trying to do is impossible."

"Like how Dad never gives up and buys a new net?" I raise a brow, a smirk on my face.

"Exactly." Her hand pats my head. "You'll find a way."

I stare at her a moment. "Mamma... What if I fail regardless of how many times I try, or I don't get another chance?"

Her smile falls slightly, her gaze shifting to the liquid left in her cup. "I guess then you can say you at least tried. Even if we fail, oftentimes we still make a difference. We learn from it, show someone else there is still hope, or make things slightly better than they would have been."

My voice rings out, a crude note, but the ocean rocks the boat, knocking us all off our feet.

"What are you doing?" Renna shouts, glaring towards me and drawing her cutlass.

"I'm not giving up." I smirk.

The notes escape my lips, the ocean spilling onto the deck, bringing Colby to my side, and barely missing the swing from Renna as she tries to cut him as he crosses her path.

She can threaten me all she wants, but I am not going to let her set the terms this time. Thanks to her desire for what I can do, I can use it against her. I'll show her that all of her training and torture wasn't for nothing. It'll be why she loses this deal with the Domi Nostrae, why she couldn't keep Colby or me by her side.

The boat continues to rock as I cut his bindings. "Still wishing I had just run?" I tease.

He scoffs, leaning against me so he doesn't topple over. "Shut up."

Calling to the aid of the sea, I have us pulled down the gangplank and the moment we hit the dock, our feet sprint down the straight. All eyes are on us, the sudden waves putting everyone on alert and our running drawing attention.

"Pirates!" I scream, pointing back to where our crew was now following after us.

The sailors around us don't hesitate to intervene, making threats and drawing their own weapons, all while Colby and I slip away from Renna's grasp.

Keep running.

As our hasted steps pound against the wood of the deck, we notice a small group at its edge. Hope flutters in my chest as I see Kellen standing with her boss.

"Something isn't right," Colby says, his pace slowing down.

As we approach, Kellen's brow is knitted together as she glares at her boss. His weapon is already drawn, along with the other guards he brought with him.

"Sorry, Mazu, but right now, this city needs all the contributions we can get." The man who is in charge of Berkin's security and safety, has just sold himself to a group who will see it destroyed.

This can't be happening.

THEY ARE SEPARATING me from the ocean. Showing me they really know what they are doing. My connection to the Seasire means nothing if I am not near her creation. The skies above us have turned grey. Storms are common during this part of the year, but there is comfort in feeling like the Tempest's will is purposefully matching my mood.

Kellen hasn't been able to meet my gaze since we were forced up onto these horses. Her boss had stopped the outraged sailors from attacking Renna and her crew.

I recognised some of the ships and their captains as they watched the four of us get detained. Perhaps word will spread and we might actually survive this.

"Is that it?" one of the guards asks, pointing out towards a grouping of tents.

The head guard who is riding with me in front of him replies, "Yes. We just need to hand the girl off."

"What about the rest of us?" Kellen asks what we are all thinking.

Maybe the Domi Nostrae will have mercy if I just give in to them.

No one answers Kellen, mainly because I believe they don't even know the answer to it. All of this is simply to put money into Berkin. They will turn us over, people they have known for their whole lives, just to help the city.

Love is seriously one messed up ideal.

As we approach, a few cloaked individuals are standing outside the tents. Renna would be close behind; having grabbed her carriage from the housing warehouse she apparently keeps it when she is not on this end of the realm.

A woman steps forward with a soft smile, her hair short and

greyed. She has an ornate brooch pinned to her cloak, her hands tucked into the sleeves in front of her.

"Welcome," she greets us, as we all dismount from the steads.

The head guard shoves me forward ahead of everyone else, and I nearly trip, but recover mere inches from her.

Her head tilts as she looks down at me. I'm pretty confident in saying she must be taller than Colby.

"You must be Mazu... We've heard a lot about you." Her voice sounds kind enough. "We're sorry about the means in which you were brought here. I hope they were not too rough with you."

I scoff, looking at her with utter disbelief. She has no idea the utter agony my life has crumbled to. Sure, the first half had nothing to do with her or this cult she's in, but Renna is happy and eager to be working with them, which means they are far from people I would want to be tied to.

Kellen comes up from behind, sticking close to me. "Rough is an understatement."

The woman's smile doesn't falter. "My name is Dasha. I'm one of the priestesses of the Domi Nostrae."

Does she want me to shake her hand or something?

Thunder rumbles through the air, the vibrations resonating in our chests. The wind is picking up as we are high up now, just outside the Cliff Keep's district. My eyes drift towards the cliff edge not far away from us.

"You have no idea what your cooperation means to us," Dasha says.

Colby chuckles to himself, shaking his head as I glance over my shoulder at him. "Cooperation? You mean compliance. Trust me, I would know the difference."

Dasha doesn't seem phased by his words, but instead steps towards him. "We only have the best intention here, I assure you. We will bring back the age of magicae, bring salvation to our realm."

Fen hides behind Colby, their eyes wide at the words. "The only salvation is the one from being trapped here with you," Colby says.

"We will see about that." Dasha chuckles, and a shiver runs through me.

Threats already.

Another group of horses sound from behind us, Renna's carriage coming into view with the rest of her crew.

Now we're all here.

Colby wraps his arm around Fen's waist while I reach for Kellen's hand. Once the deal is struck, this might be our last moment together.

There was so much more I wanted to do with my boring life. I wanted to see Ari grow up, to sing and write songs, to have more fun with my friends. To explore things with Kellen.

Renna gets out of the carriage, Vince offering her his hand to step out. She approaches our assembly, greeting Dasha with a warm smile.

"It's a pleasure to see you again." Her voice is excitable.

Dasha nods her head. "Yes, we are looking forward to finalising this deal and moving to the next stages of securing the doorway."

My eyes dart between the two of them, squeezing Kellen's hand tighter as Dasha turns towards us.

"As for the two of you." She points out the two non-magicae users in our quartet. "We will have no need for either of you."

The words fall from her mouth so casually. Colby instantly reaches out, blinding the crewmate closest to him, grabbing their short sword and dagger from the sheaths. Kellen looks towards the guards, kicking behind his knees, making him fall forward. She kicks him in the face to snatch the lance in their hands. She whirls it around, cutting down one of the Domi Nostrae's men as they approach. I grab his sword, and we all start running for it. Those who were inside the tents, spill out hearing the commotion, cutting us off from the other side of the cliff.

"Don't run from your destiny!" Desha calls out.

I glance back at the crowd charging towards us as we are getting pinned between the cliff edge and them.

This is it.

My eyes go to look towards my friends, droplets of rain beginning to come down. We turn to face them, causing them to slow their pace.

Lightning splits the sky, illuminating the chaos about to erupt. The first clash comes from my left side – a Domi Nostrae soldier lunges forward, blade aimed for Fen. Colby intercepts with a roar, his sword clanging against the attacker's.

"Get the hell out of here!" Colby shouts to Fen.

Both sides immediately leap into action. The sound of metal on metal, war cries, and grunts fill the space around us.

Fen hesitates, looking at all of us, their hand gripping on the dagger Colby handed them. "I-I can't leave you all."

"Now!" he shouts, leaving no room for them to argue as he pierces his sword through the enemy that had rushed him.

He kicks them off his blade, gearing to defend from the attacker that is right behind him. Fen's eyes widen at what they just witnessed, the dagger slipping from their grasp. They take off, running back towards the horses, avoiding the fray as Colby makes a reckless move of charging into the Domi Nostrae's space to draw their attention to him versus Fen.

Kellen pulls me back, and I nearly trip over my feet as I'm barely missed by a large man about to tackle me.

Yeah, I should focus on what's going on with me.

She acts before I do, twirling her spear around her back

before bringing it forward to impale the enemy while he is still down.

"Mazu!" Kellen scolds, only glancing at me before moving on to the next person charging.

Commotion from the other side of the group has half of them turning around, my heart swelling at the sound of a horn.

Cray.

Sailors are hastily making their way towards us. The relief that washes through me is immense. Tears nearly springing to my eyes.

With a blink of an eye, Dasha is in front of me, her hand gripping my throat. My eyes widen as I gasp, my legs flailing as she holds me up with her one arm.

What the infernum?

"You will help make this world a better place." Her docile look still plastered on her face.

I use my foot to push myself out of her grasp just as my vision blurs. My body hits the ground, and she's already reaching down towards me. Bringing up the sword, I shove it at her chest, but she grabs the blade with her hand, snapping it.

Did I just try to kill her?

Kellen comes up from behind, but Dasha must have seen my eyes dart, and she moves out of the way to avoid the puncture. Dasha stands upright, using the broken part of the blade as a dagger, and slashes towards Kellen. I move, wrapping my arms around Dasha's legs.

"Ungrateful youngin!" she yells, grabbing my hair.

Kellen uses this as her moment to lunge forwards once more. The imposing priestess letting the lance rip through her extended hand, a bellowing scream erupting from her chest. Even Kellen's eyes widen from watching the scene before her.

Dasha uses her other hand to break the shaft of the lance before pulling it out of her flesh and tossing it to the side.

"Run!" I scream, but Dasha grabs Kellen, slamming her back down before she has a chance to even think about it.

My hand grasps around the hilt of my broken sword, standing quickly. Kellen takes a sharp intake of air, struggling to fill her lungs back up from the impact she just took. Dasha stands upright, and I don't hesitate to force the blunted blade through her back.

"No!" Renna shouts from somewhere in the crowd.

Dasha coughs up blood, looking down to where the jagged edge of the blade she broke had plunged through her.

Kellen groans as she sits up and watches this. "Mazu..."

Tears well in my eyes, but I rip the sword from the back of her abdomen.

"Don't touch her." My voice low, as Dasha stares at me from over her shoulder, crimson liquid running down her chin.

Her knees buckle from under her, the light fading from her eyes. The sound of fighting envelopes me, a ringing in my ears. Kellen stands, moving towards a fallen crewmate, grabbing their sword. She has little time to react, though, as someone comes at her.

"You!" A fist connects with my face, sending me to the ground.

I hold my cheek as I turn to face Renna, who's already swinging again, connecting to my nose. Reeling back, I cry out. The tears I had brimming, now spill from my eyes.

Renna charges me. She rips the necklace from my throat, tossing it to the side as we collide with the ground. The air in my lungs escapes me, my eyes bulging as her weight stops me from being able to gasp.

"You... ruined... everything!" she screams, spit hitting my face as her eyes glare and teeth sneer at me.

Renna grips onto my hair, standing up and dragging me towards the cliff's edge. My hands come up and try to pry away as the pain in my scalp earns a whine now that I can breathe.

I feel the ground leave my back, my grip moving to hold on to the ledge. "Stop this! There's no point!" She isn't really doing this to win anything, but to get back at me.

"No point?" she whispers, her foot coming down collides with my chest, making me tetter over the edge more. "You have stolen my dream! You ripped away everything from me!" Her voice cracks, tears starting to stream down her face. "But now... my only solace will be watching you die!"

She puts her full weight onto me, my body now sliding over the edge, my hands grabbing at her ankle, but she pulls her foot away in time to avoid my grasp.

Renna did what she set out to do.

My eyes water as I stare up at Renna, her hand covering her mouth as tears stream down her face. In the end, I was the one to break her.

A smile crosses my lips.

She made me into someone I don't entirely recognise.

KELLEN'S POV

SHE'S ALWAYS SO RECKLESS.

Wanting to protect everyone, help others even at the cost of herself. Of course, it was only natural she took it upon herself to be Ari's surrogate mother versus his sister. At least that's what she thought. A part of why I love her so damn much.

Never needing to be asked, but does what's right without hesitation.

For the better part of our lives, I've been telling myself that the feelings I had for her were just platonic – something anyone would feel for their best friend. Mazu was always there. Saw me through the dark moments of my father; helped keep me on the right path when I thought it was pointless to be anything other than a waste of space. When I felt like my whole world was just turning into one messy blob of black and white shapes, she brought the colour back into it. She dragged me everywhere with her. We didn't need to talk about it or anything at all, which I was thankful for. All she did was be there. Remaining by my side regardless of how childish or callus I would be. Most strayed their path because my stoic appearance isn't always approachable, but she seemed to enjoy the contrast to her normally smiling face. There were more times than not that the only reason it remained there was out of muscle memory.

Once the commotion from the strange light and quake died down as it seemed to not impact us directly, I was dismissed and without a second thought, my feet carried me to her house. Sleep never even crossed my mind as I waited for her to return. After a few hours, the only thing I could think of was something bad had happened. I ran around Berkin, checking in to see if she had stayed with Mehl and Lip, with the Relchs. Checking all of our normal spots, and she was not at a single one of them. So, when I found my way back to her place, I felt helpless. Though a thud against the door brought me back from the hole I was slowly falling into, thinking about needing to file a missing person's report.

Seeing their rugged states made me realise that I wasn't worried for nothing, and I hated that I was right. Those two had gone through something, and I wasn't there. I didn't protect her. The exhaustion was written all over her face, but the moment her arms wrapped around me, I felt myself relax.

Right then was the moment I swore I would not let that happen again. I was going to be there. Even if I ended up failing at saving her, I knew all I needed to do was remain by her side.

When her lips connected with mine, it was the first time I had ever felt complete. The world felt like it made sense, and that all the denial I had been feeding myself over these years was no longer necessary. I was relieved. The feelings I had weren't delusional. Even though I could see the battle behind her eyes, whether she was going to fulfil my needs, there was no doubt in my mind that I finally had everything I had ever wanted. The only thing I would ever really need is for her to remain by my side.

I kick a guy off my spear, scanning the chaos quickly, my mouth running dry as I see her stuck between a monster and a cliff.

Mazu tips over the edge; my heart plummeting with her. Renna is gripping the only thing that would ensure my love's survival. My feet rush me towards the edge.

I understand it now; why you followed after Ari when he was thrown.

"Mazu!" Her name escapes my lips as I dive off the side, her eyes wide as they meet mine.

Extending my hand, and she follows suit, that damn pathetic smile she wears so effortlessly gracing her beautiful face. Pulling her closer to me, my other arm wraps around her, and uses the shift to place myself beneath her so my back faces the water.

"You're such an idiot..."

I'll stay by your side, Mazu. It's the only place I have ever wanted to be.

CHAPTER
TWENTY-SEVEN

COLBY'S POV

"Renna!" my voice bellows as I charge towards her.

She turns, the tears streaming down her face. It's a sight I've never seen, but I won't let it stop me. This is it. Years of her abuse; the anger and hatred I have for her stealing my life away simply because she had an issue with being told no.

I raise my sword; she doesn't meet my act of aggression with a defence, but simply closes her eyes.

No. I won't let you just slip away peacefully.

The sword slips from my grasp. Instead, I throw her to the ground, and I straddle her, my hands wrapping around her throat.

"You always had a thing for this..." My words are strained as my grip tightens.

She gasps, her fingers wrapping around my wrists, her legs kicking out from underneath me.

"You've made me hollow." My voice breaks. "Carved out the future Fen and I had planned with one another."

Renna's eyes bulge, her lips turning blue. Drops of water splash against her cheek. It must be raining.

I want to see it – the light fade from her eyes – to see her limp and unmoving, knowing she can never touch me again.

There is no coming back at this point.

Fen was right; I won't recognise myself after this, but I knew that a long time ago. The baker's son, the person who enjoyed making sweets, reading in the afternoons, drinking tea on the balcony of my childhood home that Fen and I were going to live in once we were married. I'm not that person anymore. Where there was baking is now smoking, drinking tea swapped for rum. I try to remain gentle around Fen, but I'm terrified that all they would have to do is push me far enough, and I'd snap.

The grip of Renna's hands on me starts to loosen, the spazzing from her body coming to a rest. Her copper eyes unfocus as every muscle in her body relaxes.

"WE'RE HERE." The servant's words bring me back to the present.

My eyes glance out the carriage window, golden fleches taking my immediate attention. The Fosa Castle doesn't look like it was built for the simplicity of beauty or to display wealth despite its expensive adornments, but out of intimidation. Sharp edges, tall structures, and Fel Watch flooding the place.

Not warm and welcoming.

They might want to take a lesson from Yral on feeling a tad more pleasant.

I had heard plenty about the old king and the Torrin family lineage. A once proud family that had built up one of the strongest and prosperous countries in all the realm had nearly crumbled under the hands of the Tyrant King. I only know the basics of who King Felguard is, that he is the king for the people. Changed the Torrin name that has ruled over this country for five hundred some sidereal years to reflect that it is not his lineage that makes him king, but the will of the people.

A little too poetic for me.

"Thanks for the ride," I mutter, opening the door as the carriage comes to a halt.

King Felguard could have just teleported me here like he did with Mazu, but no, apparently I'm not important enough.

One of the Fel Watch, with their tall frame, marches over to me. They look to the servant who is still atop the box of the carriage. He hands the guard a slip of paper, which they look over before handing it back.

"Sir, please follow me," they state, turning around and heading back towards the castle steps.

I follow their expectations, falling in step behind them. "So, I get to meet the big guy. Is this something that's rare?" I ask, but don't even earn a look back from the armoured individual guiding me.

Rolling my eyes, I do a quick look around the grounds. It's well landscaped, flowers, bushes, all the pretty things most places with money have.

"Be careful!" one of the men shouts as they are handling a statue. "We're to take her to the gardens."

My eyes take in the figure of stone, a stunning woman reaching out towards me with the way she's angled. It's odd they wouldn't have made it with something more materialistic, like marble. The level of detailing is actually very impressive for it being made of rock.

A part of me wants to take the statue's hand. She is just that compelling. No doubt why she was this creator's muse.

Something about her...

"This way," my armed escort calls out to me, forcing me to look their way.

I nod my head and give the statue one last glance before heading up the stairs and into the castle. The large doors open for us after a patterned knock.

How cute.

A mopy blonde-headed man smiles at me brightly, but as a well-seasoned liar, it's not hard to pick up on how forced that smile actually is. "You must be Colby."

I give him a smirk. "I must have gained some popularity or something."

The man nods his head, gesturing to the grand foyer we are standing in. "Very little is unknown in these walls." He tilts his head. "Or, that's what it seems like. I'm Vasile. Mazu informed us of who you are."

Well, that could be a good or bad thing. Despite warming up to her, we never really had the time to establish what it is we are to one another. Enemies, acquaintances, friends, or just a temporary truce.

"How is she?" The tone in my voice is a little more taught than I would have wanted.

She wasn't even conscious when Shaw took her. It was lucky Cray still had some boats in the area that came and pulled her and Kellen out of the ocean.

Vasile points in a direction with his head. "Come see for yourself," he says before making his way towards where I am assuming Mazu is.

Paintings, vases, sculptures, ornate weapons, all decorate the halls as we walk. The number of things this family must have collected over the years, and having the means to preserve and safeguard them... No wonder they are just decorating the halls with some of it.

"She's been in and out for many mooncycles, but we think

she is finally turning a corner in her healing," Vasile informs me.

Mazu has really gone through it, and I don't know if she knows yet. There was hardly any time to process what was happening before she was taken from all of us.

"What have you done?" Fen asks, their gaze looking down at me as I still straddle Renna's lifeless form.

After a moment, I take them in, my vision blurry.

My brow furrows and I stand, rushing towards them. "What the infernum are you doing here?" My gaze looks around as the fighting persists. "It's not safe!" They flinch at my harsh tone, but I grip onto their arm, picking up my sword, before I start dragging them away from all of this. "I told you to stay—"

"Colby!" they protest, ripping themselves free of my grasp.

I whip my head to look at them, and tears stream down their face, hands shaking, lip trembling.

They aren't safe.

My hand reaches out to grab them again, but they smack my hand away. "We need to move."

"I really don't know you anymore..." Their voice is soft. "You would never have done something like that." Fen raises a finger to point back at Renna.

"She deserved it," I state firmly.

They shake their head. "She deserved to be punished, but what you did, that was vengeful."

I scoff, taking in the area again, ensuring no one is getting too close; my grip on the hilt of my sword tightening to be ready. "Let's talk about this later. We need to go find Mazu."

"Crey's people are already on it," Fen mutters, looking

down and just past the cliff, a dingy already lowered and on its way towards the cliff.

Nodding my head, I extend my hand to them, and they hesitantly take it. We hastily make our way to the horses, who are riled up from all the commotion. I settle my stead before helping Fen up onto it.

I know I've changed, but my feelings for them haven't.

My heart tightens as their arms wrap around my waist once I am on. Whipping the reins, the horse bolts off, away from the fight and towards the docks. We bounce on the horse's back as we gallop as fast as it will go.

She will be alive.

I have to believe she is going to be okay. The weight of her necklace feels heavy in my pocket. Even without it, there is still a chance for her to survive, for her to make it through this just fine. I can only believe that because of her. When I thought that there was no way for us to get Fen and Kellen out of Liberta, we pulled it off. When Renna first stated she wanted Mazu on the crew, I didn't think she had what it took to survive on the ship, but she didn't fall apart or break down like I thought she would. When I met her, face to face, on that cliff, no one would have been able to convince me the sniffling girl, who I had thought was now tightly secured under our thumb, would jump to her death just so she could have been with her brother in those final moments.

"Over there!" Fen shouts, my eyes scanning in the area they are pointing to see the ship that had gone after them.

My mind was so derailed I hadn't realised just how fast and long we had been riding for. I steer the horse in the direction, slowing down as we start to enter pedestrian walkways.

"She's just right in there. I'll be out here if you or Mazu

need anything," Vasile says, opening the door to the healers ward.

I give him a nod and head in. White beds line the walls, but only one of them is being used at this moment. A navy blue sheet covers her body, her curls are matted from being laid on for so long. Her normal caramel brown skin seems more ashen. The door closes behind me as I step forward to her bedside. I pull over the small stool I see and sit.

"Let me see her!" I shout, shoving a tall man to the side as I make my way aboard the ship.

Though my haste is halted when my eyes actually take in the two bodies laid down on the deck of this ship. A woman comes up with her blade drawn, but I just kneel down next to Mazu.

"Shit..." My voice is hoarse.

Some of their limbs are bent in unnatural ways, blood seeping out of Kellen's nose, eyes, and ears. Neither of them are awake, and I can't even tell if they are breathing.

Fen gasps from behind me.

Hurried steps sound from the gangplank, drawing all of our attention to them. Shaw crests the edge of the ship and my brow furrows.

"Move," she states as she makes her way to Mazu's side, kind of forcing me to lean back and out of the way.

"She's severely injured," the woman, likely the captain of this ship, says as Shaw reaches down to hold on to Mazu's arm. "You can't move her."

Shaw looks over at Kellen for a moment, but shakes her head. "Come to the Felguard Country," she mutters to me and just like the first time, I blink and they are gone.

The whole ship silences as they witness the little vanishing act for the first time. My gaze shifts to Kellen to try and see what Shaw was trying to search for in that brief moment.

Mazu's eyes open slowly as I mutter her name. She glances around with her eyes first before actually moving her head to the side so she can spot me.

"You've looked better," I tease.

She smiles softly, though she coughs a bit as a chuckle tries to escape her. I look around and grab the glass of water sitting on the bedside table. Mazu takes a moment to collect herself to quell the fit, taking a sip from the cup.

I notice how dry her lips are, how the hair near her face is damp and clings to her face. Vasile mentioned her finally turning a corner, and if this is better, then she must have been in a great deal of pain since coming here.

Once she sighs, she lays her head back down and hands me the water. "You are still an arse, bringing up an injured girl's appearance like that," she claims, making me smirk at her.

I raise my hands in mock defence. "Woah, I was just being honest. If you're telling me to lie, I have no problem with that." My smirk returns. "But I'm telling people you're the one who told me lying is okay."

She shakes her head; her smile returning to her lips. "I'm glad you came." Her gaze looks to the door for a moment before coming back to me. "Where's Fen?"

I run a hand through my hair as Fen and I get checked into an inn for the night. The day has taken everything out of me. I can hardly stand, my muscles screaming at me from how far I pushed them today. Setting my sword down at the foot of the bed, I quickly shed my jacket and boots.

"You're bleeding." Their voice is soft.

I glance down and see where I had been nicked by some-one's blade. Nothing deep, but I should probably clean it.

"Just a scratch," I mumble, walking over to the pitcher of water resting on the table in the corner of our modest accom-modations.

Fen offers me their handkerchief and I smile at them as I take it to help clean the wound.

They walk over and sit on the edge of the bed. "Is this what your life has been like the past three years?"

My eyes observe their tense posture, eyebrows knitted together, how they clutch onto their knees. "Kind of," I answer honestly. "It was a hard adjustment at first, but I learned to adapt."

Fen shakes their head, tilting their chin down, making their hair drop a bit in front of their face. When Mazu first revealed to them what I had done to her and her family, there was so much fear behind their eyes. I don't know if that had been fear towards me, or the people who had been forcing me to do it. Either way, they have been more timid.

Maybe I should have explained the details sooner.

The water I had soaked the handkerchief in begins to drip from one of its corners.

"Colby... the look you had on your face. I—" They bite their lip, maybe trying to hide the soft shake to their voice.

I walk up, kneeling in front of Fen. "Hey..." I bring my hand up to push the hair out of their face.

"Don't," they whisper, making my hand stop its approach. "Why didn't you tell me?"

Dropping my hand, a sigh leaves me as I stand back up to join them on the bed. "Would you really have wanted to know? You were locked up, with nothing to do but be with your thoughts and the books and trinkets Renna allowed me to give to you. I know you, and all you would have done is sit and torment yourself about what it was I was doing."

They raise their gaze to meet mine. "Maybe I could have saved you from killing the man I love." A tear drop slides down their cheek, leaving a trail in its wake.

Kill the man they love?

My heart squeezes at hearing their words. "I'm not dead... and now that we're free, we can go back to living our lives."

"We were free the moment you and Mazu got me to Berkin, off of that ship, away from Renna." Their voice is low. "But you chose to go after her, chose to kill her versus running after Mazu immediately."

I shake my head, not understanding what point they are trying to make.

They bury their face in their hands. "You said you were being selfish... that all of this was because you wanted to keep me safe."

Leaning in closer, I want to hold them, but I know it's not what they want from me right now. "Yes..."

"Why do you call that being selfish?" Their voice getting even quieter.

To spare them the guilt.

"To spare me the guilt?" Fen says. "That's what I bet you're thinking right now."

Well, they got me there, but I don't want to admit it because I have a feeling they are about to call that bullshit.

"Fen..."

"No!" They sit upright. "It wasn't to spare me the guilt, Colby. It was to justify what you were doing."

"And if I wasn't protecting you, what was I doing?" I furrow my brow at them as they glare at me.

"Surviving."

I scoff, standing up and taking a few steps away from them as my hands clench and unclench.

They have no idea what it was like over these last few years. Watching the colour fade from their skin, seeing the bags deepen under their eyes. I wasn't just doing Renna's biddings, but doing what I had to in order to earn her trust.

"You didn't want to just protect me, Colby. You were using that ideal as a way to survive yourself, to put the blame on me whenever you were feeling bad about the things you've done," they claim.

"I regret NOTHING!" I shout, bringing a fist to my mouth to try and calm myself down. "Everything I did led to us being here. Free, alive, and together."

"And fractured." The word makes my head spin as it leaves their mouth.

Fractured?

Do they truly believe the words they are spewing? That I've been blaming them, or using their existence to simply survive?

Taking a few steps forward, I say, "Fen, listen to me... the things I've done were for you... for us. There was no other motive than I lov—"

"Don't use that word right now..." they interrupt. "Don't use it as a way to convince me that hurting people, throwing children from cliffs, killing someone out of vengeance is all okay just because you are doing it for someone you love."

I stare at them, mouth agape and eyes wide.

Makes me think to their words back when we were in their room. How they were scared that I was destroying myself, that I would become unrecognisable.

That's what Fen meant when they said I had killed the person they love.

They no longer see me as that person.

"I think you're self reflecting..." I mutter, "Claiming that I'm the one pointing the blame."

Fen balls their hands into fists as they sit in their lap. "For me... for us... you're putting the lives you ruined on the love we shared, Colby."

With everything I've done to get us here, I didn't once think that they would be unhappy about it. They have always been a delicate soul, which is why I never wanted to share with them the details, but I didn't expect them to see me as the bad guy.

"So what do I do?" My voice trembles. "How do I fix this?"

Their eyes widen a bit, and it isn't until I feel the tears drip from my chin that I realise it's because they are seeing me cry.

"I don't think you can."

No.

My feet carry me to them, falling to my knees as I wrap my arms around their waist, and place my head in their lap.

"Don't say that," I plead as I cry, dampening the fabric of their trousers.

Their hand rests atop my head. "Colby..." Fen chokes out. "I'm afraid of how far you are willing to go..."

My grip tightens around them.

So this is as far as their love goes.

A part of me can't accept this, not after everything I've done, now that we are finally free to be together. Though, the other part of me respects it. How true they have remained to themselves. The way Fen is unwilling to bend their morals, like Mazu.

"You're only saying this because you're blaming yourself for the things I've done, but you don't have to," I state, lifting my head up.

Their body shakes. "You said I could be selfish when all of this was over." I pull away from them slowly as they speak. "I can't be with someone who does the things you do and justify it with love." My arms fall from their waist. "I don't want to be responsible for making you into a monster."

Wow.

I fall back onto my heels as I stare up at them.

"They weren't up for the trip," I lie, but putting on a smile despite that wound feeling way too fresh, even after a few mooncycles.

Mazu looks me over, her own smile faltering. I get the feeling she knows, but she doesn't call me out on my dishonesty.

Clearing my throat, I ask, "How is the kid?" turning the attention on her.

"Good, I think. He's been having fun running around the castle, but he's getting annoyed with me still being in bed." She sighs. "He's been quieter... he's changed."

Haven't we all.

I nod my head. "He's safe though."

She looks at me with a furrowed brow, and I match her expression, not sure why that statement brought about such a tense look.

"Every time I ask, they say they don't know... but I need an actual answer, Colby." Mazu's eyes dart between mine. "Is Kellen alive?"

My heart breaks for her. I can tell they likely were pushing off letting her know because of her health. With everything she's been through, I want to tell her good news, give her hope and something to hold on to.

"No." My voice is soft, trying to counter the blow I just delivered.

The soundless gasp she takes makes my jaw clench, seeing her clutch at her chest with her unbroken hand. She's stopped breathing, her eyes wide as they bore into me, and I feel like I want to die just seeing her in this kind of pain. I know she must have already guessed it, but hearing me confirm it – it's broken her.

Mazu wails out, her scream reverberating through the room. The door swings open. Vasile quickly storms in with his swords drawn, but his fighting stance drops as he sees the scene before him.

I look back towards my friend, as she sobs; the arm wrapped in a cast is now draped over her face.

"She showed you how far she was willing to go..." I whisper, though I'm not sure if she can even hear me.

"It was all for nothing!" Mazu screams, her fist slamming into the bed.

Yeah, I know how that feels.

Her necklace glows, though there is no seawater for her to manipulate. It seems like a useless trinket at this moment.

Closing my eyes, I listen to her fall apart.

Neither of us got our happy ending.

Epilog

KAGE'S POV

Renatus said the legends would be meeting here, but he left before I could obtain the time frame, though I doubt he would have been able to give me an exact one. My leg bounces as my mind thinks on his words. The possibility of *my* Xylia returning to me after all these years. After so many attempts and false hopes. Ren would be able to do what I have failed to do.

I clench my fist, thinking perhaps Codrin isn't far from the surface of Renatus' mind. Either way, once Xylia is awake, it'll be me who she is returning to.

A knock on the door pulls me from my mind, a sigh leaving my lips as my eyes open and turn to see Zain peeking his head through the crack.

"Your cousin," he states, opening the door wider, letting me see the dark curly hair of Mazu.

Rising from my seat, I walk around the desk and greet her

with a smile, pleased to see one grace her features as well. "Mazu..."

She tilts her head. "Been awhile there, Kage." Mazu takes a peek behind her; a tall and lanky young man walks in. "You remember Ari."

I blink a few times, remembering the small boy I had taken in over two decades ago. "I don't know what you mean, he is far taller than I remember."

Ari chuckles and extends his hand to me. "I never did thank you, for what you did for me and Mazu back then." The sweet voice he had now a few octaves deeper. "Not that I had any idea of what was really going on, but I should have thanked you sooner."

I take his hand in mine, giving it a firm shake. "Nonsense. I was happy to do it. We're family, after all."

Zain disappears into the hall for the moment, but I maintain my focus on the ones in front of me.

Mazu leans in a bit, her eyes looking me over. "Man... you look rough."

A laugh escapes me. "Well, you have a few assassination attempts, you'll see how it wears on you."

The tone of my voice was lighthearted, but those words are anything but. Last we saw of each other, she had a performance here, and we were able to grab dinner together before she was back on the road.

"What brings you here?" I ask, pulling the conversation to a better topic than the threats on my life. "I'm guessing the war has been harsh on your tours."

She chuckles with a nod. "You have no idea... but I'm here because I got an invite." Her statement brings a frown to my brow as she fishes for the paper in her back pocket. "Says you need my help."

Mazu hands me the parchment.

Ms Hali,

Due to your involvement with the fight against Domi Nostrae in their attempts to secure the Southern Territory's Doorway, your presence has been requested as we find the war falling in line with those who wish to see our realm destroyed.

We ask that you make your way to the capital of the Felguard Country as we are looking to gather those who are willing to fight to maintain the peace.

Attached is a slip that will grant you a seat with the King of Felguard, who is heading a special task force.

The Legends of Limoria.

A knock on the door sounds. Zain walks in once more, but with him his father, Renatus, and a man that looks familiar.

"Done catching up?" Mazu asks as she turns to face the dark-haired man.

He smiles down at her as he reaches her side. "The blonde wouldn't shut up."

Vasile shoves him a bit. My memory starting to recall.

"It was all for nothing!" Her scream rakes through me as those words take me back to that night.

My confession to Xylia, the one I wish had never left my lips.

I hasten my steps and walk into the healers ward, my cousin sobbing. Vasile is watching the same scene unfold in front of me, and a tall young man staring down at her.

"Colby, correct?" I ask, extending my hand towards him.

He nods his head, taking my hand in his before giving it a shake. "Honoured to be recognised by royalty."

Though it took me a moment, I remember him being at the dinner with us as well, but he had excused himself early as one of the other members in Mazu's band had someone bothering them at the bar. He's their bodyguard of sorts, as well as her friend, from what she had explained to me.

Renatus steps forward. "Now that we're caught up, I think we should gather in the war room. Our last legend should be joining us shortly," he says, gesturing for us to walk towards the door.

"Hold on," Colby mutters. "What is this about a war room?" He looks down at Mazu with a glare.

She just shrugs. "I figured you've been bored watching me sing."

The man rolls his eyes. "So, you're purposely getting us into a fight?" His arms cross over his chest.

A small smile graces my face as I watch them, reminding me of how Xylia and Vasile would act together.

Soon.

"My gift to you." She chuckles, offering him an imaginary present.

He knocks her hands away with a laugh before lazily mimicking Ren's early gesture towards the door. "Then shall we?"

Renatus starts to lead them out, my head turning to look out the window towards the garden before I follow them.

All of this is for her.

We will bring her back, destroy the Domi Nostrae, and finally be together. We will rule this country with peace and prosperity. She will finally become what she was always meant to be.

Our queen.

269

INDEX

Berkin - Capital of the Southern Territory.

La Regina - 'The Queen' in Italian. The title that those who live in Lardo in Aumento have given Renna as she is the primary founder of the pirate haven.

Lardo in Aumento - Thief Rising in Italian. The name of the group of pirates that are most prevalent in Limoria's Eastern Oceans.

Liberta - 'Freedom' in Italian. The name is to signify the freedom of the rules and social standings that exist in Limoria, where the strong rule versus the wealthy or hierarchy. A clumping of islands separated by canals. They created a support system to creating a floating city that is anchored into the clay/earth that is under the sandy seafloor.

Sit tibi terra levis - Latin word for a traditional burial peace bringing, 'may the earth be light on you.'

Trabucco - Italian fishing shack that is on a pier far past the shoreline with giant nets.

Waterform - A creature made of the sea itself. They are vengeful embodiments of Haldoris' rage from when the doorways were sealed off. They attack anything that comes across their paths.

Acknowledgements

I seriously can't believe that the third book is FINALLY OUT!

There are so many people I am thankful for, as without them, I don't think I could have.

Chelsea, at the start of this year and well into it, our Wednesday writing sessions were the lifeblood of getting the majority of my writing in for this year! Thank you for always supporting my work—professionally, as well as a friend.

Shawna, my ever trusted reader! Thank you for allowing me to force you to read and reread this book just so I can get every ounce of your enthusiasm and critique on it. Your feedback always helps uplift my writing.

Jeri 'Red' Shepherd, for being my biggest supporter this year and such a source of inspiration. Thank you for uplifting me and my creative career! I cannot wait to see what our future holds with our creative pursuits.

My readers, for always being excited and eager to dive into the craziness, love, and passion, I pour into my world. Without you, I wouldn't be able to do this.

My friends and family, for being so understanding and supportive of what I do. I know it's not always easy for you as I pursue my dreams, having to sacrifice some of the time we have with each other. Love you all!

I cannot wait to get you the next book in the series~Daughters of Mira!

OTHER WORKS BY T R NICKEL

THE LEGENDS OF LIMORIA

Light of Evanora

Apparatus From Aruna

Songs From Haldoris

"The Maresal"